ADVANCE PRAISE

"From the shadows that dwell gifted minds around, emerges a skulk across the footplate of liter. *gencies* is the cloak thrown over th   , ᴗᴗ ᴊ̣ᴏw us that in darkness we can still find beauty, and will forever serve as a keepsake to great writing."

—**CRAIG WALLWORK**, author of *The Sound of Loneliness*

"Ah, do you feel it? That's the spectrum of neo-noir passing over you. It's wide, wider than you are It's tall, taller than you are. And it's got colors we haven't exactly named yet. Its source is a book, the book you hold in your hands. *Exigencies* has it all. Some of it's cold, some of it's funny. Some of it's strange, a lot of it's possible. We've all heard of the type of man who 'can get you things.' Richard Thomas can get you things. And his specialty is short, scary stories. Just like the addict in the alley searches for voices he can trust, I listen when Richard Thomas says it's a good story. 'Here,' he says, 'you're going to like this one...' And I listen."

—**JOSH MALERMAN**, author of *Bird Box*

"These pages house some of the most exciting writers you've never heard of—yet. They make the mundane terrifying, the poignant macabre, the violent touching. The only thing you won't find is the expected, because these stories will move the ground beneath your feet. Brace yourself."

—**NIK KORPON**, author of *Stay God*

EXIGE

DARK HORSE PRESS

NCIES

EDITED BY RICHARD THOMAS

PUBLISHED BY DARK HOUSE PRESS, AN IMPRINT OF CURBSIDE SPLENDOR PUBLISHING, INC., CHICAGO, ILLINOIS IN 2015.

FIRST EDITION
COPYRIGHT © 2015 BY RICHARD THOMAS
LIBRARY OF CONGRESS CONTROL NUMBER: 2014959397
ISBN 978-1940430492

EDITED BY RICHARD THOMAS
COVER ART BY DANIELE SERRA
INTERIOR ILLUSTRATIONS BY LUKE SPOONER
DESIGNED BY ALBAN FISCHER

MANUFACTURED IN THE UNITED STATES OF AMERICA.
WWW.THEDARKHOUSEPRESS.COM

FOREWORD

Why do we do it to ourselves as readers?

By which I mean, why do we read this kind of work? Why open up the pages and pick the rotten meat from these strange bones—what is it about noir?

I know why we do it as writers. We write the darkness onto the page because it's clarifying. Detoxifying. The bleak, black stories we write—like the stories found in the pages ahead—are an act of us writer-types sucking out the snake poison and spitting it onto a window for the world to see.

The question is, why do readers read this stuff? Why do they allow themselves to be immersed in all this nastiness? Why do they—or, we, really, since I'm a reader of this work, too—stand there admiring the spatter of expectorated poison on the glass? I mean, you read most stories, sure, you're going to get conflict. You're going to get a touch of darkness. A straight and simple line does not a good story make. But in most of those you get your happy endings, or at least endings that constitute the beloved-by-me Pyrrhic victories (*oh how much we've had to sacrifice to win this day . . .*). But what follows on these pages is not that. What follows forth is some bleak, soul-cracking blackness. It's not just fakey-fakey playtime darkness: the characters in the stories in this book are losers, failures, sometime-monsters, and they're caught up in situations that'll have your nether-hole closing up so tight it could snap a broomhandle.

Is it rubber-necking? Is this the equivalent to us driving past a car accident and goggling out the window at the broken glass, the sheared metal, the bodies on the asphalt? Idle curiosity, the safety of our own cars, the ability to speed on when our eyes have had enough of the horror just over there?

Or maybe it's a kind of catharsis. Could be that reading tales of the truly dark is equivalent to writing it—a way to excise poison, to experience the tumult and tangle of the human spirit in a safe space before strangling it with a hemp rope and kicking its ass off the edge of the boat into the churning waters below.

Certainly the world we live in is a dank, fucked-up circus. Watching the news for 45 seconds will crush the spirit of even the most stalwart viewer in ways the stories you'll find in this anthology never would or could. (Because at least the stories in this anthology possess beauty, too. They are told with great care, the narrative given shape and grace, the darkness given form and face and motive. The news is just noise; the stories here are all signal.) Maybe reading these stories helps us give context to the news we see during the 24-hour cycle. Not just a litany of horrific events, but characters and stories—a sense not only of what, but of who and why.

Hell, for all I know it's because we're all screwed up and we like reading about screwed up people. Maybe we're all closeted monsters and want to dive into the dark and the dirt and get it all over us. The darkness within us calls to the darkness of these tales and this is just us rolling around in it like a dog.

I have no damn idea.

What I do know is that you're about to take the deep dive.

Sadness and scars.

Back roads and broken noses.

Sex, drugs, and dollhouses.

The luckless and the lustful, the empty and the addicted, the lost, the never-wanna-be-founds, the dead and the dying and the wish-they-were-deads.

(Hell, you'll even find *saurian matricide*.)

These writers have spat the poison on the window.

Take a look.

Lick the glass.

—Chuck Wendig
November 10, 2014
In the forests of Pennsyltucky

INTRODUCTION

f you're done licking the glass and want to skip ahead to the stories, by all means do that. But I wanted to take a moment to talk a little bit about these stories, the authors, and why I selected the fiction that I did.

In 2014, Dark House Press published *The New Black*, which was my first anthology as an editor, essentially my "Best of Neo-Noir" from the past 5-10 years. These were all reprints, stories that I had discovered over the years, tales that stayed with me, scarred me—leaving an imprint on my mind, body, and soul. The minute I sent the book off to the printer, I knew that I wanted to do this again, but with all original fiction. 400 submissions, and a year later, *Exigencies* is what came of that desire.

This was a very hard book to put together. I rejected many talented authors, and many fantastic stories. Why? A couple reasons. Neo-noir (which just means "new-black") is a distinct voice, one that in my head may sound very different than what's in yours. Like art, or pornography, you know it when you see it, right? There were stories that were noir, but not neo. There were stories that were too classically rooted in fantasy, science fiction, or horror. There were stories that unfortunately were submitted after very similar ones had already been accepted. (If you wrote a story about cameras, you were out of luck—I took TWO as it stands.) I rejected science fiction that was too hard, and horror that wasn't horrific enough. Anything that felt too familiar, or too formulaic—it also got a pass. Anything that was too far in the past (and therefore, not new)—pass. There were some amazing stories that pained me to say no. But they just didn't fit. It's all so subjective, but I can honestly say that each and every story that made it into *Exigencies* did something for me, resonated in a powerful way—had something unique to teach me, or confess.

As I read through this anthology over the last couple of weeks, taking notes, making edits, putting the stories in order, meditating on the art that should accompany each tale, I was thrilled to see that they all held up, they all still gave me a thrill. There are stories in here that lean towards fantasy, science fiction, horror, Southern gothic, magical realism, transgressive, the grotesque—you name it, but all with that neo-noir flair, that literary bent. In the year since I accepted these stories, I've seen many of the authors in this group go on to sign with agents, to publish books, to place stories in elite magazines, and it always makes me proud. This anthology is one small way for me to say, "Look world—this is the next wave, this is the evolution of neo-noir, this is the new flesh." Long live the new flesh.

I hope you enjoy reading this anthology as much as I enjoyed putting it together. Hopefully, if I do my job right, and we find "our people" out there in the world, there will be more anthologies like this from Dark House Press. Come along for the ride. It might get a little bumpy, you may want to look away—but don't. Because right there, in that pulsing abyss, that endless yawning void—there is a tiny light shining, and it's trying to communicate, signaling something, beckoning us closer. Who knows what it might reveal?

—Richard Thomas
November 14, 2014
Chicago, Illinois

CHUCK WENDIG IS A NOVELIST, SCREENWRITER AND GAME
DESIGNER. HE'S THE AUTHOR OF MANY PUBLISHED NOVELS,
INCLUDING BUT NOT LIMITED TO: BLACKBIRDS, THE BLUE
BLAZES, AND THE YA HEARTLAND SERIES. HE IS CO-WRITER
OF THE SHORT FILM PANDEMIC AND THE EMMY-NOMINATED
DIGITAL NARRATIVE COLLAPSUS. WENDIG HAS CONTRIBUTED
OVER TWO MILLION WORDS TO THE GAME INDUSTRY.

RICHARD THOMAS IS THE AUTHOR OF SIX BOOKS—
DISINTEGRATION AND THE BREAKER (RANDOM HOUSE ALIBI),
TRANSUBSTANTIATE, HERNIATED ROOTS, STARING INTO THE
ABYSS AND THE SOUL STANDARD (DZANC BOOKS). HIS OVER 100
STORIES IN PRINT INCLUDE CEMETERY DANCE, PANK, GARGOYLE,
WEIRD FICTION REVIEW, MIDWESTERN GOTHIC, ARCADIA, QUALIA
NOUS, CHIRAL MAD 2, AND SHIVERS VI. HE IS ALSO THE EDITOR
OF THREE ANTHOLOGIES: THE NEW BLACK (DARK HOUSE
PRESS), THE LINEUP: 25 PROVOCATIVE WOMEN WRITERS (BLACK
LAWRENCE PRESS) AND BURNT TONGUES (MEDALLION PRESS,
WITH CHUCK PALAHNIUK AND DENNIS WIDMYER).
IN HIS SPARE TIME HE WRITES FOR LITREACTOR AND
IS EDITOR-IN-CHIEF AT DARK HOUSE PRESS. FOR MORE
INFORMATION VISIT WWW.WHATDOESNOTKILLME.COM OR
CONTACT PAULA MUNIER AT TALCOTT NOTCH.

EXIGENCIES

WILDERNESS

LETITIA TRENT

The airport was small, squat like a compound, its walls interrupted in regular intervals by tall, shaded windows. When Krista looked out the windows, the sky seemed slate-gray and heavy, but when the front doors opened, she remembered that it was really blue and cloudless outside.

She was early for her flight back to New Haven. She liked to arrive at the very earliest time the flight website recommended. She was prepared to wait, liked it even. It was calming to have nothing to do and nowhere she had to be. She had brought a book about the history of wilderness and America, something left over from college that she had never read. She liked the cover, a picture of a Pilgrim family, small and sickly, their clothes black and heavy on their bony bodies, facing an expanse of trees so tall and green you could see nothing beyond them. She underlined phrases in the book out of old college habit: *Wilderness remained a place of evil and spiritual catharsis. Any place in which a person feels stripped, lost, or perplexed, might be called a wilderness.*

She shared a red, plush armrest with a large woman who had

almost incandescent, butter-blonde hair. Her skin was so tan that it reminded Krista of a stain. Coffee on blonde wood.

The blonde had apparently just come from a trip to Maine. She told an older woman next to her—an even larger woman with tight pin-curls and wire-rimmed glasses, wearing those boxy, pleated shorts that middle-aged women often wear on holidays—about her trip. The blonde had stayed in *the cutest hotel*. Her entire room had been *done up all nautical*. The other woman nodded in agreement with everything the blonde said, as if she had had an identical experience.

Krista watched the airport attendants and one airport policeman patrol the area. They sometimes stepped into the waiting room and observed the crowd with what appeared to be either worry or constipation (they pressed their lips together, their hands on their hips, and blew the air from their mouths as if making silent raspberries). They had a vague air of agitation. She watched them carefully for signs of what might be wrong, but they revealed nothing in their pacing. Nobody else seemed to notice.

On Krista's left, opposite the blonde, was a family, a mother and two children separated from her by one seat. The mother was thin and loud and wore shorts with many utilitarian pockets and a simple tank shirt without a bra. She seemed infinitely capable, as if she ran her own business or perhaps even managed some kind of sports team. Krista admired thin, efficient women like this, women who wore comfortable, rubber-soled sandals and clothing with enough functional pockets. The woman and her children all spoke on their individual cell phones, all telling somebody variations on the news that they would arrive soon, that it was only thirty minutes until boarding.

An announcement crackled over the loudspeakers, the sound delivered in one chunk of indiscernible static.

Krista looked around the room, hoping for the scraps of somebody else's conversation to explain what had just been said.

Plane's delayed for an hour, the blonde said to her husband, who had also missed it. Storms down in Boston.

A general grumble rose. People shifted in their seats and took out their recently stowed cell phones. The blonde woman called her husband's name, which Krista immediately forgot.

Phone me up a pizza, she told him. I won't eat that shit from the vending machine.

———

As it grew darker in the waiting room, Krista struggled to make out the print of her book. The primary row of fluorescent lights hadn't been turned on, but nobody else had complained about the dark yet. She wouldn't be the first. She read until she had to squint in the darkness at the small, cramped words.

As she tried to concentrate on the increasingly turgid prose of her book (pages and pages about national forests, conservationists, things that Krista wasn't particularly interested in, though she knew that she should be), the blonde woman spoke energetically about her two dachshunds, Buckeye and Alexis. They liked to eat the carpet, she said, so she had soaked the edges of the carpet in Tabasco sauce, which was, incidentally, the same color as the carpet. The pin-curled woman asked how they managed to walk on the carpet if it was soaked with Tabasco sauce. The blonde shrugged, as if this were a mystery to her as well, though a boring one that she had no interest in pursuing.

Krista gave up on her book.

The mother and her children slept on the carpet below their chairs, their bookbags slung up on the seats above them, the fabric of their bulky *Plymouth Rock* sweatshirts bunched under their heads as pillows.

Krista wished that she could step outside and occupy herself with a cell phone, as many others did, but she didn't have a cell phone (she had canceled it when she'd left her job) and had nobody to call. Nobody was waiting to meet her in New Haven, and nobody was worried that her flight was late. She stood up and let the cheese cracker crumbs gathered in the folds of her t-shirt fall to the carpet.

Krista stood in the fluorescent lights of the bathroom, listening for shuffling feet, a toilet paper roll spinning. She was alone. Her stall door wouldn't shut completely (how did doors come unlined from their frames? She didn't understand what would cause it, other than a fundamental shifting of the floor), so she kept one hand on the door as she pulled down her underwear. A bumper sticker on the inside of the door said *Republicans for Voldemort*. She had never seen a Harry Potter movie or read one of the books, but she vaguely knew who Voldemort was. She was in on the joke.

She put her hand on the sticker and tried to keep the door closed as she eased her jeans and underwear down. It was just as she'd thought—in the middle of the bone-colored strip of fabric, a slight red stain. She peeked out her door into the empty bathroom: no machines.

Krista stuffed a ball of toilet paper between her legs and pulled her pants back up, letting the door open slightly, as she needed both hands. As she did this, just as the door swung open and she saw a middle-aged woman in the bathroom mirror carefully applying liquid eyeliner, the bathroom lights cut out. Nothing hummed or whirred and she could hear people in the hallway shuffling and speaking.

She buttoned her pants in the darkness and stepped into the bathroom, lit only by the dusky light seeping through the high, small window above the sinks. The woman applying eyeliner hissed *shit* and left, slamming her purse or hip into the plastic trash barrel as she left.

Before Krista even had time to panic or feel anything but mild interest, the electricity came back on again. The fluorescents above her buzzed with the effort and her blue-lit face appeared in the mirror. She was alone again. She washed her hands and pressed her wet palms over her face.

———

Ladies and gentlemen, a police officer said, shaking the flashlight in his hand in time with the syllables, sorry for the inconvenience. He and one of the nervous attendants stood before the check-in desk.

It's only a temporary outage, the officer assured them. Nothing serious.

Krista made her way back to the waiting room, stepping over legs and bookbags.

The news drifted into the main room, where Krista's jacket was twisted around one leg of her chair, her carry-on bag placed on her seat to save it. The blonde next to her watched the progress of her bag as she removed it and sat down again. She knew that she shouldn't leave her bags unattended—signs on every wall said so in bold, red letters. All she had in the bag were dirty clothes, a brochure about Maine blueberries that her mother had given her, and a business card from her father's company with a telephone number scrawled on the back. Nothing she was afraid of losing.

Her parents wanted her to come back home to Maine. She

hadn't told them yet that she wouldn't. She was jobless now, that was true, but it wasn't as they feared—she wasn't beyond help. She had skills. She imagined herself combing through the classifieds in a coffee shop, circling job after job, making cheerful telephone inquiries, putting more action words in her resume (*implemented, facilitated, utilized*). The idea didn't scare her. It seemed liberating. Fun, even. She remembered several cheerful montages from romantic comedies that included these very scenes. They had to have happened to somebody.

Did you hear what he said back there? The blonde demanded. It was a rhetorical question, since she obviously knew. Krista nodded and told her anyway.

So what's the problem? The blonde asked. She was suspicious, if not of Krista, then at least of the policeman's words.

Storms. Storms are the problem, Krista repeated.

The woman sniffed and shook her head, kicking off her pink flip-flops. Storms. I bet.

It was completely dark out now. Somebody had put the lights on in the main room, so Krista could no longer see the parking lot and tree-heavy outskirts from the window. The pizza delivery car had taken forty-five minutes to reach the airport. He had reported heavy wind and rain somewhere close and coming toward them. The woman and her husband ate an entire large pizza all by themselves. Krista didn't want any of their pizza, but she found it rude for people to eat in the presence of others who were not eating.

She couldn't concentrate on her book. She put it away and tucked her luggage under her seat. She stood up, feeling the blood rush back into her legs. She'd go outside—the air in here was stuffy, full of the smells of powdered cheese and industrial cleaning liquid.

The glass doors folded away instantly for her, as if she had bid them to do so.

Outside it was still, but the streets were slick, as if it had recently rained, though she had seen no rain. A group of men stood by the doorway, talking about a sports team that she didn't know.

He could really fucking get that ball across the field, he said. That boy was something else. This was from an airport attendant, one she had not seen before, a young man with a slightly fat, womanish body—large hips and a round ass. The other men nodded in unison. They made brief eye contact with Krista and nodded in turn, as if she were a visiting dignitary, somebody who needed at least a modicum of acknowledgement. She smiled and looked down, the proper response.

The streetlights reflected back against the cloud-covered sky, giving it a uniform orangey, sick tinge. Shallow puddles of water collected at the edges of the lot. The entire parking lot was lit by rows and rows of light.

Out beyond the parking lot, Krista saw a paved footpath from the airport to a big, empty industrial complex next door. The flight, according to her blonde neighbor, was delayed for another hour. She had time for a walk.

She set off across the lot, hoping that the men on the steps were watching. She didn't want to be stranded if the plane happened to arrive early and everybody boarded without her. She imagined coming back to find the waiting room empty, her piece of luggage the only sign left that the place had once been inhabited.

The air was humid but cool. A cold sweat gathered on her bare throat and forehead as she pumped her arms and walked fast to reach the walkway. She wanted to be far away from the airport, to be able to see it from a distance. As a child, she had often fantasized about opening the car door and just running into the woods that lined the highways in Maine, disappearing from her parents and never arriving at whatever place they'd intended to take her. She often had a desire for literal distance from places, to see them in perspective to the sky or horizon.

She crossed the wooded median and broke through to the parking lot of the complex. She turned around. The airport looked small in comparison to the huge building next to her, which had at least a dozen stories and was completely made of glass.

A light swiveled continually from the airport's roof. From a distance, she could see the people inside the building below the fluorescent lights. The blonde chewed a piece of crust. One of the men outside lit a cigarette. The match flamed in his hands and then disappeared. She sat down on a bench facing the airport, and then rested her head on the slats. She was tired, she realized, and the swampy air increased the feeling. She would only close her eyes for a while.

———

Ma'am. Ma'am! The voice woke Krista immediately. A flashlight bobbed around her face. She tried to speak, but only a low moan came out.

Are you hurt? Are you all right, Ma'am? The policeman (Krista could see his badge and recognized his slick black hair from the airport) flashed his light into her eyes. She sneezed, then sat up, wiping her nose on the back of her hand.

I'm fine, she said. Is something the matter?

The policeman stood up from his crouching position. He towered over her as she sat, stood too close. Her nose was level with the brass button on his pants. She stood up.

I'm supposed to get everybody back to the airport. Storm coming. The flight is delayed for another hour. He jerked his head toward the airport. The men over there said you'd walked out thisaway and I came to get you. The policeman turned and started back toward the airport, so Krista followed.

I'm sorry to trouble you, she said to his back. She hadn't imagined somebody would come to get her—why would he do that? Had he been watching her?

His shoulders were very broad. She liked how every policeman called every woman Ma'am, even if the woman was clearly younger than he was.

The policeman shook his head. No trouble. He didn't turn to look at her.

Krista wondered when the storm would come. The sky was still a strange, flat, orange-black.

When Krista entered the room, the blonde woman and her husband looked away.

Found the last one, the policeman announced to the airport attendant.

Go ahead and take a seat, he told her.

It seemed to her that the whole room watched as she walked to her seat, removed her luggage, and sat down. Some of them didn't take their eyes from her even as the airport attendant began to speak. She looked at the floor.

It looks like we'll be keeping you for another hour, ladies and gentlemen, he said. The airport attendant looked around the room nervously, his hand rested on the top of his walkie-talkie. He wanted to leave, Krista could tell. He placed one foot behind him, ready to pivot him away. The flight is having minor technical difficulties, which should be resolved within the hour. He took a breath. But we got one request from the local authorities—you all must stay inside until the airplane lands.

At the word *authorities*, the room's temperature changed. The blonde's husband sat up straight in his seat and began to protest, as did several other men. The children looked at their mothers. The mothers pulled their children close.

What *authorities*, exactly? A few voices asked, stepping closer to the front counter.

Krista watched the airport attendant's face. He put his hand up and grimaced. I don't have any information beyond what I have given you.

Safe from what? What kind of danger, exactly, might we be in? A balding man in khaki pants stepped forward. He stood with two children—a boy and a girl of seemingly equal age, both thin and uncannily poised, their hair long and neat and pulled away from their faces. They looked just like him, tall and thin with large, bony elbows and hands.

The attendant shook his head. Sir, I only know what I've been told. All I know is that you are not in any immediate danger, as long as you stay in the airport.

Krista felt her stomach pang. She'd been outside. Was she in danger? Or was it only right now that the outdoors was dangerous? She turned and tried to see outside the windows, but she could only see the reflection of the group on the glass.

Listen, another man said, we need to know—but the attendant's walkie-talkie crackled and he held his hand up, pressing it against his face. He spoke into it, a series of yeses and nos. The attendant held up one finger to the crowd, indicating *just a minute*, and returned to the gated doors that separated the waiting room from the security check.

When he left, people looked around, dazed. Some began to speak to each other, to people they would not otherwise speak to. Fear, Krista saw, made them trust each other with their own fear. They turned to each other and said plainly *I am afraid*. Not in those words, but in other words and in the angles of their bodies, in how much closer they leaned, how much more quickly they spoke.

The skinny mother with many-pocketed pants called *hey, hey* in Krista's direction, and she gradually realized that the woman was speaking to her.

Did you see anything while you were outside?

Krista felt the attention of the room turned to her.

She shook her head. Nothing. I didn't see anything. It was completely calm.

The blonde's husband snorted. Calm, he repeated. Krista looked at him, not sure what he meant. Did he think she was lying?

Did you see any people out there? The woman asked, her eyes darting around Krista's head.

No, nobody but the policeman. Krista didn't like the way they watched her. Their eyes narrowed as if they couldn't quite get her into focus.

The police arrived thirty minutes later. She could see their squad cars' headlights momentarily illuminate the otherwise black parking lot. They did not have their sirens on, but when they emerged from the squad cars, they were wearing masks. It was difficult to see exactly what kind of masks (she had only the light from their headlights to see by), but they seemed to be gas masks—a thick tube like an elephant tusk hung down from each policeman's mouth and nose.

One of the children said *His mask is scary*. He pointed, and they all looked out the window, some running up to press their hands and faces to the glass. The entire window was covered with people trying to see through it. Krista remained seated. She'd seen the masks and didn't know how it would help to see more. She could also feel that she was bleeding and was afraid to stand up.

Fuck this, said a young man, one of the people pressed against the glass. He was handsome in a slim, well-groomed way that made Krista nervous. Men like this didn't notice her unless she was doing something for them—putting their call through at her office, for instance (her *former* office, she reminded herself), or reminding them to sign a form. They might reply *thank you*, while looking right through her. This man was dark-haired and wore a t-shirt of a solid, rich color—a brownish brick. He looked as if he'd stepped from an Eddie Bauer catalog. Krista's mother got an Eddie Bauer catalog every month. She remembered admiring those outdoorsy people, thirtysomething, financially stable, wearing primary colors and sturdy shoes. They had formed her idea of what it meant to be a happy adult.

I'm going to see what's going on here, he told the room. People around him nodded, even the mothers, who Krista thought might be offended by the fact that he had just said *fuck*, but maybe they excused the language in an emergency situation.

The man walked up to the glass accordion doors. Before, they had immediately opened when anyone stepped close to them. Now, they didn't open. They must have cut the power to the doors. For the first time that night, she began to understand why everybody else was so frightened. It had taken her longer, she thought, because she only had herself to be afraid for.

The Eddie Bauer man pounded lightly on the glass doors, which shook under his fists. They were not very solid. He could have broken them if he wanted to.

Give us some fucking information! He screamed at the plastic seal in the middle of the door. Krista had an urge to laugh, but she turned it into a cough. She didn't want to offend the man, who had done nothing to warrant unkindness.

It must be chemicals. Some kind of chemicals outside, the blonde said. Then she repeated it, looking around the room for somebody to tell. It must be chemicals. We've been attacked with chemicals and we're stuck here. Her husband nodded.

Some of the men, older ones with children, went to look for the airport attendant and the policeman, who had all disappeared during the half hour before the police in gas masks had arrived.

Did you smell any gas out there? The blonde turned to Krista. This is important. Did you smell anything?

She wanted to help the woman. She tried to remember smells. The hedges smelled like pine. The bed of flowers around the industrial complex smelled like fresh manure and maple syrup.

No, I didn't smell anything unusual. Krista shifted in her seat and felt her stomach heave and salt at the back of her throat. She was going to be sick. But she couldn't be sick here, not with them all looking at her, thinking she'd been poisoned.

The blond shook her head and turned from Krista, done with her. I don't want to die in this goddamn place. I don't want to die.

Her husband gathered her in his arms and pulled her away from Krista. He shot her a look of mild anger, as if it were her fault that the woman was upset.

Krista stood up, hoping to leave the room for a while, to go to the bathroom and rest her cheek against the cool stall door and be away from the constant noise, the questions.

Mommy! A girl raced down the hallway, almost colliding with Krista as she ran. Mommy, the water hurt me! The little girl's mouth was red with blood. It smeared her lips like lipstick. At first Krista thought it was lipstick, but it was wet on her hands, too, which she held out before her.

What did you do, baby? What happened? This wasn't the many-pocketed mother, but a more frantic mother, one who wore a jumper and a headband. She was as upset as the child.

What hurt you, baby?

Krista stood in the hallway watching, like everyone else, waiting to hear what was wrong. She stood perfectly still, afraid that moving would collide her with whatever had hurt the child. The child sniffled and hiccupped, but eventually, she managed to get something out. She had only taken a drink from the water fountain. It had cut her, and she had come back here to tell her mother about it.

As the mother wiped the child's mouth clean with a napkin from her purse, they heard a rustle from the front of the room— the security door opened and the attendant stepped out, his walkie-talkie crackling.

Good, you're all here, the airport attendant said, surveying the group. He did not seem to notice that they were gathered together strangely, turned toward the mother and child in the middle.

You might have noticed the police presence, he said. They are here to secure the airport. He held up his hand when somebody spoke, the tone angry, though they were not able to get out a word. The plane is scheduled to leave in thirty minutes, it has just landed. We've put a plastic tunnel from the door to the plane so you don't have to go outside when you board, just as a precaution—understand? He paused and looked at the bulky, digital face of his watch.

The blonde jumped in, ignoring his still-raised hand. What's going on? Have we been attacked? She held a paper towel to her eyes and dabbed beneath them where her eyeliner bled.

The attendant shook his head. No Ma'am, no evidence of that. The FBI determines that. You'll know as soon as I know. The man nodded at them all, and, as the questions began, as the mother with the bloody-mouthed child tried to bring the child forward, a paper-towel held against the girl's still lips, the man walked fast—almost jogged—back to the gated security area, slid through the smallest possible sliver of open door, and then locked the door behind him.

The crowd was still for what seemed like a very long time to Krista, though she knew it was probably only a few seconds. Then, the Eddie Bauer man ran up the slight slope to the locked entrance and shook the gate like somebody in a prison movie or a primate behind old-fashioned zoo bars.

We've got a kid bleeding in here. We want to speak to somebody in charge. His voice echoed in the empty security area and bounced back down to the crowd.

The mother held her daughter and began to cry. The child was dry-eyed. Everyone was speaking but Krista. Unlike the others, she was uncoupled, without a child or a traveling companion. In Victorian novels, women always went with traveling companions, maiden aunts or cousins to keep them safe from the influence of crowds and sinister men. They also served another purpose, one which Krista had not thought of before—they were for company, somebody to be with, a buffer against loneliness beyond the everyday loneliness of being in one's own head. She usually enjoyed her own company, but her alone-ness oppressed her here. Even now, people did not usually travel alone, at least not the way she was, aimlessly and with nowhere to go, no one to care if she arrived or not.

She imagined that the others sometimes looked at her sideways, never directly. Krista wasn't sure if she was exaggerating their glances—her mother said that she tended to suspect dislike where it wasn't present. *You were always a fussy, fearful child*, she'd said during her latest visit, after Krista had explained what had happened at her job, with her boss, how she had been shamed into leaving, how he had never called her again. *I'm sure it would have blown over if you'd just waited. If you'd just been a little more goddamn calm about it.*

Being fearful makes people want to hurt you, her mother had said. *When you shrink away, people want to give you a reason to shrink.*

Krista tried to breathe deeply to calm herself. She opened her bag and took out her book. She had read only one half-sentence (*Wild animals added danger to the American wilderness and here, too, the element of the unknown intensified feelings*) before she felt her stomach tighten. She had the urge to stretch out on the floor until the sickness passed, but she couldn't. She put her book away and rose. As she stood up, the blonde, now sitting with her head between her hands, the empty pizza box occupying the seat next to her, turned to watch.

Are you sick or something? The woman looked at Krista, though she kept her head in her hands.

I'm ok, Krista said. Just had too much water.

Her mother had always called her period her *monthly friend*, and Krista had been encouraged to adopt similar euphemisms for bodily functions. *Going number two. Making water. Making wind.* She couldn't imagine answering the woman's question truthfully.

The woman pursed her lips and nodded, but turned to Krista again, her face still blank. Sure you didn't pick up something from outside? You went farther out than any of us. As she said this, the woman weeping on her bleeding child's blonde head looked up.

Did you drink out of the water fountain? Did you get something from outside on the fountain?

Krista shook her head, rising again. No, no. I have my own water. I swear, there's nothing wrong with me. Nothing was wrong outside when I was out there. She looked at the two women, both staring at her, their mouths hardened, their teeth not showing.

Excuse me, she told them, as if ducking away from a dinner party. I have to use the restroom.

In the bathroom, Krista leaned her warm forehead against the bathroom stall, then thought better of it and pulled away. She didn't know it was safe to touch. Maybe she was getting poison on everything she touched. The woman's fear was convincing.

In the stall, she knelt and rested her head in her hands. Her head ached dully. She couldn't take one of the Tylenol she'd brought in her carry-on bags—she didn't have any water left in her bottle. She knelt until the sickness passed. But she had to go back. She couldn't hide.

Before she left the bathroom, she caught a flash of light in the small window above her eye level. They were just outside, the men in masks. Krista wondered if she could see anything—maybe something she could tell the others about, gain their favor with—through the small, rectangular window in the bathroom. She turned over the bathroom's metal trash can and climbed on it, holding the wall for balance, until she could see outside.

The window looked out onto the front law of the airport. She saw three figures in jumpsuits gliding their flashlights along the lawn. One seemed to be examining the grass. Another seemed to be looking at the edge of the building, where the foundation met the ground. Another was farther off, sweeping his light in the little stand of trees between the airport and the industrial complex. Their motions seemed cursory, almost mocking, as if they were only putting on a show of searching, and not even a very convincing one.

Looking for someone you know? A man's voice surprised her, and Krista turned on the trash can, almost falling. It was the blonde's husband. He wasn't wearing his baseball cap and his reddish, curly hair was flat and greasy against his head like a stack of smashed bread.

You scared me, she said, not sure how to understand the man's presence in the women's room. Is something wrong with the men's room?

The man shook his head. I just came to make sure you were all right. You were taking so long. His voice was wrong; it didn't match his words. He smiled at Krista and motioned for her to join him.

Come on back out here. We've all got some questions.

Krista nodded, though she didn't understand what he was saying. Questions for her? When she entered the waiting room, she saw that her baggage had been opened. The Eddie Bauer man had her book in his hands. He wore rubber gloves. Krista wondered where he had gotten them—*did he pack rubber gloves whenever he traveled?*

What are you doing?

The people around him looked up at her. They had all let him do this, she could see. They all approved.

We found this, the blonde said, pointing at Krista's seat. The red seat was stained black in a neat, tea saucer-sized circle. You're bleeding. Why didn't you tell us?

They think I'm sick, she thought. It isn't— she began, but the woman with the many pockets interrupted her.

You haven't spoken, and you're traveling here alone, she said. You go outside right before the attack. You visit the restroom five or six times after. You don't call anyone to let them know what happened. You don't ask any questions, and you don't seem to be phased by what's happening here. The woman held her hands up, palms to the sky. What are we supposed to think?

Listening to the woman, Krista almost felt convinced of her own suspicious behavior. She was vaguely afraid that they would find her out. But there's nothing to find, she soothed herself, there's nothing wrong with me. I'm only alone. There's nothing wrong with that.

You can't do this to me, she said instead, the words surprising her. How dare you do this to me? The words seemed familiar, like something she had seen on television, and they made her feel powerful. She wanted to hit the Eddie Bauer man and take back her book. She wanted to make the blonde stop smiling or smirking or whatever she was doing with her mouth.

What, do you think you are some kind of important person? That you're better than the rest of us? This was from the blonde. She crossed her arms over her chest. Krista imagined that this was the way she stood when scolding her children.

I am important, she told them, not sure what she was trying to say. *Tell them about your monthly friend*, she told herself and almost laughed out loud. I'm as important as—

She stopped when the lights went out. A few of the children screamed and the mothers hissed words of comfort. Krista didn't move. It seemed safer to stay where she was. No need to drag it out. No need to make things harder on everyone. Though it was dark, she could hear the rustle of someone moving toward her.

LETITIA TRENT

'S BOOKS INCLUDE ECHO LAKE (DARK HOUSE PRESS) AND
ALMOST DARK (OUT IN 2015 FROM CHIZINE PUBLICATIONS)
AS WELL AS THE POETRY COLLECTIONS ONE PERFECT BIRD
(SUNDRESS PUBLICATIONS) AND YOU AREN'T IN THIS MOVIE
(DANCING GIRL PRESS). HER POETRY AND PROSE HAVE
APPEARED IN BLACK WARRIOR REVIEW, FENCE, SOU'WESTER,
PSYCHOPOMP, AND SMOKELONG QUARTERLY, AMONG OTHERS,
AND HER NON-FICTION HAS BEEN PUBLISHED BY THE
DAILY BEAST, THE NERVOUS BREAKDOWN, AND BRIGHT WALL/
DARK ROOM. SHE HAS RECEIVED FELLOWSHIPS FROM THE
MACDOWELL COLONY AND THE VERMONT STUDIO CENTER.
TRENT CURRENTLY LIVES IN COLORADO WITH HER
HUSBAND, SON, AND THREE BLACK CATS.

MONSTER
SEASON

JOSHUA BLAIR

My brother showed me how to make a tattoo gun before I became the only son my parent's friends know about. During that short window between statutory rape and aggravated assault, he said to start with the plainest toothbrush you can find. None of this stuff with angled necks or soft rubber grips. What you want is just a stick with bristles at one end.

He said you cut off the head of it, so all you have is about six inches of straight plastic.

He held his old toothbrush, which he hadn't used for the last six to twelve months, in the light that shone through the open kitchen windows. The fingers of his other hand, wrapped around the knife's handle, looked like an old man's. Long. Bony. Veins crisscrossing under the skin like a map of Los Angeles freeways. Mine would look the same by the time I grew to be nineteen.

If your eyes traced a straight line down from his fingers, you'd see the slow build of thin black patterns that followed him home from prison. They started with spider webs in the elbows.

He would tell you, "Your elbows are nothing but a thin layer of

skin over bone. That's why it hurts so much there. That's why so many people get them done."

He'd say, "Tattoos on your elbows are a way of telling everyone else that you're some kind of monster."

This was back when you didn't need to be a millionaire to have a real backyard in California. This was back when people didn't mind having linoleum floors or shit-brown carpet. It was around the same time that people started repainting their homes, because of a rumor that said Richard Ramirez, the Night Stalker, only killed people who lived in yellow houses.

My brother worked the knife back and forth, sawing the head off his old toothbrush. He said, "If none of your buddies have kitchen duty, you could bite through the plastic, but it takes some time and could leave your mouth cut up for a few weeks."

He tossed the bristles into the trashcan under the sink.

This was during that one summer when, no matter how hot it got outside, everybody slept with their windows locked shut. The same summer that the girl who cut my hair leaned over me and whispered, "One of the women I work with, her neighbors were killed a few days ago."

She brushed away the little wet shards of hair that were stuck beside my ear, saying, "The Night Stalker cut out the husband's eyes so he could have sex with the empty sockets."

That Saturday, my dad and my uncle were out renting a paint sprayer.

My brother pulled a lighter out of the small pocket of his jeans and then sparked a flame a few inches beneath the toothbrush. Thin wisps of white smoke floated away from the plastic, with a smell that reminded me of burning tires. When the plastic started bubbling tan at the middle of the brush, he stopped to roll it against the tile countertop. He bent it ninety degrees, then watched it flex almost all the way back to normal as it cooled.

He said, "Right now what we're making is the body. What holds everything all together."

Then he heated it again, to the very edge of boiling, and then rolled it against the counter. Each time it left a little more plastic melted to Mom's tile. He said, "You're done when it's a right angle, like the number seven, and it doesn't bend back when it cools."

You could hear Mom at the front of the house, holding swatches of color to the stucco walls. Holding different colors to the wooden trim. Her voice wafted in over the hot summer breeze while she and my aunt discussed paint schemes that wouldn't get us all murdered.

Even further out, where you should have been able to hear little kids yelling and playing, there was just wind and leaves. The wet summer heat was pressure-cooking us inside our houses.

I think my brother was the only person in our neighborhood who would go outside alone at night, and I only knew he left because he would wake me up. His face was just a shadow in the night outside our window. "Close it," he said, "and make sure you lock it."

I asked where he was going, once, and he only smiled. I didn't do the math until a couple years later, when I realized that the first night he left was on Lucy's eighteenth birthday. The night she stopped being a felony.

"Grab me your tape player."

I went to my room and brought back my Walkman. It was a big red clunky thing with blue buttons. Yellow headphones. The colors of my Superman pajamas.

He took it in one hand and slipped the blade of the knife deep into the seam between the body's two halves. One quick twist and mystery bits of the machine tinkled to the linoleum. He walked over to the kitchen table and worked at pulling it all apart with his hands.

The inside of a tape player looks like a pulley glued to a green computer board. Take out the pulley and you've got a little rotary motor with a pair of wires coming out. He said the best batteries were nine-volts—the kind that would zap you if you licked one end. You touch the red wire to the simple looking terminal; touch the black wire to the crazy-looking terminal. That's it. You have the spinning heart of a tattoo gun.

The trick, my brother said, is converting rotary motion to the linear up-and-down motion of a tattoo needle.

He said, "You're going to thank me for teaching you this after you go to jail too."

"Yeah right. I'm not going to jail."

"That's what everybody seems to think until they get thrown in."

The trick, he said, was jamming a piece of cork around the spinning part on the motor. Dead center, you jam the cork on the spindle, or you glue on a pencil eraser. Anything round and soft enough to poke a guitar string through, but strong enough to hold it in.

This was during that one summer when, after sunset, our family would sit on the couch in our living room watching the evening news. We'd hear the stories of people getting slaughtered worse than animals. People like my hair-cutter's friend's neighbor. We'd sit there knowing that, even as we watched the stories, that guy was out there, maybe in our own neighborhood, looking for an open screen door.

Governor Feinstein got on TV and told us how he operated. How he was a Satanist and he drew pentagrams in lipstick on the dead thighs of women he'd raped. Criminologists talked about how most killers were slowly made that way, but sometimes you got one that was pure. A monster born, rather than a monster evolved. Think of the difference between Mr. Hyde and Frankenstein.

The news said to keep your doors and windows locked. Buy an alarm. Consider painting your house brown, with green trim.

The voice of my mom came carried by the breeze, saying," I think I like forest green more than eucalyptus, but I don't think it goes as well with sandstone."

And my aunt's voice came, "Don't you think sandstone is too close to yellow anyway?"

She said, "At night, you probably couldn't even tell the difference."

My brother quietly said, "If any of these people spent a day in prison, they'd know the best security they could get would be to paint a giant pentagram on their garage doors."

He used electric tape to attach the Walkman motor to the bent toothbrush, arranging it so that the spindle was in line with the leg that went down. He said, "Innocence is what makes you a target."

If your eyes traced a line over the patterns of his skin, starting with his elbows, up to the part hidden under the sleeves of his shirt, they might have spotted the bottom leg of a swastika. Thin and bent like the number seven.

After my brother got home from prison he never got out of the bathroom after taking a shower unless he was fully dressed. He never went to the pool, or to the beach, or did anything that'd let you see the marks on his body.

He taped a nine-volt battery to the inside leg of the toothbrush thing, beneath the motor. When the wires bumped into the battery's terminals, the little spindle twirled a hunk of cork, big around as a dime.

He said, "Grab me a pen," and then used his front teeth to pop off the little cap that sealed its back end. He pulled out the thin little tube of ink. He cut the tip of the pen off so the ball at its point rolled out. Dark blue stains rolled out behind it on Mom's table.

I got a handful of paper towels and began cleaning it while he walked into our parents' room. He came back with his hands full of stuff he took from their bathroom - things which he arranged into a neat row on the kitchen table. Cotton balls, baby oil, mirror, shampoo, cough syrup. He added an empty coffee can from underneath the sink.

"The ink in those pens is no good for tattoos," he said, "so we have to make our own."

He soaked some cotton balls with a few drops of baby oil, set them on fire, and then dropped them into the can. He set the mirror facedown over the can so that the smoke would darken the glass.

After the fire burned out, he turned over the mirror. "See all this black? That's carbon. That's our black."

He took the cap from the cough syrup bottle and turned it over on the table, then used the knife to scrape fine black powder off of the mirror and into the cap. Then he began mixing baby oil in with the soot. "To thin this out, just keep adding more oil," he said. "Or, if you need to thicken it, add some of that shampoo."

He gently swirled the cap between his fingers. "I've seen guys mix oil and cough syrup to make red ink. I thought about trying it now, but, nah."

He said, "Now, grab me your guitar."

That summer, on the nights when my dad wasn't home from work and my brother was out late, Mom would make me fall asleep next to her on the couch in the living room. All the shades would be drawn but all the lights would be lit. She'd have the TV on loud enough to be heard from outside. The news anchor saying, "There's something about the summer months that draws these guys out of the woodwork. Ted Bundy. Son of Sam. The Manson murders. We're always talking about July and August."

I sat on her left, because she'd be holding a hammer in her right hand. She always held it backward, so if she was attacked by the killer, she'd bury the forked part in his brain. The way my brother showed her.

My brother, who took my guitar and started twisting the tuning peg of the high e-string. The lightest string on the guitar. He kept twisting until the string when slack, and then he pulled it out of the turning peg. He pulled the pin out of the bridge and the string came free.

He said, "So have you figured out what you want me to put on you?"

Me, all of twelve years old, I said that I wanted Superman's "S."

He grabbed the knife and cut off the twisted end of the string, then pulled it through the hollowed-out pen. He bent the very tip of the guitar string to a right angle. The number seven. Then he shoved the bent part through the cork, just off of center.

When he briefly touched the wires to the battery, the cork began to spin and the guitar string reciprocated up and down through the pen. "There," he said, "rotary to linear."

He electric-taped the pen to the toothbrush, down the leg of it. He made a final cut so that the end of the guitar string became a needle point sticking about an eighth of an inch out from the pen.

He said, "The Superman 'S' huh? No pentagrams? No devil faces?"

He dipped the needle into the ink concoction and said, "Okay, so where do you want it?"

And I said, "On my elbow."

He smiled.

My aunt's voice drifted in from outside, saying, "If we ever buy another house, it's going to be as far from the freeway as I can get it."

And my mom said, "You live in Southern California, doll, there's no such thing as a house far from a freeway."

"Well, maybe I could find a place that isn't right in the middle of so many."

By the time I was nineteen years old, I could use the veins on the back of my hand to find my way to the old house. It was a freckle off the fifty-seven, between the ninety-one and the twenty-two.

My brother told me to fold one of my arms so that my hand gripped the shoulder. He said to put my elbow on the table. He said, "This is going to hurt."

He said, "A lot. Try not to scream or we'll both get in trouble."

That summer some guy came in from the street and slept on our couch. Someone my brother knew. This guy, he had stubble poking soft and blonde through his scalp.

He slept on our couch that night because he didn't have anywhere to go, and it was monster season outside. If you traced a straight line up from his hands, you'd find large patches of cough-syrup red beginning just beneath his elbows.

My brother saw the new tattoos and asked, "Does the red actually cover up the other stuff?"

The man replied, saying, "Some of the smaller things, yeah. I had to use black for the worst ones though."

My brother closed his hands over his shirtsleeves. His gaze lingered on the fabric, as if he could see the marks that his clothes kept hidden.

The man rubbed his scalp. The television droned on. Then the man spoke softly, "He's out now."

"Who?"

He nodded at my brother's arms. "You know who. The artist. Aaron."

My brother looked at him for a long time before giving a slight nod. He asked, "Where is he sleeping?"

"Far as I know, he doesn't."

And my brother said, "I wouldn't either."

Back in the kitchen, my aunt's voice floated in on the wind. She said, "You ever been to Chino?"

And my mom said, "The prison."

My aunt said, "Of course. Sorry."

My brother got up and slid the window shut, locking their voices outside. He sat back down across from me, taking the tattoo machine in his hands. He stared at me for a long time before saying, "Kid. If you put a person in the wrong place, at the wrong time, in the wrong state of mind, you can turn them into anything."

He said, "If you saw the way they train dogs to fight, you'd understand."

He said, "Now, if you ever do this to someone, never, ever, forget how bad it hurts."

Then he wrapped the wires around the battery and started tracing lines of ink into my elbow. I bit down so hard I could hear my molars groaning over the dull buzz of the needle. Flecks of black spattered over my skin as blood began weeping from the tattoo. The blood and ink mixed into shades of purple while the needle burned. The pain was worse than all the times Mom had to pour peroxide on my scratched-up knees. It was worse than the time I sliced my palm open on the lid from a can of cat food. It was as if

33

every bump and scrape I had accumulated over my twelve years was condensed to a fine point that was now slowly gouging a new wound into my elbow.

Just a rectangle of skin over bone.

My brother stopped long enough to touch my wet cheeks with two of his fingers. He said, "You're okay, kid. You're doing good. We're halfway there."

He said, "You're tougher than everyone in Chino."

Then he sank the needle back into my skin. Carving the diamond shape around the Superman logo.

When he finished the tattoo, it didn't look like much. A black smear that went purple in parts. Small enough to rinse off and cover with a Band-Aid. By the time I'd be nineteen, it would be less than that. A memory of a Saturday instead of a tattoo. A light blue haze to remind me of the summer that the Night Stalker murdered an old woman in our neighborhood.

A woman who lived in a yellow house so close to all those freeways.

The summer when I asked the girl who cut my hair, "What does 'sodomize' mean?"

The summer that my brother still hasn't come back from.

The Band-Aid on my elbow was already catching blue lint that night. After he climbed through the window, after he popped the screen back in, my brother spoke to me through the plastic mesh. He said, "I might not be back before tomorrow morning. Tell Mom and Dad not to worry about me."

And then he said, "Love you, kid. Stay out of trouble."

I shut the window and locked it.

That night my dreams were all about my brother getting caught by the killer on his way to Lucy's.

That summer, that night, my brother borrowed someone's truck and drove the freeways. He went past the dairy fields of Chino and up into parts of Ontario where they collected broken trucks and burning tires. If you were tracing the veins on his hand, you'd follow the fifty-seven, to the ninety-one, all the way to the fifteen.

Now it could be a neighborhood full of track homes and high-speed internet. Back then it was a baked field with corrugated-metal shacks where people would do speed and shoot at the stars. It was where someone named Aaron would sleep, surrounded by his gang of neo-Nazis.

That summer, that night, while the killer was sodomizing the old woman down the street, my brother was carrying the tattoo machine we had made. The next morning my dad would say, "Have you seen the cough syrup?"

And my mom would say, "Do you know where Jack is?"

Somewhere between driving down the freeway and a fifty-year prison sentence, two bodies were found: The old woman that Ramirez had murdered, and a skinhead named Aaron. A man who we later learned had a reputation for torturing other inmates at Chino with a home-made tattoo gun.

When they found him, his eyes were tattooed through their lids. The head of his dick was shriveled up and mangled like hamburger meat. The circle around his asshole was traced cough syrup red. Every part of him was covered in fresh tattoos, down to the last square inches of flesh covering his elbows.

Just skin over bone.

And when they found him, my brother was still on top of him, squatting over his body with the tattoo needle shoved up Aaron's nose, almost deep enough to reach his brain. Bubbles of blood foamed out from his other nostril while the man screamed as loud as the shredded remains of his throat would allow.

Even today, you can still see my tattoo. A black smear that was supposed to be the Superman "S." Most of the time when people ask about it, I just tell them it's an old scar

Ask me if it hurt and I'll tell you yeah.

Yeah, it hurt. Sometimes it still does.

JOSHUA BLAIR

STUDIED WRITING UNDER CHUCK PALAHNIUK, CRAIG
CLEVENGER, AND WILL CHRISTOPHER BAER. AS A
JOURNALIST IN SOUTHERN CALIFORNIA, HE'S INTERVIEWED
ROCK STARS, PROFESSIONAL ATHLETES, AND THE HIGH
PRIEST OF A SATANIC COVEN. HIS THREE NOVELS ARE
RESURRECTING DAPHNE, MARTYR, AND THE DANCING WILLOW.
HE'S CURRENTLY RESEARCHING STANDUP COMEDY AND
THE DEATH OF ELISA LAM IN PREPARATION FOR A NOVEL
TENTATIVELY NAMED FIVE MINUTES ON THE DEAD GIRL.

CAT CALLS

REBECCA JONES-HOWE

The girl is on the Skytrain again. Her red raincoat always pulls my gaze. She smiles through the window. Today her dark hair's tied back. Her lashes are curled and her eyes are lined in black, catty. My fingers tighten around the handle of my briefcase. I swallow before I board.

"You're wearing those pants again," she calls. "I always thought they defined your package real nice."

The other passengers look up. They look at her and then at me, at my black pressed slacks. My throat tightens. My gaze drops to the floor and I take a seat. I set my briefcase over my lap.

"Why don't you sit over here?" the girl asks.

The train starts, its moan filling my ears. It always sounds like a ghost getting off. I lean back against my seat and stare out the window as the train passes through the city and the rain. Then the bells chime and the speaker announces the next stop.

The next station is New Westminster.

The girl gets up. She's all legs under her raincoat. Her thighs are smooth and her calves are lean. Her platform heels click across the floor.

The bells chime again and the doors slide closed. The train starts. The moan continues.

"You never want to talk," the girl says.

My fingers tense and I meet her gaze. "Look, I'm married, alright?"

"That's okay," she says.

"It's not okay," I say. "You've been bothering me all week. I'm just, I'm not interested."

She puts her hand on her hip and her raincoat rides up, revealing the hem of her dress, floral fabric with blues and yellows, baby bedroom colours. She steps forward and straddles my leg. Her thighs rub against my slacks.

The next station is 22nd Street.

The girl leans forward and pushes her knee against my briefcase. The handle digs into my stomach. New passengers board the train, their eyes immediately on me.

"Maybe you should move your briefcase," she says.

I shift and draw a breath, looking up. Her eyes glisten. She bites her lip.

The next station is Edmonds.

"There's a war in your head, isn't there?" She braces her hands over my shoulders, pushes me back against my seat. "It's okay to admit it," she says. "There's a war in every man."

The train slows and I turn my head. Outside, the rain patters against the glass.

"You get off at Commercial-Broadway, right?" She massages my shoulders, her grasp tight, kneading pressure, an ache in my head.

I tighten my fingers around my briefcase.

She leans in closer, her breath hot against my ear. "You wanna get off now, don't you?"

At work, the reception area is decorated with balloons and banners. Everybody jumps out from behind front desk and they yell, "Surprise!"

I hold my briefcase in front of me like I'm still on the train.

Everybody sings Happy Birthday and they give me a card filled with handwritten jokes and sentiments about being over the hill. At lunch, they serve cake in the break room. I bring a slice back to my office but I eat my sandwich instead.

Dick walks past the open door. "Are you not going to eat that?" he asks, looking at the cake on my desk.

I shake my head and he takes the plate. He slices a fork through the red velvet and talks through mouthfuls. "Leslie have plans for you tonight?"

"I don't think so. She's been so preoccupied with that house lately."

"The heritage Victorian on Fourth?"

"Yeah," I say. "She showed it to some buyers who seemed interested. She's been spending all her time working things out."

"That'd be a nice present, hey? A big commission check."

"What do you mean?"

"She must make more money than you, Jason. You can quit your job and live like a kept man."

"That's not funny," I say.

He laughs anyway, and I look over at the phone, remembering how Leslie used to sound when she called, the need that registered in her voice after the failure to conceive, the IVF treatments, the miscarriages, the debt. She used to spend every day at home in her blue bathrobe. It used to be I'd have to spend every lunch hour in my office so she could call. Her voice always shook over the line.

Just tell me everything will be okay.

I look up but Dick's already gone.

The crumbs of my sandwich fall on my lap.

———

The next station is 22nd Street.

The next station is New Westminster.

The next station is Columbia.

It's dark by the time I get off the train. On my way back to the apartment, I walk past Leslie's heritage Victorian. Her picture's on the For Sale sign. She's smiling, blonde hair curled, lips painted red, powerhouse.

My ears start to ache.

Leslie's already asleep when I get home. She's in her baby blue bathrobe, the bedsheets kicked around her feet. Her lamp's still on. It's almost like it used to be, except she's got housing contracts on the nightstand instead of the stack of pregnancy books she used to read.

I crawl beside her and kiss her forehead, her cheek. Her hair smells like lavender. I wrap my arms around her. I press my lips to her ear.

"I love you," I say.

She moans in her sleep. She nudges me with her elbow. She pushes me away.

———

I write strata notices over lunch. Dick walks in and stares at the crumbs on my ledger. "Jesus," he says. "Can't you give yourself a break? It's depressing enough just looking at you."

He drags me with him to the bar after work. He orders a round of Caesars. "If you're man enough, you don't give a shit that it's a cocktail," he says.

I stare at the glass, red thickness like clotted blood, test tube baby waste that goes down salty. Dick flags the waitress and orders us a second round. He looks her over when he orders a third, leans in too close when he orders a fourth. The taste of the Clamato juice settles in my gut.

"How's Leslie?" he asks.

"She was asleep when I got home last night."

He laughs. "You didn't even get laid on your birthday?"

"Why would I care about that?"

"Hey, before Alice and I split, birthdays were about the only time we ever had sex."

A Skytrain passes on the tracks outside the bar, its moan filling my ears.

"I don't really think about things like that. I can't."

Dick looks over.

I shake my head and blink, lightheaded. "All that shit, you know, not being able to conceive. It's kind of insulting. You just, you spend all that money to jack off into a bottle and then they just make a baby in a dish?" My throat tightens. I clear my throat. "Leslie painted the spare room blue and yellow. She always wanted a gender-neutral nursery."

Dick lifts his glass and takes a drink.

Another train passes outside, going the opposite direction. Its ghostly echo haunts like Leslie's voice when she called me at work the first time. She sounded so hollow, so dead.

Jason?

"She wasn't even herself the second time." My gaze drifts to

43

the red mess in Dick's glass. "She called me every day when it got worse, you know. Then I got home from work and she was hunched over the counter."

Dick sets his glass down. He scratches his brow.

"Seeing her go through all that, I just, I did what I could."

"She reinvented herself," Dick says, staring down at the table, his fingers flinching. "You have to, after something like that."

"Yeah." I shake my head. "It's just, she didn't even tell me about becoming a Realtor until she got her license. She just said she was going to make the spare room her office. She painted the walls grey."

I sway on the platform until the train arrives. The first thing I notice is the raincoat. The girl is slouched in her seat. She tugs at the zipper, opens her coat to reveal her tight dress, her figure. I avert my gaze and slump into the nearest seat, setting my briefcase on the floor. The train starts and the briefcase tips over. I pick it up and set it on the empty seat beside me.

The girl walks up. She pushes the case aside and sits down.

"You're drunk," she says.

"So what?"

The train is nearly empty, just a handful of students with headphones in their ears. I stare at the reflection in the window of me slouched in my seat, her beside me. She crosses her legs. Her skirt rides up. She's wearing black panties. They're lace.

"What were you drinking?" she asks.

My ears throb to the pace in chest.

"Caesars," I say.

"That's not a very manly drink."

"So?"

She puts her hand on my thigh. "I like you better this way," she says. "You're a white flag."

The taste of the Caesar lingers in my throat. "What do you want?" I ask.

Her fingers tighten. "Tell me something," she says. "Tell me a secret. Drunk men always share secrets."

My gaze drifts to my briefcase. "I turned forty this week."

She draws a breath and her grasp moves from my leg to my hand. She touches the ring on my finger. "Did your wife give you birthday sex?"

"No." I pull my hand away.

"Why not?" she asks. "Married men still like pussy."

The train turns a bend, squealing on the tracks.

She leans in, her lips against my ear again, her voice a whisper. "How big is your dick?"

My head hurts too much to answer.

The next station is Columbia.

Her fingers trace along the crease Leslie ironed into my slacks. The train slows and the doors open. I reach for my briefcase.

"You're losing," she says.

"Losing what?" I ask, stumbling to a stand.

She glances at the briefcase. "You always look so miserable carrying that thing."

I stagger out of the train before the doors close. She smiles through the window. The train pulls out of the station and I blink, trying to rid the stain of her raincoat from my gaze.

⎯⎯⎯⎯

There's a sticker on the sign in front of Leslie's heritage house, SOLD written in bold block letters. She pounces on me when I get home.

"Baby, it finally happened!" she says.

She's in black lace lingerie, but the dark overpowers her. She always looked better in baby blues. She claws at my chest, undoes the buttons on my shirt. The briefcase slips from my grasp. It hits the floor, the bang heavy in my ears.

Leslie shoves me against the wall.

You're a white flag.

"I want to celebrate," she says. Her lavender scent brings a headache.

In the bedroom, she climbs on top of me and writhes. She arches her back. She shakes the bed, moans in my ear, distorted sounds like the Skytrain.

Married men still like pussy.

My lungs ache when I inhale. My grasp tightens around her waist. She tilts her head back, braces her thighs around me. It's the way it always is now, her hands on my chest, pushing me down. She groans when she comes.

"God, baby," she says. "We never do this enough."

She makes it worse.

———

The next station is Patterson.

The next station is Joyce-Collingwood.

The next station is 29th Avenue.

The girl isn't on the train, but I leave my briefcase on my lap and I look out at every platform for her red raincoat, her bare legs.

The next station is Nanaimo.

The next station is Commercial-Broadway.

The train slows and I grip the nearby pole and stand, gravity pulling me. The bells chime. The doors slide open. The rustle of people. The city's busiest station, bodies and red all over.

You wanna get off now, don't you?

———

There's a dent on the side of my briefcase. It's difficult to get open. The papers are scattered inside, a mess of tenant applications, noise complaints and rental contracts. I work through all of it. I call references. I set up appointments. I answer every complaint with sympathy.

I'm a joke of a property manager, eating lunch at my desk.

———

There's take-out Indian food on the counter when I get home.

Leslie clears her housing contracts off the table. She lays out a white tablecloth and serves tikka masala over rice. The food burns my throat. I stare at the plate, wincing against my headache, the pressure.

There's a war in your head, isn't there?

My fingers flinch around my fork. I set it down, getting sauce on the tablecloth. "So, this is stupid," I say. "There's this, well, there's this girl on the train sometimes."

Leslie looks up.

"She just, she says things to me."

"Like what?"

I shrug and shake my head. "Just how good my pants look. She asks me how big my dick is."

"Seriously?" Leslie asks.

"It's gone on all week," I say. "It's kind of degrading, really."

"Oh, come on," she says.

"Haven't men ever made cat calls at you?"

"Just ignore her, Jason."

"What do you think I've been doing?"

"She's probably just teasing you." Leslie buries her fork in the red on her plate. She slices through a piece of chicken. "Just take the compliment and move on," she says, laughing.

———

At the bar, I empty the dregs from the beer pitcher into my glass.

"You know, the thing about Leslie?" I say. "She always gave terrible blow jobs."

"You two have a fight or something?" Dick asks.

A SkyTrain passes outside, moaning.

"Are you having an affair?" he asks.

"No," I say.

"Are you considering it?"

"No." I finish my beer, hesitating. "I still love her."

"Yeah, that's what I told myself at first," he says. "I spent years telling myself that, but with the kids grown up there was nothing to look forward to. I'd come home and Alice would have dinner ready. She'd ask me about work and I wouldn't even want to have a conversation with her. The girl at Subway was more interesting to talk to." He shrugs. "Things just happened. No sense in denying it. There was so much shit in my head."

"What about when Alice found out?" I ask.

"Honestly, it was really just a relief," he says, leaning back in his chair. He whistles at the waitress and holds up his empty glass. He thinks he's a real man, but he ogles the waitress's chest when he orders another Caesar.

———

The last train of the night arrives. The girl's there, bare legs crossed, her raincoat undone. She's wearing her yellow and blue dress. The fabric clings to her figure.

Just take the compliment and move on.

The doors slide closed behind me. The girl looks up. She smiles and my headache starts to ease. I stumble across the car, slipping into the seat beside her. I drop my briefcase on the floor.

"What are you doing?" she asks.

"I don't know."

The train whirs to life.

"I like you drunk," she says. She touches my leg, runs her fingers along the crease I had to iron in because Leslie never has the time. "You look so good in black slacks."

She takes my hand. My fingers slip between hers.

"I like men like you," she says. "I like your business wear and tear, the tortured look on your face. I like your briefcase. You always look so miserable and it makes me so wet."

The next station is Royal Oak.

She parts her legs. Her thighs are pale and she runs her fingers up. She isn't wearing panties. The train slows and she slides her fingers into her folds.

"What's your name?" she asks.

"Jason," I say.

The train starts again, its moan echoing.

The girl pulls my hand between her open legs. "Do you wanna know what I feel like?"

Her skin's warm, soft. I slide my palm up her thigh and under her dress. She's smooth, her inside an abyss, slick lips warming my fingers. I stare out the window at the passing blur of all the shitty apartments that I control.

She leans in. Her lips brush against my ear. "How big is your dick, Jason?"

The next station is Patterson.

"It's six inches," I say.

"Is that not big enough for your wife?"

My throat tightens. "It used to be."

The train shakes as it slows. I slip against her. She smells like rainwater.

People board, their gazes falling toward her open legs. She clutches my hand before I can pull away.

"Let them look," she says. "Let them think what they want. I just want you to do this for me."

The train starts. My headache starts.

"Please," she begs. "Please."

She grinds herself against my palm. My thumb slips against her clit and she moans.

"Right there," she says. Her breaths are heavy, just like Leslie's when she used to call. She grips my hand. She's shaking.

Just tell me everything will be okay.

I rub her harder, thumbing circles, pushing down, two fingers buried inside of her and she writhes in the seat. Her moan echoes with the Skytrain. I lean over her, feeling her breath against my neck. Her grasp tightens. She digs her nails into my wrist and she fills the train with her moan.

The next station is Columbia.

The train slows and I look up. The other passengers turn their heads.

The girl exhales, her chest heaving. "You're so good," she says. Her fingers loosen and I pull my hand away.

My palm's still wet, smelling of her.

I bury my hand in my pocket, leaving the briefcase behind.

———

The sun streams in through the curtains and I roll out of bed with a new headache, the girl's voice in my head.

How big is your dick, Jason?

Leslie's in the bathroom, standing before the mirror in her baby blue robe, her blonde hair tied back.

"Jason?"

I stumble into the hallway and she turns and meets my gaze. Her eyes are bright, glistened with tears. She's holding a pregnancy test and there are two red lines in the oval window.

"Can you read this?" she asks. "I need you to read this." She gives me the test and the box, even though I don't need it to tell me what the two lines mean.

I rub at the stubble on my face. My fingers still smell like pussy.

REBECCA JONES-HOWE

LIVES AND WRITES IN KAMLOOPS, BRITISH COLUMBIA.
HER WORK HAS APPEARED IN PANK, PULP MODERN, AND
PUNCHNEL'S, AMONG OTHERS. HER FIRST COLLECTION OF
SHORT FICTION, VILE MEN, WILL BE OUT IN 2015 FROM
DARK HOUSE PRESS. SHE CAN BE FOUND ONLINE AT
REBECCAJONESHOWE.COM.

CEREMONY

OF THE

WHITE DOG

KEVIN CATALANO

The egg hung in the morning air as though winter had frozen it midflight. It had funneled through the fog of marijuana smoke that ghosted over Chittenango Creek. Brett peered into this smoky cone, and saw on the opposite bank, a slowed-down Dean, unwinding frame-by-frame from his pitcher's hurl. This was Brett's moment of peace, before the world tipped into its sudden violence, and the icy egg crashed into Brett's face.

The pain blazed, every inch of him sizzled. He was positive his head was halved like a melon. He writhed on the ground and held the pulp of his face together. His legs flopped and thrashed as he swam in the bloody slush.

Dean was laughing. Brett heard the scrunch of his retreating footsteps. Then silence. Footsteps coming, and Dean's voice was above.

Don't be a pussy. Get up. Dean kicked his leg. Come on, you're not hurt bad.

Dean's breathing trembled Brett's nerves like thunder. You better not tell your dad. Or you're dead.

Dean was gone. There was only the burble of water slithering beneath crisps of ice. Brett didn't want to move. He would allow his body to empty itself into the creek and curse it.

A voice fell down on him. It was a girl's, "Hey," shrill enough to cut through the cloud of coming-on unconsciousness. But it was familiar, part of the soundtrack of his neighborhood.

Hey. And a dog barked, and Brett knew.

He heard Angela Ruggero struggle down the steep bank, cursing Cauliflower too freely for a twelve-year-old. Come on you bit-chass dog or I'll punt you into the cocksucking creek.

Don't touch me, drummed in Brett's head, hoping it was loud enough for her to hear. He felt a damp nose chilling his ear, wet hairs tickling his cheek.

Get the fuck back, and Cauliflower yelped. A pressure on his shoulder warmed him entirely. Brett? Her voice was suddenly silk-threaded as if another girl spoke for her. Can you hear me? Can you stand?

He thudded his boot to the ground, the meaning of which he didn't know. She must have taken it differently. She was tugging at the shoulders of his coat, grunting, the dog nosing the back of his head.

No, Brett managed to say.

You'll freeze. Angela yanked his chest off the snow. Her strength was unbelievable, and again, he wondered if there were two. Fucking help me goddammit.

Brett put his arms under him in a push up. Once on his knees, he expected his head to roll off his shoulders and shatter. The damage was unknowable, other than the blood goring an unsettling circumference like the inksplot of a giant pen.

Brett was on his feet, though unsteady. Cauliflower was lapping at the red snow, his white muzzle crimsoned like a clown. He felt Angela holding him, guiding him up the slope.

How bad is it? Brett asked.

It's steep.

No, my face.

As if he were a camera, her head came into frame, a close-up. Her grayish eyes squinted; her narrow nose scrunched. Puberty was shaping her—a zit on her forehead, a thickening of her eyebrows, the thinning of her cheeks. The end of a fat, brown braid was in her mouth. When she spoke, it remained tucked in her cheek like Skoal.

You look like a caveman, she said. I think it's an improvement.

Cauliflower led the charge up the bank, fighting against the leash's length. Brett focused on Angela's breathing, the occasional grunt. When he stumbled, she jerked him up and cussed. They reached the top, but they still had Russell Street hill to climb, and another block after that. Brett's face had gone numb. Blood leaked off his nose and chin, speckling the snow. He drifted in and out, held fast to Angela's shoulder.

They were on his doorstep. He couldn't remember getting there. Cauliflower was chewing bald a patch just above his tail.

Angela asked, Is your dad home?

When she again came into his camera view, one side of her knit hat and face were slathered red. She didn't seem to notice, or care. A fantastic tickle flooded Brett's chest, as though someone had opened a liter of soda inside him.

She snapped her fingers in his face. Hello? Caveman?

Brett examined his deformity in the bathroom mirror while masturbating. His reconstructed nose was purple and bloated, halved by a centipede of black stitches. His eyes were a pus color underneath, and the whites were like shitstain. His shiny-swollen brow did, in fact, resemble a caveman's.

He ejaculated without orgasm.

Brett leaned his forehead onto the mirror, pressing the thick, other-feeling wound against the cold glass until his head tingled. Light swarmed behind his eyelids, lasers and orbs.

He left the bathroom, snuck across the hall so his dad wouldn't notice, and went into his bedroom. He circled the cramped space, three or four times, like something caged. There was an overwhelming, unnamable desperation. On his desk littered with empty Skoal canisters and unopened textbooks, he honed in on a protractor, pens, and lighter. He sat and snapped a pen in half. He blew clean an ashtray, then emptied black ink into it. He lit the pointed end of the protractor, blackening the silver. The underside of his left arm was soft and pink. He pressed the point into the skin just below the wrist until the flesh popped and blood bubbled. His hand shook as he dragged the needle through. He then lifted the point, punctured a different spot near the other, and tore a second line. His arm burned as if set aflame. Blood slithered in rivulets. He sopped it with a pair of boxers, then smeared the ink into the cuts. He repeated the design on the other wrist. When he was finished, he laid his two arms on the desk, admiring the emblazoned Xs.

Brett returned to the creek in search of Dean. It was the same early morning as a week ago, the snow on the banks glowing purple. Brett would meet Dean here for their morning routine—smoking a bowl of mediocre weed, then enjoying a refreshing tobacco dip on their walk to school. Brett sat under the bridge on the cold cement landing and packed a bowl, though he had no intention of smoking. He wanted to remain clear-headed now—avoid numbness whenever he could. He itched through his coat at the crusting tattoos. Instead of the Skoal, he lit a stale cigarette he'd found in a forgotten quarter pack in his sock drawer.

The bowl was for Dean.

There remained evidence of the assault, if it could be called that. It looked like a deer had been slaughtered—brown-red smudge and the imprint of a carcass. There was no drip-trail up the bank, which Brett took to mean a part of him hadn't survived.

He didn't spend his time wondering why Dean had done it. Growing up, Brett knew Dean was different—somewhat dangerous—and that he should be left alone. Dean loitered at the Byrne Dairy, stealing money from the kids who came with hopes of buying candy and soda. He had been known to break into cars, and one time the high school, spray painting his name across the basketball court. He set the maintenance building at Sullivan Park on fire, which nearly ignited the forest.

No one at Chittenango High got close to Dean, who was a second-time senior, inching on twenty years old. Brett, a measly 9th grader, was the closest thing to a friend Dean had, and vice versa. This might have something to do with Brett's dad, and the fact that the Chittenango police turned their heads on Brett's public marijuana use, and therefore, Dean's. Brett had hoped this was not the case—that Dean saw something else. Maybe it was that Brett reminded Dean of his brother.

Ten years ago, Dean and his little brother were abducted. They were stuffed into the trunk of a car and held in a cabin on Oneida

Lake. The story—now part of Chittenango lore—went that Dean managed to rescue his brother's body, swimming him two miles through the lake. When Dean appeared on his parent's doorstep in the early morning, cradling his wet, stiff brother, he'd apparently said—though Brett had his doubts about this, "We're home."

There was a side of Dean, however, that only Brett saw, or so he wanted to think. Sometimes, out of nowhere, Dean seemed to revert back to a younger self. Brett knew it was happening when Dean got a soft, wet-eyed look, and wouldn't speak for a while. He appeared lost and quietly frightened, as though he had suddenly found himself in a different time. What triggered this shift Brett didn't know, but he liked to think that Dean was gifted, like a troubled superhero, with the ability to move through his own history with a simple glance back or forward.

Dean usually came out of this trance by punching Brett in the arm, or recruiting him to vandalize something. Or, just as often, Dean would leave unannounced, as if Brett was never there.

Out of boredom, Brett stood and began searching for the egg that had damaged him. He raked his boot across the surface of the snow, which scattered like billions of sand-sized crystals. This meant it was getting warmer—the first sign that winter might actually pass. He found nothing but some pinkish slush. So he climbed the slope, crossed the bridge, and descended to the other creek bank. There, he found a cache of eggs, plugged into a mound of snow in a neat, violent row. Brett plucked one out, harder somehow than rock. He wound up and whipped the egg across the creek, aiming for his old self. The egg smacked into the bridge's support.

Get up pussy, Brett called in a different pitch. You're not hurt.

He grabbed another one and hurled it harder.

You better not tell your dad or I'll kill you.

There were many more eggs, and endless self-loathing. But no more time.

He climbed the bank, and left the packed bowl for Dean.

⸻

His return to school was torturous. When he passed girls in the hall, they scurried from him, gag-laughing. The guys treated him like a minor celebrity, crowding his locker and seeking details of the assault as if he had fingered one of the girls from the JV soccer team. Where once Brett would have been thrilled for this attention, today he was repulsed. He might have told them, he couldn't exactly recall, that the kingdom of heaven is at hand.

Dean hadn't shown. He wasn't in the corner of the school parking lot where the smokers smoked and compared butterfly knives. Nor was he lifting his baggy jeans over his butt in the back of the football field, where the chain-link fence divided school grounds from the cemetery, the designated spot for fights. On the way home, Brett walked by the Byrne Dairy, then the creek again—but there was no sign. The bowl hadn't been touched.

He did, however, see Angela.

She was at the top of Russell Street, tugging at Cauliflower who was chewing his ass. When Brett saw her, he stopped, considered turning back. But she looked up. He pulled his hood down as far as it could go and tucked it behind his ears. He walked past her—Cauliflower nipping his boot laces—and said, Hey.

Hey? she said. I save your cockass and all you can say is *Hey*?

Brett stopped. The cool gray of her eyes seemed to reflect into her hair, giving it an unnaturally silver tint.

Want to lick my scar?

Gross.

He smiled, and she quickly added, Maybe I'll French kiss it instead.

Brett laughed before he could call it back. He didn't like to laugh.

Cauliflower saw a squirrel and growled. The dog darted for it, but Angela yanked so hard Cauliflower somersaulted. She crouched down, grabbed his muzzle, and said, I hate you, fucking dog. Cauliflower got hold of the fingertip of her glove and pulled. Goddamn stupid cockbitching . . . and that's all she had.

So you're a dog person.

He's Trent's dog. She put the icy-stiff end of her pigtail in her mouth and sucked. He's too lazy to take care of him.

Trent was Angela's mother's boyfriend who moved in a year ago. He worked nights tending bar at the Ten Pin. During the day he drank beers in the garage while painting historical murals of the village for the upcoming bicentennial. These were commissioned by none other than Brett's dad, who—like everyone else in the neighborhood—had noticed Trent's skill with the brush.

Why don't you let me take care of Cauliflower?

Angela squinted.

I'll tie his leash to the bridge and toss him over. It'll look like a suicide.

Angela's eyes got wide—with more light, the gray turned green. She said, We could give him some Tums, see if his stomach explodes.

Pour honey into his ears, then dump fire ants inside, Brett added. Watch him get eaten inside out.

Dip his paws in gasoline and set them on fire. See how fast he runs before burning up.

Brett was in love.

Cauliflower had his leg up in the air and was licking.

Well? Brett said.

Well what?

Which is it going to be?

She sucked hard at her pigtail, tired eyes staring at the curb.

Trent gives me ten bucks a week to look after shit-for-brains, she said. I'm not going to off my only source of income, not in this economy.

Again, Brett laughed. A twelve-year-old who watched the news? He wanted to make a joke about the stimulus bill or government bailouts, but couldn't piece one together. What remained was an awkward space to fill. A car drove by and a high school dick leaned out the window. Fuck her in the butt! Cauliflower barked, which, for once, was welcomed.

I gotta go, Brett said.

Yeah. Then Angela added when Brett's back was turned, If you think of other ways to torture a dog, let me know.

Will do. Brett cringed at his father's stupid expression.

———

Brett woke to his windowsill pillowed with six inches of snow. Heavy flakes fell as though the clouds had exploded into pieces. People would soon be out in this pre-coffee, heavy coats thrown over pajamas, armed with shovels as their cars warmed to escape for work.

Someone trudged through the street, phantomed by the flakes that whitewashed his form. The cigarette dangling from lips, the long skeleton stride, the hoisting of jeans up over the butt—it was Dean.

Brett scrambled to get his clothes on. He darted to the front door, jammed his feet into his boots and stumbled outside before they were fully on. The falling snow made a curtain of white and gray, impossible to see a great distance. He high-stepped down the driveway to the street. Dean's boot tracks were already filling. Brett hurried after them, but the flakes were dizzying. He could no longer tell which direction was which, whether behind him was his house, or if it was ahead. He smelled cigarette smoke. He thought he'd collide into Dean at any moment. He called to him, but the snow muffled his voice as if he had yelled into a pillow. He tried again, and thought he heard a response. He tried to run, but only advanced a few steps and fell. His bare hands were hot with cold. He tried to get up, but felt cemented. In the swirling white ahead, there might have been a figure, and it might have been coming, or going.

———

Trent tipped a can of beer into his mouth, and then went into the mini fridge for more. Brett knew it would be empty. He'd been counting on it. Trent set his brush down on the workbench and put on his Bills coat. He checked his pockets for car keys and wallet. Cauliflower lifted his head from his paws. Trent spoke to him, then got into his rusted Crown Victoria and drove off. Brett had also counted on his leaving the garage door open. The Trents of the world were predictable.

Already in his coat and boots, and with a red duffel bag under his arm, Brett hurried outside and across the street. The neighborhood was quiet, everyone at work. Brett had skipped school for this. When he stepped inside the garage, Trent's presence smacked immediately, as though he hadn't left. It felt like Brett was occupying someone else's body, a creepy sensation that nearly caused him to turn right back around.

Cauliflower watched as Brett unlatched the door of the cage. He put his hand under the dog's tender belly, lifted him out, and then placed him inside the duffel bag. Cauliflower seemed to expect this.

Brett hurried out of the garage. When he was a couple houses away, he quit his half-jog and continued casually toward the creek. He tried to empty his head. He had already convinced himself that this was the right thing. Angela needed to be unburdened, and he knew she wasn't capable of doing it herself. He could then find a job, give her fifteen dollars a week instead of ten. Hopefully, this would get her to fall for him.

The snow was wet, slicking his way down the slope. The creek had nearly overcome the ice—it would any day now. When it did, it would flow north. Everyone born here knew that. Which way other water ran in other towns, Brett didn't know.

He set the bag down on the stony bank. When he opened it, Cauliflower's twitching nose emerged, sniffing hard. Brett's temples thumped as he put his hands around the dog's muzzle. The bones pricking through the fur felt like a smaller creature's—a squirrel's maybe. Cauliflower licked Brett's palm as he squeezed. The cold gums slimed; the teeth felt like a string of wet pearls. The black, glistening eyes looked at Brett as if to say it understood why it should die, that its existence was torturous.

What you got there?

Brett fell over the duffel bag. Cauliflower barked at Dean sitting in the shadows under the bridge. A dense cloud of smoke circled his body like aura. Dean used both hands to get to his feet, then pulled his jeans over his butt. He walked dreamily forward. His eyes under his baseball cap were wide and teary. A dog? he said.

Brett was soaked from the snow. He got to his knees and held the dog's collar so he wouldn't escape. He said, It's my neighbor's.

Dean sat cross-legged in front of the duffel bag. He put a chapped, purplish hand on the dog's head. Cauliflower licked Dean's wrist and Dean smiled.

Can I hold it?

Sure, Brett whispered.

Dean pulled Cauliflower from the bag and embraced him. He nestled his face into the thick fur of Cauliflower's neck. A low purr came out of Dean. Brett remained still, mesmerized, as if witnessing a rare natural occurrence. Dean gazed into the blue, cloudless sky—or through it, into another place. His jaw was working something out, as if he was reading to himself. Brett watched carefully as Dean's eyes began to narrow and harden. His lips clenched into a thin line. He noticed the dog, squeezed him, smirked. He then looked at Brett, who could see Dean was returning from wherever he was.

The fuck happened to you? said Dean, staring a hole into Brett's face.

Brett raised his hood and tucked it behind his ears. He couldn't meet Dean's eyes. You did this.

The egg? Dean laughed. That really fucked you up.

Brett sank deeper into himself.

Dean held Cauliflower away from him and swung the dog's legs from side to side as though it were dancing. This is a shit-ugly dog, he said. What're you doing with it?

Brett wiggled a stone free from the icy ground and tossed it at the creek. I'm going to kill it.

Dean's expression froze, where Brett thought he might have been disturbed. Then, a smile crawled up into his cheeks and his eyes twinkled. He simply said, Yes.

Things began moving quickly.

Dean brought Cauliflower to the creek and kicked a hole into the thin ice. He plunged the dog in. The water was only deep enough to submerge Cauliflower's head and shoulders, while his hind legs fought against Dean's chest. Dean was unsatisfied with this, and removed him. Cauliflower licked the water from his muzzle.

Hey dipshit, Dean said, not even looking at Brett. Get me the bowl.

This wasn't going how Brett wanted, even though there wasn't a plan. At the very least, he was the one who needed to decide Cauliflower's fate—for Angela. If it wasn't him, it defeated the whole purpose. Still, refusing Dean was nearly impossible.

He brought the bowl to Dean, whose arms were full with wet, shivering dog.

Light it for me.

Brett held the pipe to Dean's mouth and fired the lighter. Brett watched Dean's sucking lips. He tried to remain casual, but his belly was flipping at the thought of how far this could go.

Dean held Cauliflower by the neck, and spit a thick fog of smoke into his face. Cauliflower bared his teeth and growled. Then he whipped his head side to side and barked in high pitches as though badgered by fleas.

Dean laughed. What else can we do to it?

Cauliflower was panting, looking in Brett's general direction, but at nothing really.

Hey Brett. Dean said his name without irony, as though he'd been saying it for years—longer than they'd known each other. As though they shared a bedroom and parents, and this was how Dean would have always addressed him.

What else should we do to this dog? asked Dean in earnest.

Brett scratched at the arm-scabs through his coat.

Zip him inside the bag, he said darkly. We'll stone him.

Dean was giddy. He pressed Cauliflower into Brett's arms and then searched the ground for rocks. The dog shivered, but was otherwise listless. Brett placed him inside the duffel bag, and felt each zipper tooth clicking in his fingers as Cauliflower disappeared.

A rock smacked the heel of Brett's boot.

Get out of the way. Dean was about to hurl another.

Brett joined him and watched as Dean missed. He tried again—throwing so hard he fell forward. The rock landed in the creek.

Dean said from the ground, You were easier to hit than that fucking thing. He smiled. I got you first try.

As though his head were stuck inside a colossal, clock tower bell at noon, Brett was deafened by a riotous clang. His body knew it, but it took his brain a frantic moment to understand how furious Dean's statement had made him. He was struck dumb by it, wrenched from the scene and ringing as he watched Dean from a distant place.

Dean brushed away snow, revealing a rock the size of a cinderblock. This will do it. He stood and bent his knees to lift. He waddled to the bag with the rock knocking between his knees. The bag bulged at one end, and Brett heard—beyond the thrumming adrenaline shaking him—the scraping of claws on nylon. Dean grunted the rock up to his chest, then like an Olympic weight lifter, pushed it over his head. Dean wavered, stepped backward to regain his balance. His boot hit Brett's, who had come up behind him and grabbed hold of the rock. Brett's hands overlapped Dean's; his nose grazed the back of Dean's neck.

The fuck? Dean grunted through biting teeth.

Brett said to the back of his head, Why'd you do it?

What?

They both wobbled underneath the rock's weight.

Did you want to get rid of me?

Dean's elbows rattled. Brett began to relinquish more weight to him.

Brett.

Did you want me dead?

Brett, please.

He let go, and the rock dropped square on top of Dean's head. What came from Dean, as if out of his stomach, was a guttural *Huhn*. He pitched backward into Brett, and both fell to the ground. Dean was face down and contorted like a corpse. Brett was strangely calm. Someone like Dean couldn't die that easily. He'd been through far worse than this, and maybe his life had already been taken all those years ago.

Still, Brett turned him and put his ear to Dean's chest. The heart was strong. It lulled Brett, softened his insides. When else had he been this close to Dean? To any other person for that matter? Brett's head gravitated towards Dean's face, the excuse being—if anyone was looking, or if Dean happened to wake—that he was listening for breath. Dean's cheeks were cool, stubbled with acne and whiskers. He couldn't smell him, but imagined that it was sharp, tangy sweat and marijuana. He positioned himself onto Dean, shivering so hard he was afraid his clattering teeth would rouse him. Brett shuttered as he grazed Dean's flaking lips with his. A blossoming in his stomach reached between his legs, into which he was succumbing, losing himself. He pressed his mouth onto Dean's, pushed his tongue inside. He ventured deeper so that their teeth clinked, so that he could lick the throat. His erection was violent, and he thrust into Dean's crotch. Not enough, not nearly. He unzipped his jeans, unzipped Dean's, put his erection into Dean's zipper, the slit of his boxers. His nudged the moist, deadened pearl-head. His jabbed and bullied it awake. His fought and fought, looking to kill and the thrill that comes from it. By the time he found resistance, he was already coming into the thick coils of pubic hair.

Brett was heaving into the hot yawn of his mouth. He tasted copper. He looked at Dean's lips, bloodied teeth marks.

He expected Dean to be awake, to acknowledge what they'd shared. Dean's arms, however, remained stretched out on the ground, palms up Christ-style. His jaw slack, eyeball whites peeking like moon slivers.

Brett draped Dean's limp arms over his back. He put his legs up on Dean's so his entire body lay flush on his. He nuzzled his head just under Dean's chin and tried to allow the slow, deep heartbeat to carry him away. It was then that Brett noticed the rock lying smack in the middle of the duffel bag. He watched it for many heartbeats, but there was no movement.

———

The doorbell. Angela stood on the front porch, manically zipping her coat up and down, chewing her pigtail.

Where's my dog?

The fear wetting her eyes, the panic raising her voice—she was still a girl. The world was still a good place. She had a long way to go to thirteen, when things would begin to unravel and the ugliness would be revealed.

A single look told he'd misinterpreted her, terribly.

You're a sick freak. She flung around, pigtails whipping dramatically. She marched down his driveway and across the street to her yard.

Brett wished he could call out to say he had Cauliflower in the house. He'd invite her in and reveal the dog, wagging its stub of a tail. Angela would give Brett a long, honest hug, then go to Cauliflower. There was a tin of cocoa mix in the cupboard left over from when his mom still lived there. He'd make some for Angela the right way, on the stove with milk, and that would be the beginning of something. It would be their strange story of how they found each other.

———

These mornings made long shadows, birdsong and mosquitoes. The moon was a milky stamp in the bluing sky.

Brett leaned over the rail of the bridge, looking down on the creek. The water had broken through the ice and foamed in its rush. A crowd of birds riddled the bank on Dean's side of the creek, pecking at the thawed, rocky ground. They fought each other for something, hopping and biting, flinging white chips like confetti. It was the eggs, broken open and runny. Brett could only imagine the terrible smell that brought the swarming fruit flies competing with the birds. On the opposite bank, a single egg was split, spilling its snotty, black innards. Three birds pecked hungrily at this rotten meal.

Brett had come back for the duffel bag, and its contents. He'd considered leaving it, fearing this return, but decided he didn't want Angela to stumble on the body of her dog. The bag, however, wasn't there. In its place was the large rock, which radiated the memory of Dean. He couldn't look at it. He hoped any evidence of the event, including that which hid inside him, had gone with winter.

Something spooked the birds on this side of the creek. Dean emerged from under the bridge. He held Cauliflower in his arms like a football. The dog was very much alive, his cottony tail flailing. Brett stepped back so Dean wouldn't see him. Dean stooped, and Cauliflower leapt from his arms and sniffed the split egg, then sneezed. He spotted the multitude of birds on the opposite bank.

Cauliflower darted into the water up to his belly and barked high-pitched and crazed.

The birds took off into noisy flight. Collectively, they skimmed the water going northward, then darted up above the budding trees. As they ascended high into the atmosphere, their shape accordioned—thinning out, then bunching—as if they were showing Brett how to breathe.

KEVIN CATALANO

WAS BORN AND RAISED IN CHITTENANGO, NEW YORK, A
SMALL VILLAGE THAT CELEBRATES THE BIRTHPLACE OF
WIZARD OF OZ AUTHOR L. FRANK BAUM. HE IS THE AUTHOR
OF THE WORD MADE FLESH, A COLLECTION OF DARK FLASH
FICTION. OTHER STORIES HAVE APPEARED IN PANK,
BOOTH, PEAR NOIR!, ATTICUS REVIEW, GARGOYLE MAGAZINE,
FRIGG, AND MANY OTHERS. HIS STORIES HAVE ALSO BEEN
ANTHOLOGIZED IN PRESS 53'S SURREAL SOUTH '13 AND IN
FIDDLEBLACK ANNUALS #1 AND #2. HARASS HIM AT
WWW.KEVINCATALANO.COM.

THE

ARMADILLO

HEATHER FOSTER

bought you a junkyard. You've said twice you want one. Texas is bigger, more lonesome than you thought. You show it nights, when we cut loose on back roads in the Chevy. We go at it so hard in the dusty bed, you shake out sand from my hair like stars, a glitter against the skin. Anything to connect, to constellate. Half of me did it because you wanted one. The other half? I thought of how much I could bury.

An old man sold it to me. "I'm asking a grand. Wife's got the cancer. Gotta let it go." He was short for a man, and skinny, mid-sixties, but blue-eyed and handsome enough to make a habit out of getting his way.

"Seven's the best I can do."

"You can't bullshit a bullshitter, lady. You got more than that somewhere." He slid off the rickety barstool, smiling and squinting a little, moving to pull the door shut. "Damn sun. Eyes can't take it." There was a rip in the black faux leather seat and someone had duct taped it. He sat again and unzipped his fly. "Seven hundred, huh?"

He threw in a blue VW van that won't run. Something about the transmission. I used to think I'd drive a van like that if my name had been Summer, if I'd had redder hair. But I'm a Sadie, through and through. Girl's choice, saddle-tough, sadistic even? Hell, it is what it is. My momma knew.

I checked the dump out after I bought it. A half dozen cars, some busted tires, a backhoe shovel. The small pond in front's full of scrap metal, nothing but turtles and algae living in it; maybe a cottonmouth when it warms up some.

The back border is marked by a hill of garbage and unmatched shoes. An armadillo lives on one side in a corduroy couch. Did you know they smell bad? Faster than shit, too. On my seventh Thanksgiving, an armadillo ran across the yard and my big brother made me chase it. I was a fat kid, did I ever tell you that? Fat and slow. The critter was long gone before I tripped over the bottom step and rolled into wet grass, before my brother kicked me in the back with his work boot. When I caught my breath, I smelled the animal's wet rot in the fog. It was scared of me, too.

———

It was somewhere around Little Rock, fourteen hours in, when I knew. I stopped to let you pee and you looked surprised it was a woman that took you.

"Ma'am?"

Listen. Right then I was still thinking of the clean wet slap of aluminum bats.

"Where you taking me?"

Seventh grade. Toby Hatton with his hand down my best pair of panties—lilac satin bikinis, white bows on the sides. I got wet and it grossed him out.

"What do you want with me?"

We went walking up the road instead—me with a dead piece of vine, him with a ball bat—bashing the heads of roadkill.

"Won't you please turn me loose?"

Your hair's got a lot of blonde in it, but it didn't show in the dark when I snatched you. I didn't like the way you looked in the daylight. Too young. Eighteen, twenty maybe. You can't fake a feeling like that. Not like I did in Macon. Fuck that.

I told you to keep quiet, and you did, turning your back and pissing in the grass behind the truck. You were trying to use your manners to get out of a tough spot. I understood. You thought you could good-boy-voice me till I gave in. But it wasn't that. I hope you know it wasn't that that did it. It was—and I didn't want to admit it till now—I was lonesome. Jesus! A girl like me, lonesome. But I was. For the first time, I'd picked one that didn't remind me of him, at least not in the light, and I should have known but I thought maybe. Maybe just a few days, just to pass the time, and then I'd move on. So I let you climb in the cab with me and you puked bile onto the floorboard and blacked out.

———

The first one I took was Jason. They say it's harder when you know them, when you see expressions you shouldn't ever see on a face you know like the crook of your own elbow. For me, it was different. Jason was easy. I knew exactly what kind of a son of a bitch he was. The farther I got from home, the less I liked it.

It was easy enough finding the Jasons—crooked grin, a little skinny, and some darkness in the eyes—the kind of boy who takes pieces of girls and never gives them back. The kind of boy who isn't big enough to make you do what he wants with just his body, so he learns all the tricks. The older boy who pretends to be your age—

you just thought he had a mean daddy—until you're gagging on his cock and he's laughing, telling you the truth as he comes in your throat. The kind of boy—and you know this is pathetic—you'd have gotten naked with again if he'd let you.

But a doppelganger isn't good enough. They can't just favor him. They have to become him. So I fuck with them, push their buttons, piss them off, and the switch flips. And then they can tell me no, and I can do what I want with their bodies.

—————

Around the Oklahoma line, you came to.

"You got sick back there," I said, watching the road.

"Where are we going?"

"You got all stirred up. Try to keep your nerves about you if you can."

"Who are you?"

"You ask too many goddamn questions. You need to eat something." I passed you the bag of chips and the water thermos. You took them.

For a while, you stared out the window with your forehead pressed to the glass. When I turned off the CB, you whimpered, "I'm Kent! I'm an only child. They'll be looking for me."

My backhand knocked you out for 30 miles.

—————

There was a rabbit, half a deer, and an armadillo. Guess which skull I smashed.

Halfway across Texas. I-40. Dust dry heat. Dusk. We made camp in the truck for the night at a KOA under the stars. You ate the chips.

"So who are you?" You wiped the powdered cheese on your pants leg.

"What a waste. I always lick it off when I eat them."

"I don't like it by itself."

"My name's Sadie." I passed you the thermos. Air whistled through the spout as you drank.

"Well just what are we doing out here? Are we running from somebody? Do you need money or something?"

Not the one you think. Trick question.

"Kent?"

"Yeah?"

"If you could have anything in the world, Kent, what would it be?"

"Listen, I just wanna go home! I've got a whole life back there. I've got... I'm an only child. They will have noticed it by now. That I'm missing." You were rubbing your cuffed wrist raw on the steel.

"What would it be? Shut up about home. Pick something real."

In third grade, I wrote a report on armadillos. When they come to a body of water, they have two choices: walk across the bottom and hope they make it, or inflate their intestines and swim across.

As if remembering being told once to cooperate with a hijacker, you settled down. "I guess a junkyard, then. See the weird stuff people toss."

"You've never been told no, have you Kent? I bet you never heard no in all your life."

⸻

The next day, we got an early start. I wanted to make it to Sedona before sunset, show you a saguaro the size of a grown man, the rocks you'd swear were painted.

It was almost like you'd forgotten about home, until we ran out of food in the truck and I had to press a .38 to your back in the drive-thru to keep you from squawking out the truth like a stolen parrot.

I drove hungry till I found a spot we could park and eat. I holstered the gun. "I hope you know I wouldn't have done that if I'd thought you could keep a secret," I said, taking a fat bite of burger.

"I'm still not sure what the secret is."

"Kent, you ever had a girl get a hold of you so good, you'd do anything for her, even if it hurt you real bad?"

"You ain't gotta hurt me like he hurt you, Sadie. Whoever it was. If that's what you're thinkin'."

I slapped the horn, "Answer! The goddamn question! I don't need a fuckin' shrink."

You kept quiet then, for a long time, just wiping the burger's mustard off your lip with the back of your hand, then licking it. "Naw," you said, staring into the rippling horizon of rocks and hot dust, "I don't guess I ever felt that way about a girl yet."

———

The scene in the truck pushed us back a day. We never made it out of Texas. That night, under the stars again, but this time in an empty field half a mile off-road, a few tumbleweeds rolling past. You said you'd only seen them in the movies.

"Kent, I wish you'd lived your whole life alone in the desert. I wish you never had to know about pain." We sat in the cab this time, till you fell asleep and I followed, lulled by the truck's Tejano static.

The next morning, we woke up with our sides pressed together, and I told you things about Jason. I put my hand high up on your leg. "No!" you screamed out twice, backing against the door, "Don't touch me!"

I slid across the slick bench to my side of the cab.

"Listen," you said, a little afraid of us both, "I'm real sorry about what that boy did to you, but you're sick, lady. You need some help." I didn't move. "You can't just go around snatching people up, driving them into the desert and shit. I mean shit!" It was happening, the thing I'd hoped would happen when I'd snatched you back in Little Rock. But this time, I was wishing like hell it would stop.

"Did you know every star has a story?" my daddy said, setting up the telescope in the cul-de-sac, "Every star has a name." I was six, barefoot on the asphalt in a white cotton gown, and I could see my breath. Our flashlight was covered in red tissue paper to protect our night vision. Bright light is hell on a stargazer.

This is the story of how we met. I tell it to you every night, like you really could remember. But it's a ritual, see. I'm a planner.

In the junkyard, we lie on the couch and get used to the smell.

I take your hand in mine and direct it. Two days—three tops—till your skin's too raw to take my touch. For now, the fires of stars are in your eyes. I'm heaven-bound. There's a harvest moon tonight. The kind of light that makes a dead man glow.

HEATHER FOSTER

LIVES AND WRITES ON A CORN AND SOYBEAN FARM IN
WEST TENNESSEE. SHE HAS BEEN A GUEST BLOGGER FOR
SUPERSTITION REVIEW AND KINDLY QUESTIONED FOR THE
CURIOUSER & CURIOUSER INTERVIEW SERIES. HER POEMS
AND STORIES HAVE APPEARED IN THIRD COAST, TAMPA
REVIEW, MONKEYBICYCLE, IRON HORSE LITERARY REVIEW, PANK,
RHINO POETRY, AND MEAD: THE MAGAZINE OF LITERATURE &
LIBATIONS. SOMETIMES SHE READS SCARY STORIES IN
BED AND SLEEPS WITH THE LIGHTS ON.

THE LAST

MANUSCRIPT

USMAN T. MALIK

"I want to live in Pakistan because I love this bit of earth, dust from which, incidentally, has lodged itself permanently in my lungs…but the fact is, Uncle, that we have so distorted our faces that they have become unrecognizable, even to us."
—Letters to Uncle Sam, SAADAT HASAN MANTO (1912-1955)

L ast night I dreamed I went to Heera Mandi again.

Past Taxali Gate I walked, one shambling step after the other, swathed in a mist that was not entirely dream, and in the way of dreams, I knew it was one. Slender, silent girls wrapped in black shrouds lay on biers and charpoys like cheap cigars on display in a tobacco shop. Their eyes were bruised and swollen, their lips tumorous. One winked a mismatched eye at me and flicked her tongue. "Want some *maal, sahib?*"

Once upon a time hurried by—before I had time to catch it, I had stopped. There were five of us—smoking pot, drifting from one rickshaw to another, whispering about a ride to the whoremarket, and one of the drivers had responded. Through orange lips shaded by a thick paan-colored mustache, betel juice trickling into the

corner of his mouth, he murmured, "Eid night, sahib. Too many policemen rounding up the girls. Cost you an extra hundred."

(And in the dream, I saw a bile-green rickshaw slumped over a fruit vendor's cart, broken splinters of wood poking out of the metallic hulk like embalmed fingers.)

Driving past the Shahi Mosque, in the courtyard of which echoes of *isha* azan had not yet died, Haider leaned out of the rickshaw. He hawked up a fat globule of phlegm and spat it across an admirable distance onto the neck of a traffic constable. We shrieked with laughter as the man in blue jumped violently and lost his hat, rubbed his neck and stared at the green mess smeared across his palm.

Circular Road became Fort Road. Past the Gate onto night-splashed streets that meandered into themselves till they became dusty ghosts shimmering with concrete and pimp spit.

The pimp looked at us, scratching the bleeding mole on his cheek, fingered it, and beckoned.

Up we went single-file behind him, clattering on wooden steps that wound behind a house with darkened windows. They slipped in one at a time, ugly little things with syphilis and venereum, so said Haider with a dusky laugh, his eyes glittering at us. Miraj and Nandoo and Rajoo and I shook our heads. "Got some that don't look like stepped dogshit?" asked Haider. When another woman came in wearing painted cheeks and a riveled ear chewed by a past patron, Miraj stumbled to the beaded curtain, thrust his face through and vomited, a stream of thick liquid with Phajja's special goat trotters swimming out in an inky waterfall.

Haider looked at us and winked. "He's never licked cunt, the bastard motherfucker," he said and moved into the shadows with one of the twitching girls.

86

My wife and I went to Pakistan in early 2012. Our two-and-a-half-year old yelled through most of the 24-hour flight from New York to Lahore, while a green-clad PIA flight attendant gnawed at her lips and fluttered between the aisles, murmuring meaningless niceties.

It was spring and Lahore was bipolar, swinging between soft shadowy mornings and hot angry afternoons. Papa and Mama picked us up at the airport. Mama burst into tears. She dabbed her eyes with the hem of her chador, while Papa crooned at Salloo and kissed the nape of his neck again and again. Salloo grinned happily at the sight of so many women wearing shalwar kameez and dopatta, a uniform he associated with his doting aunt, my sister, back home in Florida.

"Dada eats *paratha* and Dado eats *mithai*. Tell me, little Salloo, do you want *ras malai*?" sang Mama all the way home, and Salloo giggled till he became bright red, the color of my old alma mater's brick facade.

"Papa, who's Aitchison College's principal now?" I said.

He shrugged. "I know that British apple-polisher's been kicked out. I didn't follow up after." He absently tapped the abridged *Verses from Rumi* poking out from his breast pocket. Papa had fallen in love with Rumi after retirement from Pakistan International Airlines. Mama told me he had memorized hundreds of Maulana's couplets; that he murmured them daily as he walked around the neighborhood. She thought it was a newly discovered spiritual thing. I thought Papa was growing old and wary of death.

I glanced around to make sure Mama was not listening. She was kissing Salloo's nose. "Did they really find the principal running naked after a *gori* in the college grounds?"

Papa laughed. "No. That was a rumor. I do believe *that* particular gentleman was General Yayha Khan before the formation of Bangladesh. He was gently escorted by two soldiers back into his quarters, while the naked lady stayed hidden patiently behind a tall bush."

We laughed together, and in the rearview mirror I saw Hina press her lips and glance out the window, her eyes someplace thousands of miles away.

———

That night, for the first time in years, under the *hum hum hum* of a jittering UPS-connected fan, I slept like a baby. Chronic neck pain forgotten, head sunk deep into the contoured memory foam pillow, I slept with my hand kept carefully on my side of the bed, and dreamed.

In my dream I was shimmering, a waterfall of atoms and empty space, falling with the spinning earth into an ungauged black hole. One of the girls on the leaning biers stroked my hand, ghost to ghost, as I walked past. I turned and the biers were empty and the girls were gone. Heera Mandi was haunted by their absence and I knew this was not the Mandi of my youth. The shop with the fake-wood guitars and the rababs and violins was gone, as was the Sarangi Man with his twenty-six strings strumming in a halo of music that shook the plaques and arteries of this ghetto of faded courtesans.

Dead culture, faded courtesans, their blood laden with exiled royalty and slaughtered princes; these streets moved beneath my feet and I moved with them to the tune of a prostitute mother humming to the prostitute babe on her dark-nippled breast.

Once I had tried to suck one of these breasts as the pimp lay wrapped in his sentinel chador a few feet away on a blanket, eyeing us with satisfaction. It was a wintry night in Heera Mandi and the woman unzipping my jeans shivered, gently pulled away, and said, "Sahib, my baby still drinks my milk." And at the same time we were undressing each other, not making love but negotiating the youthful memory of my initiation.

Afterward I asked the prostitute who was a mother, "Will you stay here forever?"

She shook her head and pointed a steady finger past the pimp's silhouette at the curtained window. "Tibbi Gali. That's where I will go. Do you know Tibbi Gali?"

"No."

She laughed. In the dark I smelled her breath and it was fruity, not unpleasant. She'd let me kiss her lips unparted only. "Well, you're a rich boy, sahib. I saw you come in a car. You might see me there one day. This room, this place is for when I am twenty-three. Which is now. Wait till I'm thirty-three. Tibbi Gali is for the older whores with dangling breasts and stretched stomachs. One day you will find me there. I'll be cheaper then. You want to wait till I'm cheap, sahib?"

I pulled on my jeans, hiked a thumb into the belt, and hitched them up. When I said nothing, she wrapped the condom (which looked in the half-dark like a curled lizard) into a tissue paper and slipped out the door.

And in my dream a little girl slipped once. She recovered and skipped rope past a dead dog with birthday streamer intestines spilling out of a ripped belly. "Sahib-jee, Sahib-jee. Today I'm free. Today I'm free," she said as she hopped and smiled. Dream-thickened, her features blurred till a pale teenager with a strapped vest emerged, frightened and lost. "Where are the infidels?" he asked, and blew us all up.

———

"No sir. I'm quite certain we don't have any collection called *The Daroo Diaries.*"

I was standing at the oak desk of Quaid-e-Azam Library under the shade of a rusted fan that scythed the air weakly. The burly man at the desk wore piss-colored spectacles, his eyes narrowed through the thick lens. He stared at me as if he didn't know what to do with me.

"Are you sure, bhai sahib? I talked with Professor Ali Khan at Punjab University some time ago and he told me specifically that it is here in the archives."

The burly man leaned forward and smiled. His uneven yellow teeth poked through a gutter-hole lined with tobacco stains. "We don't have it," he said. "What part of that don't you understand?"

I understood. I slipped a hand in my pocket, brought a fifty out and pressed it into his palm. "Friend," I said and smiled. "That may be Manto's last collection of reminisces. You've heard of Sadat Hassan Manto, the legendary short story writer? Of course you have." I kept my voice carefully neutral. "That may be his last book—never published because it disappeared from his room after his death. I came from abroad to find that book. I'm writing an article about it."

Smiling more broadly than ever, Burly Man pocketed the money and nodded, his potbelly jiggling under his colorless half-sleeve T-shirt. "Yes, yes. Manto sahib. Great writer. Alcoholic too. Pity he died so young. This year could've been his hundredth birthday is what the newspapers have been saying." His fingers drummed on the desk. "Pity we don't have that collection here. You may want to try the Punjab University library or Karachi University."

"What do you mean you don't have it? You must have some sort of catalogue of books housed in Pakistani libraries." My voice was rising. I felt the familiar neck pain stretch across my shoulder and press the bad spot behind my right ear.

His smile vanished. "Sahib, keep your voice down. This is not your house. It's the public library."

"Damn right it's the public library and I'm the public. I want to find that book."

"Then go find it." The smile returned. He glanced at my collectible Disney watch with Mickey and Minnie holding hands, looking deep into each other's eyes, while Pluto grinned in the background. *I know all your secrets*, said that grin. It was a birthday gift Hina gave me a few years back when she was still giving me gifts.

"What are you, a child, sahib?" Burly Man laughed, putting up his hands behind his head. "You must be an expatriate from England or America, am I right?"

I flipped him the finger slowly, deliberately. That damn smile never left his face. I turned to go.

"Fuck you too, *chootiyay*," he called from behind; then: "Welcome to Pakistan. I hope someone kidnaps you."

———

Haider lit the joint and held it out. I shook my head. He raised his eyebrows. "*Abay gandoo*, you're serious, aren't you?"

I nodded. "Told you, man. Quit all this shit some years ago. I got a family now."

"What's the harm in a fucking *kathee*?"

"I don't like the taste. It nauseates me."

He leaned back, holding the joint between his thumb and index, and took a drag. The afternoon was surprisingly mellow for Lahore, and quite a few couples and teenagers were hanging out by the pool tables or the Shisha bar. I glanced around. "It really has changed, hasn't it?"

Haider was staring at a thin twenty-something girl wearing a red sleeveless T-shirt proclaiming *If you're lookin', keep looking, pal*, her bra strap visible on a tantalizingly brown shoulder. She sat alone, puffing on a hookah pipe, looking at the teenagers without interest. "What has?" Haider said.

I sipped my Coke and said nothing.

"Where are *bhabi* and Salloo?" he said, still eyeing the girl who'd caught his glance and was looking back at him, a trace of a smile on her lips.

A sense of déjà vu. He had always been good at that. Young or old, they always responded to him.

Got some that don't look like stepped dogshit?

"Out shopping at Siddiq Center."

"How're things at home?"

"Good."

"Good." Haider waved at the waiter, turned back and fished out his wallet. "You know I envy you."

"Yeah?"

"Yeah. Good-looking wife. College Queen," he said, not looking at me but the thin girl. "Decent paying job in America. Nice family life. What more could a man ask for?" He never smiled at the girl. Just looked at her with those blue Pathan eyes of his. "And here I'm stuck in Paki-land doing the same old Dad business shit." He brought his black leather Montblanc watch close to his eyes. "Shit. Okay, man. I gotta hit it."

He smacked a five-hundred-rupee note down on the table, and my half-empty Coke overturned, the dark liquid sloshing over my white shalwar. "Oops. Sorry, man."

"It's fine," I said automatically and grabbed a few napkins to dab at my wet crotch. How many times had I said that to him over the years? *It's fine and It's okay and You go ahead. I understand. Yeah, I'm sure. We're not dating anymore. So why the fuck not?*

"How're Miraj and Nandoo?" he said as he got up and stretched. When I didn't respond, he glanced down at me. "You met them, right?"

"No."

"Why the hell not?"

"I'm here on official business for my magazine. Not on vacation."

He shrugged. "Nandoo works for Depilex. He may be able to help you out."

"What's Depilex?"

"Some sort of beauty magazine. He knows people in the business, or so I hear. He may be able to help you with that...that article or whatever."

"You got his number?" I said, and wished I hadn't. Now he would know I hadn't been in touch with the others for a long time. Hell, he probably already did. He was an asshole but not a dumb asshole.

Haider held my gaze for the briefest of moments. Then he flicked his iPhone's touchscreen and rolled his thumb around, swiping and circling. "Ready?"

I nodded. He gave me the number and turned to face the thin girl. Paused. "How long you in town, Jamal?"

"Two more weeks."

A shadow swam overhead: cloud cover across the hot Lahore

sun. Haider looked like he wanted to say something. Something played in his eyes. Then his shoulders slumped. He smiled, a full wide smile I remembered from a time when the world was not so full of misery or hollowness. When the French fries from a lean, sunburned vendor tasted better than McDonalds. "It's good to see you again, you dick."

"Sure," I said, not sure that it was. Not sure in fact whether this encounter in the heart of New Lahore was real or meaningful at all.

He flexed his back, stretching out the stiffness from sitting. "Yeah, whatever. Gimme a call before you leave, okay?" Without another word, he went to the girl, his tall, broad, toned silhouette moving gracefully against the sun.

I got up and left Mini Golf. As I passed them sitting together, the thin girl smiled up at me.

Haider didn't smile again.

"I told you I didn't want to come, didn't I? I told you."

Little Salloo was screaming, his left cheek bright red. Slapped-Cheek Syndrome, the short, acne-pocked Punjabi doctor had called it when I took a limp, febrile Salloo to him. Nothing to worry about. Common childhood virus. Take a few days to go away.

"He said it could have happened at daycare too," I said, but Hina still glared at me as she patted Salloo on the back, which my little one took for encouragement to bawl even harder. "It's a common childhood virus."

"I don't care." Her lower eyelids were red, the way they turned sometimes when she was tired or depressed. "Those damn cousins of his gave him that."

"Be reasonable, Hina," I said, hoping she wouldn't do the opposite. "Are you taking your pills?"

She flinched. Salloo stopped crying, startled by the motion. Hina stared at me, her hawk nose flaring. "How dare you," she whispered. Her voice rose before I could hold up a hand in explanation. "How dare you make this about me. My son is sick. He's sick, you hear me, Jamal? Your son is sick. And what do you do?" She smiled, baring her teeth. "You run all over town, partying with your dirty, filthy friends."

"Gimme a break, Hina." My neck was throbbing. There it was, the familiar buzzing in my right ear when the muscle stretched taut and pulled at my uncinate joints, or so the neurologist I'd seen in Orlando said. A *wisha wisha wisha* of tinnitus that played like a phantom surf inside my head. "I haven't seen those guys in a long time. They're my friends."

"Yes. They are, aren't they?" she said, and Salloo squealed in her hands. Hina looked down, surprised. She was clenching his butt too tightly. She turned him over and patted him. "Friends are as friends do. And Haider with his mean weird eyes…" She stopped, breathless, holding Salloo hard against her breasts. "He brings back bad memories. I don't want to see them again."

"You won't. We're done hanging out."

Her eyes were unreadable, but when she spoke, the vehemence had left her. For the first time in months there was something other than death and dullness in her. "You remember when we were in college? All of us together? Such a long time ago." What was that in her voice? She looked around at the room, her eyes wide as if seeing everything for the first time: the mahogany headboard of the ancient bed my mother brought in dowry; the bare walls with the PIA: *Great people to fly with* clock hanging like a dead thing, its metallic tongue lolling; the shod carpet with the corners lifting up; the old mirror smeared with juices of dead mosquitoes and flies.

Hina sighed, a sound that filled the room like a soft, sad dream. Salloo rocked in her hands. The PIA clock ticked loudly. We looked at each other through slitted eyes.

Hina turned and drifted out the door.

———

Saadat Hassan Manto and I were walking the streets of Anarkali. It was early morning and the cockerels were still crowing. A soggy fog drifted in the alleys. Somewhere a donkey brayed.

"It must have seen me," said Manto sahib and turned to me with that mustached smile of his. "They say donkeys bray when they see the Devil."

I said nothing. In this place and time I was content to let Manto sahib lead the way. The alley twisted and we found ourselves in front of an old bookshop. Manto sahib turned the knob of the screen door. It opened. Without glancing back he entered. I hesitated, then followed.

Manto sahib was lying on a jute charpoy with a broken post. The charpoy tilted vertiginously. His face was jaundiced, his eyes yellow like egg-yolks sitting in a spoilt omelet. His hands twitched and flapped weakly. A moonshine bottle lay lidless on the floor near his hand; it swayed in an unfelt wind. The dark glass reflected his face, twisting and wrenching it into a grotesque mask.

When I entered, he looked up and tried to smile. "You made it," he said, his voice hollow as if sighing through a reed flute.

He was naked except for a loongi that covered his crotch and thighs. His chest was caved in, but his abdomen was bloated, the navel popped out like a floating cork.

"I'm dying," he said, and his lips and tongue quivered. "But you can save my soul. Uncle Sam, save my soul." He managed a weak grin. "Have you read my *Letters to Uncle Sam?*"

I nodded, my eyes burning, heart thudding in my chest.

"This country has gone to cunt-city," he said. His eyes rolled up and he died, one finger lying gently on the bottle rolling back and forth on the phlegm-covered floor.

———

We went to Shalamar Bagh.

The van ride was bumpy and hot. Salloo cried most of the way. When we got there, the Mughal gardens were covered with thin and fat Lahorites, their half-naked spawn jumping up and down in the piss-yellow fountains. The oak and banyan trees were stained with white slugs and slug-juice. Papa and Mama walked Salloo up the marble steps leading to the terraces. Hina and I held hands tentatively, looked at each other, and smiled.

Haider and Nandoo showed up around midday. A silver Land Cruiser screeched to a halt in the graveled parking lot, pluming a rooster tail of red dust behind it. When Haider stepped down, his sunglasses glittering, Hina turned to me. Her eyes were frantic and furious. I shrugged. They had called me and wanted to meet one last time. She jerked her hand away.

Nandoo and I walked side by side, our first meet in ten years. His hairline had receded more than mine, and his face was chubbier, but otherwise it was the same old Nandoo. We had talked on the phone about *The Daroo Diaries*, and Nandoo sounded delighted to hear my voice—although he regretted to say he had bad news for me.

"It's a fake manuscript," he said.

Two college kids at the National College of Arts had prepared it. The fabrication had been exposed months ago and hushed up by an embarrassed academia. There was no last manuscript by Manto.

No unfinished business in Lahore for me.

"How's life, Jamal?" Nandoo said now, smiling that easy smile, that brave smile in the face of our youth's adversities. Dear old Nandoo who had never refused me anything. Who always ran to fetch my kites when they floated like giant wasps on steamy, blindingly white summer days.

"It's good, man."

We walked in silence for a while. A fruit vendor yodeled his wares. Two brown children cut across our path and a tall swarthy security guard paced the garden, his AK-47 slung over a thick shoulder.

"Why'd you never call?" he said at last. "I tried to stay in touch, you know. You didn't."

I scratched the back of my hand with a fingernail. What could I say? That time is a dying snake eating its own tail? That years come and come and we move through them like unhappy ghosts in limbo? That my wife looked at strangers in the park near our suburban Florida home with more clarity in her eyes than at me?

"I'm sorry, I guess."

He laughed. "Same old Jamal. Your ass is sorry and you don't even know it."

Awkward, I laughed too.

We turned a corner, and came upon Hina and Haider. They were sitting together. He was gesticulating wildly. She was gazing at the ground, but her face glowed. Oh, how it glowed. Brighter than this hot miserable day from hell. Her eyes were dreamy and they were clear. Her T-shirt was mussed up, its tail out of her jeans.

When they saw us, she jumped away from him, stumbled to her feet awkwardly, and walked quickly toward us.

"Where's Salloo?" she said, breathless. Then, "I'm going to get him." She turned and fled.

Haider came toward me, his eyes hidden beneath gold-rimmed Police sunglasses that I could never have afforded when I was young and penniless in college.

"How's it going, boys?" he asked and smiled.

I was confused. That smile.

Nandoo hawked and spat a creamy wad at Haider. The spit landed at his feet. "You're such an asshole. Is that why you came here?"

Haider looked at the spit. Looked up. His sunglasses slid down his nose, and his eyes were defiant and blazing. "What the fuck are you talking about?"

Nandoo glared at him. Wordlessly, he turned and pulled me away. "Let's go."

I stumbled after him, not knowing what to do.

———

That evening, without telling anyone, I went to Heera Mandi.

Past Cuckoo's cafe I walked, looking for Tibbi Gali. It was there, a narrow lightless alley bulging with a dozen or so fat hookers. They wore cheap and gaudy clothes, and huddled together like bloated factory-farmed chickens in a coop. They smiled and pawed at me, and I stopped and moved and paused again. I didn't see her. That sad dusky face with the fruity breath. What was her name? In sudden despair I ran down the alley, and a pimp sidestepped, startled and wary.

She was not there. She must be thirty now, mustn't she? She'd said thirty-year old fat whores went to Tibbi Gali.

But Tibbi Gali was empty of her, barren and silent.

We left for the U.S the next day. Mama and Papa stood waiting at Lahore Airport as I talked to the attendant at the desk. I came back, sporting a wide smile on my face. Mama sobbed, and Papa held his book of Rumi poetry in his hand. Salloo goggled at them both and my mother kissed the top of his head. Her tears gleamed in his brown hair like pearls.

"*Listen to the story told by the reed,*" said Papa. I noticed something I hadn't before. The hair on the back of his neck had turned white; it stood out in wilting bunches. "*Of being separated. Ever since I was sliced from the reedbed, I have made this crying sound.*"

Hina handed me Salloo's stroller. I slipped Salloo inside and fastened the belt.

"Anyone separated from someone he loves," said Papa. Mama looked at us, her face lined, her black liner smudged down her cheeks in rivulets of grief, "understands what I say."

I moved forward and hugged my parents one after the other. Mama hugged me frantically, and I felt her bones pushing through her doughy flesh. When I embraced my father, he kissed my cheek and my earlobe. He whispered, "Remember what the Maulana says, son. Few will hear the secrets nestling within the notes. May you be one of the few."

"Yes, Papa," I said, pulled away gently, and smiled at him.

We turned and walked down a milling space toward a dark tunnel into the heart of the airport.

Last night I dreamed I went to Heera Mandi again.

And in my dream the five of us were watching a cricket match on a broken black-and-white TV in front of a paan-shop in the whoremarket. Wassi Bhai bowled to Allan Lamb on the brain-gray Melbourne Cricket Ground, and Lamb lifted his bat and swung it at Wassi Bhai's head. Brain gray and red floated on a sea of scarlet, and Captain Imran Khan lifted Wassi Bhai's skull and waved it proudly at the maddening crowd. The '92 World Cup was ours and we stood and cheered, as Haider came out from a dark room and wiped his lips.

Once upon a time I went to Heera Mandi with my best friend. "Ammi, we'll be back before dusk," said my best friend, taking the money for his first acoustic guitar from his mother's purse. "What times have come that a son tells his mother before going to Heera Mandi!" said his mother, and we all burst out laughing.

Once upon a time I dreamed I went back.

But then youth, dream, and the reed flute were shattered; and I opened my eyes to find myself in sunny Florida, browsing the Escort ads on Backpage with my pants unzipped and my hand coiled around a lifeless object.

USMAN T. MALIK

IS A PAKISTANI WRITER RESIDENT IN FLORIDA. HIS
FICTION HAS APPEARED OR IS FORTHCOMING AT TOR.
COM, STRANGE HORIZONS, AND BLACK STATIC AMONG OTHER
VENUES. HE IS A 2013 GRADUATE OF THE CLARION WEST
WRITERS WORKSHOP. IN WINTER OF 2014, ALONG WITH
MAN ASIA LITERARY PRIZE NOMINEE MUSHARRAF ALI
FAROOQI, USMAN LED PAKISTAN'S FIRST SPECULATIVE
FICTION WRITING WORKSHOP IN LAHORE. DROP HIM
A LINE AT WWW.USMANMALIK.ORG.

$INGLE LENS

REFLECTION

JASON METZ

From across the field, Daniel Blakesburg sits at a picnic table studying his subject, waiting for an opening. He sizes her up, guessing she's in her seventies. She has a slight hunch in her back, but still buzzes around the playground. She doesn't wear eyeglasses. When she pushes the boys on the swings, they scream in delight.

Experience says the old lady is a simple mark, that it's easier on his nerves. Sleepless nights disagree, the job tormenting him all the same.

She sits on a bench, pulls a thermos out of a canvas tote bag, and he moves in.

"Ms. Bitoni," asks Daniel.

Startled, she looks up, glances over to the boys, then back to Daniel. "Yes," she says, as if she has the same question. "May I help you?"

Daniel reaches into his backpack, pulls out a thirty-five millimeter and raises it in her direction. Seated, she grips the armrest, recoiling into the back of the bench.

"I was hired to shoot you," he says.

The assignment arrived in his post box just like all the others, an off-white 3x5 postcard–a photo of an hourglass on the front, his subject's name, location, date and time on the back.

"I was told I'd find you here," he says.

He brings her into focus, snapping off shots in rapid succession, framing her just right, not the least bit concerned about her facial expressions. She looks like a hound dog, jaw dropped and hovering above her chest, pulling her wrinkles down with it.

"Perfect," he says, putting the lens cap on and shoving the camera into his bag. "You're as beautiful as ever. I'll have the portraits in the mail tomorrow morning."

"Portraits," she asks, inching forward on her seat, looking over her shoulder at the boys, laughing, the swings creaking. She turns back to Daniel, cocks her head to the side and raises an eyebrow. The hound dog is trying to understand.

"Oh, it's not their day, ma'am."

He's gained a dozen or so pounds since his college days, but he's fifty yards away by the time she calls to him.

"Sir," she says. "Sir?"

He hits the parking lot, turns to see her rounding up the boys, and he ducks behind an aisle of cars, slinking into his tiny blue Honda. He drives out of the lot, slow and calm. By the time Ms. Bitoni is calling the police, he's out of focus, miles down the road.

———

In his laundry room, Daniel unscrews the standard light bulb and replaces it with a red one. He picks the negative he's most partial to, the hound dog impersonation, and drops a single sheet of paper into the developer tray, enlarging it to an 8x10, rocking the tray gently, side to side. He slips the paper into the stop bath, then into the fixer, waits a few moments, hangs it on the clothesline, then retreats to his living room.

His living room is lit by the cool blue overtones of a reality TV show. The show is about those who've held a winning lottery ticket, how it changes their lives. He stands watching from the tile that separates the kitchenette from the living room while two slices of meat lovers supreme spin in his microwave.

The reality show completely misses the point.

The microwave beeps, lukewarm slices, limp and soggy, satisfy his cook-for-yourself resolution. He falls into a faded plaid love-seat, kicks his legs over the arm rest, plate on his gut, and considers the concept of a lottery. The camera only follows the money and what came after it, for better or worse. What the camera doesn't show, what it seems no one wants to say, is that it all ends the same. He chews, slow and thoughtful, until it's gone.

Daniel wakes the next morning lying in the same position, the TV still on, a grease pocked paper plate resting on the coffee table next to a twenty-four ounce can of Pabst Blue Ribbon. He stands in front of the mirror and runs his fingers through his thinning hair. His eyes are dark, too heavy for a man who's yet to reach his fortieth birthday. The stubble is grey and there's a suggestion of a deliberate design. He splashes water on his face, pops a mint into his mouth, slides his feet into a pair of flip flops and walks to the coffee shop. He grabs the morning edition of The Globe, orders a small black coffee, smiles at the girl behind the counter with the dimples, and stuffs a ten dollar bill into the tip jar. He finds an empty table next to a group of clean-shaven men dressed in neatly pressed shirts and slacks. They're eating Cobb salads, talking about eating stock and using terms like Angel Investor and Drag-Along Rights. One man says he's starting a start-up that helps build start-ups. He says that this is his golden parachute.

Daniel unfolds the paper and finds the obituaries.

After coffee, he stops by the post office. There's another postcard in his box. On the front, is a picture of an hourglass. On the back is an address. The address belongs to Martha Bitoni.

He gets home, goes into his laundry room, and swaps out the red bulb for a soft white. He grabs the picture hanging from the clothesline and studies his work. The hound dog face is replaced by a young woman's face, perhaps fifty years younger. She is standing by a swing set. Standing alongside her is a handsome man with jet black hair, slicked back. The man is holding a baby girl.

This is how Daniel's photos develop. These are the moments he captures. These are the reminders he's agreed to deliver.

Sliding the photo into a manila envelope, he can no longer allow the beauty to overwhelm him. If his job had an actual training manual, he doubts this would be a part of it. There is no mentor. The colleagues are unknown. His tolerance is not what it used to be.

On the envelope, he's writing the name Martha Bitoni, followed by her address. On the top left corner, he doesn't write a return address. On his way to his bartending gig, he drops the envelope in the mailbox.

The process is this: he waits five days from the completion of his last assignment. He goes to the coffee shop, tips the girl with the dimples ten dollars, finds an open table, and turns to the obituaries. Today, he reads the following:

Martha Louise Bitoni, 76, of Boston, MA, died on May 25, 2012. She was the wife of the late Henry G. Bitoni. She was the daughter of the late Lawrence C. and Helen DiLorenzo of Topsfield, MA. She is survived by two children and five grandchildren. A memorial service is to be held on May 29 at 10:30 a.m., Forest Hills Cemetery.

Daniel finishes his coffee and stops by the post office. In his box is a manila envelope. In the envelope is a stack of bills. In his apartment, there is a small silver safe in the back of the closet. He opens the safe and puts the new stack of bills next to the others, closes the safe, then the closet door. He puts on black pants, a white shirt, then a bow tie, and takes the train to an upscale restaurant where he tends bar, practicing small talk. After his shift, he sits alone at a booth by a window in a diner where he watches taillights fade into dawn.

———

The back of the post card says the name Derek Nichols. The assignment is for the following morning, 8:11 a.m., Florist, Boylston Street train station.

At 8:05 a.m., Daniel is standing by the stairs near the florist, just outside the stop. He cannot afford to be late. There are no sick days in Daniel's line of work. There is no getting out of the contract. He remembers the deal he made all too well and the repercussions of free will. He mumbles under his breath, rehearsing his approach. As the minute hand moves closer to 8:11, Daniel's stomach churns, nausea sets in. He takes the lens cap off the camera.

A tall, white male in a light gray suit, perhaps in his late thirties, comes up the stairs and buys a bouquet of yellow daffodils, hints of an early New England spring. As he puts the change in his pocket, Daniel approaches.

"Mr. Nichols?" he asks.

The man does what most of them do. He pinches his eyes together, looks down at the camera, then meets Daniel's eyes. He half-smiles and cocks his head to the side.

Most of them say, "Yes?"

Mr. Nichols is no different.

Raising his camera, Daniel says, "I'm with Hourglass Photography, I was told I could meet you here." Before Mr. Nichols can react, Daniel is hitting the shutter release. By the time Mr. Nichols is asking, "Who are you?" Daniel is smiling, putting the lens cover back on, and putting the camera in his backpack.

Before Daniel can say, "Perfect, I'll have them in the mail by tomorrow," a woman comes from behind Mr. Nichols and wraps her arm around his. She is brunette in her mid-twenties, her hair pulled back in a bun, a quick study in natural elegance. Mr. Nichols asks if she hired the photographer for their anniversary. Daniel is pivoting on his heel at the same time she shakes her head, "No" Mr. Nichols grabs Daniel's camera bag and spins him around, asking him who he is. Daniel swings his arm, hits the bouquet of yellow daffodils, sends the daffodils into a cup of black coffee, sends the coffee onto the front of the woman's white cotton single-breasted coat.

Daniel screams, "FIRE! RAPE! FIRE! RAPE!" and runs. He does not look back when he hears the repeated slap of wing tips on the concrete. It's been a while since his college rugby days, but his Nikes put enough distance between him and the slaps. He allows himself a look, sees Mr. Nichols slowing up, yelling and shaking his fist. Daniel ducks into the subway, pushes through the morning rush, and waits behind a pillar for a train that comes two minutes later. He is not concerned in what direction the train is headed.

When he gets home, he preheats his oven to 350 degrees, takes a pre-made breakfast burrito out of the freezer, turns on the TV, and develops the photos just as he's done so many times before.

———————

It is the final gasp of winter. Daniel is sitting in his booth. He has some time to kill before he has somewhere he needs to be. A tired waitress fills his cup for the fifth time. He slides a twenty to the end of the table. The waitress calls him honey.

Outside, there are flurries. They fall from the heavens, hang around for a little while, and melt into the sidewalk. He catches one with his gaze, freezing it in time. In this fleeting moment, he sees its shape, like none that came before it, and none that will follow. He watches as it falls to the ground to melt with the rest.

Beyond the flurries, a woman is standing on the sidewalk. She is looking through the window into the diner at the booth where Daniel sits. She walks in, ignores the hostess, and sits down across from Daniel.

"I've been searching for you," she says.

When Daniel starts to get up from his seat, she threatens to scream fire and rape. Daniel sits back down and listens to the woman.

The woman takes off her wool beanie and sets it beside her purse. From her purse, she pulls out a photo. On the photo is a picture of Derek Nichols. In this photo, he appears to be dumbfounded.

"Who are you," she asks.

Daniel doesn't answer. He looks around the diner and takes stock of who's sitting nearby. The waitress who calls him honey puts an empty coffee cup in front of the woman. The woman looks up to the waitress, nods and smiles, has her cup filled. The woman pours in two creamers and one artificial sweetener, stirs it twice, and lets it rest.

"Derek said this was the most beautiful picture he's ever seen."

Daniel looks down at the photo, Derek Nichols confused, the lighting awful. It may be one of the worst pictures he's ever taken. He looks across the table at the woman whose lip is beginning to quiver. Her face turns flush, her eyes water.

Daniel doesn't talk.

"He said he's never felt so peaceful," she says, her voice breaking. She buries her face in her hands. Daniel takes cheap, thin napkins out of the metal container, offers them to the woman. It is the best he can do.

"Who are you?" she asks again.

He's been asked this question before. He's even seen a woman cry. But never both at the same time. This is a scenario he has not rehearsed.

"I'm the photographer," he says.

"He's gone," she says.

"I know."

It's two cups of coffee later before the woman speaks. She asks him once again, "Who are you?"

Daniel has questions of his own. This is the only way he can answer her. He asks, "What do you want to see before you go?" She stares back at him. Her eyes offer no response. He says, "It's random you know, when your time's up."

He motions for the waitress to pour another cup of coffee. He asks for two slices of pecan pie. The woman initially says no but Daniel insists. He slows down while eating his slice, keeping pace with her.

When they're finished, he says, "Before they go, not everyone gets to see themselves in that way."

She wants to ask him again, she wants to know who he is. She wants to know what he is. He can tell by the way she's trying to force out the words, her voice trembling, failing her.

"I took a job, a long time ago," he says. He looks at his watch and puts his hands in his pocket, traces his finger around the outer edge of the post card. "I have to go."

"Derek . . . was he happy?" she asks. The woman is staring up at him as stands to leave, pulling a twenty out of his wallet. Her eyes, full and green, are watery, running mascara. In them, he sees his own reflection. In it, his wrinkles are gone, the face smooth, a thin smile, his own eyes, wide and bright, are staring back at him.

"Very much so," he says with a smile, climbing back into the booth.

They sit quietly for a bit, until the sun comes through the window, sending a shard of light that cuts across the table, dividing the two of them. He rubs the post card in his pocket, looks into her eyes and asks if she can stay. She shakes her head from side to side and smiles ever so slightly. He reaches across the table, wipes a tear from her cheek and says, "Thank you."

She doesn't have any more questions.

He's found an answer.

She leaves.

He misses his appointment.

Daniel steps out of the diner into the snow and puts his hand above his eye, staring up at the sun. This moment is interrupted by another man. The man is asking the name, "Daniel Blakesburg?" Daniel cocks his head to the side and flashes a smile for the camera. The man tells him he should have the photo in the mail by tomorrow morning.

Daniel says he won't need to see it.

JASON METZ

AS OF 2015, JASON METZ IS ENTERING HIS FINAL YEAR OF
STUDIES AT THE UNIVERSITY OF CALIFORNIA RIVERSIDE
PALM DESERT LOW RESIDENCY MASTER OF FINE ARTS IN
CREATIVE WRITING AND THE PERFORMING ARTS AND
HE CAN'T HELP BUT WONDER, HOW WILL THEY GET ALL
OF THOSE WORDS ON THE DIPLOMA? IN ANY CASE, JASON
CANNOT WORRY ABOUT THE WORDS OF OTHERS AND
TRIES HIS BEST TO STAY FOCUSED ON HIS OWN. SOME OF
JASON'S WORDS ARE ONLINE AND IN PRINT IN PANTHEON
MAGAZINE, AS WELL AS OTHER STRETCHES OF THE
INTERNET AND BEYOND. HE CAN BE FOUND IN SOMERVILLE,
MA SITTING BEHIND A SMALL WOODEN DESK ON THE THIRD
FLOOR OF A TRIPLE DECKER OVERLOOKING THE BOSTON
SKYLINE, HIS BULLDOG KARL LYING BY HIS FEET, QUIETLY
DREAMING. YOU CAN FOLLOW HIM ON
TWITTER @WORDOFMETZ

THE
MOTHER

NATHAN M. BEAUCHAMP

The warmth of her presence radiates through the membrane and into my tiny body. Wriggling, weightless, I drive my cutting horn forward, thrusting, desperate to reach her. A tear opens. Fluid whooshes through the gash and the membrane collapses, weighty and terrifying. Claws slashing, I shred the remnants of the pod and push toward murky light. Cool air fills my lungs and rushes back out in roars of pride. I shake my head and the final chunks of the pod fly free and the world swims into focus.

A massive face descends from above—knobbed scales, dark eyes, slightly parted jaws. My eyes roll in their sockets. Tongue lashing against baby teeth, love and terror overwhelm me—love and terror for The Mother. I skitter over sand and nestle against her side.

I soak in her warmth, eyes trained on her face. The sound of cracking and the sharp odor of blood fill the air. Others spill from the mound of pods, a living flow—thick with mucus, trembling. In turn they see her and swarm forward. Exhausted, we lay in piles, masses of claws and scales. But it was I who first broke free from my pod and looked upon The Mother.

We eat what she drops from her massive jaws and drink from the stream where the drying pieces of our pods litter a small nook of raised earth. We crowd against her for warmth in the dark, and fight over food in the day. Largest and strongest, my cutting horn lengthy and sharp, I dominate the rest of the brood. I eat the choicest portions and then take from the weak. Slamming into their soft sides, I drive them away from globules of still-warm fat that coat my throat with hot grease.

The Mother watches impassively. Fifty times our size, as tall as the trees that line the stream, covered with thick plates, her tail lashes with enough force to cripple the unwary. I wish for her to notice me—my size, my dominance—but if she notices, I cannot tell. I will grow bigger still, and when I am able, I will show her my worth. I don't know how, but in the way of knowing, which led me to destroy the membrane, I know that soon her great, shining eyes will rest on me.

We spread over the stream bank that separates water from the great, green deep where The Mother goes to hunt, but we are not allowed. The first time she rises to hunt, some of us race after her. She stops and lowers her head, bellowing heat and the smell of rot into our nostrils. All of us stop except a single, foolish youngling. She pounds the ground and raises a footpad, claws extended. Swift and graceful, she dips and catches hold of the youngling and flings him back towards the brood, a chaotic scramble of teeth and claws. Before he strikes the ground we catch him in our jaws and devour his flesh.

None of us try to follow The Mother again.

The weakest have died. Some from lack of food, others cut open, a few broken by The Mother's lashing tail. The food she drops has changed from scraps to whole animals—things with tan fur and branching horns, useless for fighting. I slice through a ribcage and bury my head, pulling out the soft things within. Rising on hind claws, shaking mouthfuls of the pulsing flesh, I bellow my gratitude to The Mother but she does not respond. Why does she ignore me? Doesn't she see that I am special?

I watch her carefully, anxious to learn. Each day she lumbers into the green deep and returns with dead things clamped in her jaws. Where does she find prey? I have never seen one of the soft-horns except those The Mother drops for us. How does she hunt them? Will she take me with her one day? My jaws are strong and my horn long. Why does she delay? What must I do for her to take me with her?

While she hunts, the others lie atop the shale at the edge of the river. They have grown lazy. With only four of us left, hunger never sinks into our guts the way it once did. The Mother brings enough food that we no longer bother to rouse ourselves and fight.

Great, whirling birds circle in the blue. What do they see? What does the below look like to them? My eyes see poorly—far things clouded like the fog that rises off the stream in the early morning. The breeze carries a thickness of smells, as varied as the spread of color made by light caught and thrown by water—bringing no picture to my inside eyes. I have seen so little and know so little. I root in the moldering thickness at the edge of the green deep, unearthing squirming things full of bitter juices. I carve marks high into the trunks of trees, slicing through their skin and releasing golden resin. But I dare not go into the green deep and instead travel far along the bank of the stream.

The flat where the husk pods have dried to powder disappears. I follow the stream until the sweet bloom of purple and orange flowers overpowers the scent of my kin. Stalks line a pool where the stream slows. Beneath the surface, a flash of movement! I plunge my head into the water. Silver fish dart over gray pebbles and dodge between reeds. Two fierce warriors battle over a gray fish carcass, their claws locked in combat. Rich with happiness, pleased by their display, I watch them grapple until my air grows short. Rising, sucking air through nose holes, I trumpet happiness into the blue.

I return to the sunning stones and close my eyes but my inside eyes replay all that I have seen so that I cannot sleep. How can the others sleep when such wonders exist? What does The Mother see when she goes off to hunt? If I want to learn, I must risk following her. Then I will learn where she finds prey and how she kills. Together we will make many kills and eat until swollen. Perhaps she and I will never return to the stream. We will travel on and on and we will create trumpet sounds for everything that we can scent and taste and kill.

The next time the Mother leaves for the hunt, I follow. The sleepy ones watch absently—they don't desire the attention of The Mother or care about what lies in the deep. They are like the fish that school in the pools of the stream—happy to eat and grow—content, wanting only food and a place to sun themselves.

I keep downwind of The Mother. I slide between trees without cracking them, claws retracted, footpads light over the spongy undergrowth. Brightly colored birds flit through the treetops and call out angrily as I pass under them. Soon I will see the soft-horns that she brings to us, sometimes still alive, their eyes full of dread as we scissor them open. Saliva drips from my tongue and I tremble with anticipation.

She shows no sign of noticing my presence. I stay far from her, trusting that her eyes see no better than my own, until the sun slides high into the blue and we reach a wide expanse of wet and mud. At the far edge of the wet, another green deep begins—strange and shimmery, like light over water. I hide at the edge of the mud, eyelids retracted, tongue extended, scenting the air. Scenting . . .

What?

Not The Mother, my brood, prey or anything I have smelled before. My plates flatten against my back and I root the air, eyes swiveling. The smell comes from the shimmer—I do not like the smell and I do not want her to go near it. I choke down a trumpet of warning, afraid that if she finds me she will break me with pounding feet and lashing tail.

The Mother thumps over the mud flat. As she nears the strange shimmer I see another Mother! The second mother looks like The Mother and moves towards her, stride for stride. Their noses touch and the new mother swallows The Mother and she disappears.

I charge forward, rage escaping me in a terrible shriek. My claws dig the muck, plates plowing the mud. Ahead, a heavy-skulled brood mate rushes towards me, head lowered for battle. Where did he come from? How can this be? I stop and the other stops. I blink and the other blinks. The smell of the shimmer burns harsh in my nostril holes. And then I understand—the shimmer is like the surface of the pool. In it I see my reflection. My muscles quiver and my tongue buries itself in my throat and I back away, ashamed of my fear until I remember how I submerged my head in the water and discovered silver fish. This shimmer might contain a pocket of life as well—a different sort of deep hidden away, known only by The Mother. If I can breach the shimmer and find her there—perhaps that is what The Mother has waited for. A brave one—a finder.

I paw the mud and trumpet my intention to the brood at the edge of the stream, to all of the creatures in the deep green, and most of all to The Mother. I charge, all four of my legs trembling with their strength—leaping, head extended. I slam into myself. A crack rips the air. A jolt of white agony travels down my horn and I fall backward into darkness.

I wake to the haze of a night sky obscured by mist. I ache with pain like thousands of wounds beneath my plates. The shimmer ripples, impenetrable. How did the mother enter it? Is her strength that much greater than my own?

Again I throw myself against the wall. Crackling heat sears into my bones. I roar and slam into the wall, again and again. Blood and chunks of shattered teeth fall from between my gaping mouth. I turn towards the wall once more and fall, heavy, unable to move. Flat on my stomach, I press my face into the mud. The Mother is gone, dead—swallowed by the wall like I swallow the flesh of prey.

I am lower than nothing. The Mother. Oh, The Mother.

From within the rushing blackness I feel distant vibrations rising from beneath me. Trumpets of joy, teeth, and ripping, sounds from the stream bank. Have my siblings grown so hungry they have hunted on their own? Cold and weak I rise up and thrash back to the stream.

Buzzing black flies circle a carcass picked free of meat. The others lie on the flat stones, soaking in the lingering warmth. And there, amongst them, head resting on fore claws, is The Mother. How can she have survived the fury of the shimmer? Did she slip past me while darkness filled my mind? Did she not see me, alone on the mud flat?

I roar and paw the ground and shake my head. The others rise up to look at me and then slump back—prey consumed, they have no interest in my challenge. I sidle up to The Mother, my head turned, one black eye level with hers. The eyes look dead and do not move, as if she cannot see me, pressed against her body. My trumpeting becomes plaintive—mournful, sounds far beneath me, but I cannot stop. The pain I feel is worse than the shimmer wall, worse even than the belief that The Mother had died.

I will make her respond.

I thrust, pushing my horn between two belly scales—a small wound, painful but quick to heal. The liquid oozing from her side smells wrong. I know our blood smell—I have tasted it! The others rise, suddenly alert, three pairs of eyes watching intently.

I push farther into her flesh. How I wish that The Mother would turn on me and attack with her terrible strength. Run my body through or stamp me into the ground. In death, knowing that she knew me the way that I have known so many of my kind—their taste and essence merged within me, intoxicating. Instead, my horn slides easily inside her, meeting no resistance from a ribcage. Then my head presses against The Mother's side.

I lift and The Mother rips open.

Empty.

Her body splayed like the clams I hunted when very young. No pulsing organs, no entrails. Her arms and legs kick wildly, her head rolls on the end of her neck, and her tail lashes, useless. Black juice spurts thin and reflective, nothing like blood—nothing at all. Something crackles inside of her chest and a hot smell like the shimmer fills my nostrils, acrid and foul.

The others set upon me. I whirl and strike at them, a flurry of blows, but they do not turn back. They rage and bellow, blind, unable to see that the thing writhing in death is not a mother and was never a mother. It is an empty husk. I hate it with the intensity of the midday sun.

Claws grip my plates and teeth sink into the soft places underneath. Bucking, biting, crushing, I lose myself in the fury of battle.

The brood is dead. The Mother is dead. And soon, I will die as well. I crawl over the ground, thick with blood, and stare at the empty eyes of the false mother. I will do one thing before my blood leaves me. With great effort, I slice downward, severing the false mother's head from her shoulders. I lift her head on my cutting horn and turn my back on the dead.

The shimmer reflects my broken body, the false mother's head mounted on my cutting horn, and her unseeing eyes. She never saw me. She never saw anything. But soon I will know what is on the other side of the shimmer, or the shimmer will bring swiftness to my passing.

The shimmer ripples like water, opening before the false mother's head. Forward into a feeling of suspension, weightlessness, bound on all sides. I remember this feeling. I remember the time before I learned to love The Mother when all I wished for was freedom and the light. I push and the shimmer dissolves into warmth and dazzling brilliance.

Whirring and clicks sound from above, and when my eyelids finally retract I see the mothers. Many, many mothers, identical to mine, motionless, rest on shaped stones the color of moonlight. Beyond them, many great spaces full of herds of prey. Streams of the grey material run outwards to green spheres that hang like droplets of water suspended from blades of grass—larger than the sand flat or the green deep and as high as the birds that wheel in the sky.

I whip my horn from side to side until The Mother's head flies free. Rising on foreclaws, I trumpet long and deep. I keep bellowing until the sound becomes a rasp and then a gurgle and a great many pink, hairless things swarm out of an opening like ants from their crushed nest. Tiny eyes peer up at me and then they scatter—running, frantic.

All but one. Soft and pink, it approaches, forelimb extended. I lower my head and root the air but the pink one doesn't stop. It chirps like a tree bird and moves closer, closer, a clawless paw extended.

Warmth spreads where it caresses my flank. I slump unto my belly, weak and dying. The eyes of the pink one move rapidly. It chirps away, paw stroking my neck, tiny blue eyes flitting about as it looks at me—sees me. My trumpet of surprise comes out as a mournful sigh. Before my eyes close, the pink one leans in close. Wetness forms in its eyes, suspends from lashes, and finally breaks free.

NATHAN M. BEAUCHAMP

WRITES SPECULATIVE FICTION RANGING FROM HARD
SCIENCE FICTION TO TRANSGRESSIVE HORROR. HIS WORK
HAS APPEARED IN PANTHEON MAGAZINE, UNDER THE BED,
AND A NUMBER OF THEMED ANTHOLOGIES. HE ATTENDS
WESTERN STATE UNIVERSITY WHERE HE IS EARNING HIS
M.F.A. IN CREATIVE WRITING AND WILL GRADUATE IN JULY
2015. HE TEACHES ENGLISH AT CONCORDIA UNIVERSITY AND
LIVES IN CHICAGO WITH HIS WIFE AND TWO YOUNG BOYS.

EVERYTHING
IN ITS
PLACE

ADAM PETERSON

Watched from a far enough distance, it's difficult to know who anyone truly is. It's not the silence, but the bodies. Without words there is only the bracing of shoulders and the shifting of weight from foot to foot. From a far enough distance, any person can appear beastly. Take this boy. He jumps from the black car the moment it stops, too impatient to wait for the garage door. It's a beautiful afternoon and he's only minutes out of school. He is free and he is home and his yellow home is bright and big with love. He skips. From a far enough distance, it looks like the best afternoon of his young life. But his father. Take this father still in the idling car as the garage door opens to reveal a dollhouse, a blue dollhouse, occupying an entire stall. The father could pull forward into the other stall and be done with it. Instead he rolls down the window and says something that stops his son like a bullet just as the boy hops up the last step of the porch. The boy turns, his smile gone, the reprimand greying his face. He sulks back to the car and throws himself into the seat before the car moves forward and the garage door swallows them up. Across the street I watch from my truck, and I would swear the boy might never recover.

So it is important that I'm careful with what I write in my notebooks. I have to remind myself that I do not know the man. Or at least I know him like I know the stars by studying the night. I know only what shines—not what's there, not what's died.

Near the end, my wife told me she did not know me at all. I told her I knew her better than I knew myself.

"How?" she asked.

"I watch."

We were going to have a farm, my wife and I. We bought a place far on the opposite side of the city from the man's yellow house. With only 10 acres, calling it a farm was a joke between us. On our backs in bed, we would dream of all the things our farm would someday have.

"Goats?" my wife would say.

"Of course."

"And apples. Maybe peaches, too."

In the morning, we would wake up and make coffee and look at each other like we'd done something shameful the night before. The very sight of the other would make us both blush. Anyone watching us would have thought we were not in love.

So I am patient with my understanding of the man. His name is Jones. We did speak, once. It was on the third Tuesday since I began watching him. On Tuesdays and Thursdays Jones leaves work early to pick up his son from school. His son's name is Jacob. The rest of the week, his wife does it. His wife is younger and far more attractive than the man, and she seems completely happy with their life. Or at least that is how it looks from across the street. She sparkles. Her name is Alice.

Four times I had followed the man and watched as he led his son back to the car. Twice they had held hands. Twice they had not.

I think about this while watching the sleeping house. In the starlight, the yellow house looks purple and deserted, as if all the light bulbs have died or, like a dollhouse, it never had any at all. I think about how on the third Tuesday, I left the man at work and drove to the school early. It was a risk, but I wanted to get closer. Around me, mothers put hands behind their children's heads and guided them home without ever touching their hair. A female teacher in a blue sweater supervised the departures. All of the laughter and movement made me nervous, and I suspected the teacher knew I was not supposed to be there. My shirt did not look like a father's shirt. My eyes were not searching for threats. Maybe I was the threat, and she knew.

Jacob was alone on the cement steps stealing fearful glances at the street. I wanted to tell him I was afraid, too.

"I'm sure your ride will be here soon," I said.

He tightened and loosened the straps of his backpack and checked the line of cars. The teacher glanced in our direction.

"My dad is always late."

This, I knew, was a lie. In all of the Tuesdays and Thursdays, this was the first time Jones had been late.

"I know he'll be here," I said to reassure him, but this only made him more worried.

Only a few students remained when the black car swerved into the school parking lot. Jones took the corner so fast the tires squealed, and the man nearly ran from the car. My heart raced as I tried to think of what I should say, but luckily he spoke first.

"Thank you for keeping my son company," he said. His voice was high-pitched and thin. It was shocking when unexpected, like hearing your alarm clock in the afternoon. His maroon tie was loose and his hair stuck up from running his hands through it. He appeared too old to have a son so young, but from a distance he had always seemed younger than I knew him to be, a very distant star.

"I'm waiting for my own son," I said. "The teacher held him after class. Simon."

The man paused but then lost his nerve and said farewell. In my truck, I check to see if I made a note about Jacob's face as the man pulled him roughly away by the hand, but I see I only noted the man's: flushed.

Jones was born on a farm. College brought him to the city. More than one person I spoke with said he keeps the city running, that without him everything would go to ruin. He is respected and even feared. Before his marriage it was said he never arrived at or left the office unless the stars were out. Some would arrive early and see him on his second cup of coffee. Some would stay late and he would tell them that he would lock up as they left. His superiors joked about his country work ethic until he became a supervisor himself. A co-worker described his wedding to Alice as beautifully perfunctory—everything in its right place. A doll wedding. I'm sure Jones does not think of it that way. Most of my notebooks are full of details about how happy his family looks through binoculars.

Which is why it is a surprise when he disappears.

I follow him to work. It is a Thursday, a week after he yelled at Jacob for jumping out of the car. We both put our visors down to block the morning sun as we drive east into the city. At a coffee shop, he orders his usual, and I order an ice water. I do not care for coffee, not anymore, but he drinks many cups throughout the day. I see him go to refill his "World's Greatest Dad" mug through the glass walls that surround his office. At this distance, his job for the city does not seem so special. His office is one of many. His chair is not from a well-known designer. His screensaver is the seal of the state university he attended. He is only one more man in a dark suit.

When I get disappointed, I get sloppy. I stare too intensely at the back of his head. A secretary across the hall has been watching me. I know because I know. She looks away too quickly when I turn in her direction. When watching, you have to hold a person's gaze long enough to seem confident but not long enough to be remembered. Like patience, it is an essential skill when watching someone. I leave for my truck to change my shirt and put on a baseball cap. I am only gone a moment, but when I return he has disappeared.

I will never see him again.

Almost as soon as my wife and I moved to our farm, the city came. We had one year of nights dreaming out loud before they built a highway along our back fence. In that time, we had not planted any fruit trees or bought goats. We did have a golden retriever, Simon. My wife took Simon when she left. Or at least that's how I see it. If you ask her, she will tell you I left. But she would be wrong. I am still here.

It is a strange place to live. Because we never worked the land, the grass grew high. Because the grass grew high, strangers feel like they can pull over on the highway and dump unwanted items. There are rusted refrigerators and old television sets hidden in the grass. Nights, the metal winks back at the stars.

This is where I go after I realize I've lost Jones. I never expected him to disappear, but maybe it was inevitable. Every day he was so precise, so perfect. Had he known about me? It's possible. The first time I took my eyes off him, he was late to get his son. The second time, he disappeared. But when we met at the school, he had not recognized me or been afraid to see me with his son. If anything, he had been curious, like he wanted to ask me a question but could only think of statements. If I had known he was about to leave, I would have stayed away from his son so the boy would have been prepared. I will not always be there to wait with Jacob. From this day on, he will always be waiting, and because of me he knows nothing of patience. This is what keeps me awake in my bed.

My home is modest, a bachelor's home now that my wife has gone. In my cupboards, there are old spices for recipes I cooked only once, if I cooked them at all. Some may have been there for nearly a decade. Somehow, time goes quickly for me here even if day-to-day life feels torpid. Just like those stars throwing old light, thousands of years can pass in an instant if you look at it from far enough away. But for the stars, they still have to shine, day after day, until they can do it no more.

I realize my dog is probably dead. Poor Simon.

The next day there are no police cars in front of his yellow house. The day after there is one. The day after that there are three. One of them is black and does not have lights, but the men who come from the car are clearly detectives. The holsters on their hips clip their gates. Their upper lips look like they only recently lost their mustaches and might miss them. It is a Sunday morning, and their suits have just been lifted from the church pew. Alice greets them at the door and they disappear inside. Jacob is in his room. Every so often he peeks through his blinds as if he will see his father's car squeal around the corner.

In a week, the police rarely come by and neither do I. Maybe I am not so patient. My wife used to say that I experience power surges.

"Like when lightning strikes the power lines," she said. "There's no predicting it."

"Isn't it good?" I said. "Otherwise I might have too little power."

I said this to give her an out to make me feel better. I did not like thinking of myself as someone who blew light bulbs and sent people scuttling to buy new appliances. I knew what became of the old ones.

She appeared to think about it.

"Maybe. But you get bored waiting for the lightning."

This was only days after I purchased the farm for us. I told myself she was angry and taking my rash purchase out on me. Now I don't know. She was so thrilled with the house and the land and our imaginary farm. I don't remember her being angry at all.

But without Jones, I really am bored. Alice has not come outside since his disappearance. A neighbor from across the street carries casseroles and plates of cookies to the yellow house. She is a young woman trying to help, but after a while she looks exhausted. There is nothing to be done about someone else's tragedy. After a time, you want to grab the victim by their shoulders and shake the grief out of them so you can tell them about your own.

To pass the time, I look for new items that have been left on my property. I find a broken shopping cart and a microwave that appears to be in perfect condition but is an unfashionable color. It takes time to remember how to sleep in my bed. The sound of the highway never fully dies. If anything, it gets worse past midnight when it is only big, lonely trucks. Sometimes they seem to blow their horns just to see if anything will blow back, like whale song.

"The secret is to think of the sound as angels going by," my wife told me once.

"Where are they going?"

"To perform miracles," she answered as if she had thought a lot about it.

I nodded, even though it was dark and this would never be my solution. The sound is too sharp, and I don't believe in angels.

My solution was different. I never told my wife, but she knew I found one when I began sleeping through the night.

"The angels, right?" she said.

I smiled.

It was partially her idea: I think of the hum of the highway as light, as electricity. I imagine it coursing through my body and keeping me alive. In the dark, I concentrate on the sound until I know that it is light and not blood in my veins. I know this because when I close my eyes so tight that I feel like my head will burst, I see not darkness but stars.

Three weeks after Jones's disappearance there is a knock on my door. I have not left my home to sit outside the yellow house for two days. Stupidly, I think it might be Jacob at my door. He will demand to know why I abandoned him. Instead it is a very short man in a blue suit. He is years older than Jones and at least a head shorter. It is hard to tell for certain because he wears a grey fedora. It appears to be a nice hat, but it is not one you see much anymore. When men wore hats like this the city ended miles from here and my farm really was a farm.

"Is this about Jones?" I ask.

The man tilts his head to the side like Simon used to do when he didn't understand something.

"No," the man says. His voice is deep and slow, as if he's struggling to pull it up from somewhere hidden far inside himself. "I do not know Jones. I'm here with an odd request. My wife, you see, she threw away something that means a great deal to me. Perhaps she did not know how much. I only recently discovered what she had done. After a great deal of questioning, she confessed to having driven by your property and thrown it from the car. I did not understand why she would throw this item on a stranger's property, but now I see why she might do such a thing."

"Yes," I say, "People do it often."

The man takes off the fedora and squints at a skeletal antenna someone has propped against my fence. It is a hot afternoon and there is a whisper of breeze swaying the grass.

"I would like your permission to search for this item. If I find it, I will pay you for it, of course."

"Money is no matter," I say. "I'll even help you look."

The man purses his lips and places the fedora back on his head. He says, "I do not mean to be ungrateful, but I would prefer to search alone."

I tell him he is welcome to search for as long as he likes. I show him the hose he can drink from and offer to take his coat and hat, but he declines and says he would like to get started.

He is a patient man. On the first day he walks the property at random. He walks north for twenty yards then abruptly turns to the east before cutting back south and so on. It is a romantic way to search, to hope that fate will bring the item back to him. Lovely but ineffective and after the first stars come out the man leaves without a word. His white pants are torn and sweat has soaked through the brim of his hat.

The next day his search begins early and is scientific. I watch him scratch a grid in the dirt. For three days he walks the grid until it's exhausted. Next he climbs trees and looks down into the grass from above. The man must know I am watching, but he does not seem to mind. Nor does he ask for my help. He arrives before the sun rises from behind the road and leaves after it falls into the city's skyline. When he goes I step out into the night and search myself. I think maybe if he searches with the sun and I search with the stars one of us will find it. I find broken baby carriages and old mobiles but not what the man seeks. I am certain I will know it if I see it.

After his 18th day of searching the man knocks on my door. I have been watching him, but I count to 20 so he thinks I came from deep inside the house.

"I knew that if I did not find it on the first day I never would," he says. The search has aged him, made him smaller. He turns from the sun like it is now his enemy. "There is a time when patience becomes blindness. I believe we are at that time. Farewell."

I will never see him again.

That night there are not many trucks on the highway, and I feel like my battery is nearly dead. When I close my eyes so tight it feels like my head might burst. I do not see stars. It is as if they all burnt out years ago and only now am I discovering that their light has gone. Since I cannot sleep I drive my truck to the yellow house for the first time in weeks. All of the lights are on but no shadows move behind the curtains. I enter without knocking. It feels like my own home. The walls are white and the floors are oak. Everything is meticulously clean and silent except for a familiar hum coming from upstairs.

There, Jacob sits on the floor of his room taking a toy racecar on laps around a blue rug. The car makes the sound of an engine traveling at a much faster speed. Jacob does not look surprised to see me, but he does not look happy either. I ask him where his mother is.

"She's here," he says. "In her room. I think she comes out when I'm asleep. That's why I'm trying to stay awake."

Every door in the hallway is open except the set of double black doors at the end of the hall. I knock softly. I wait as long as I can manage, but I am tired. I knock a final time but there is no response. When I walk back down the hallway I see that Jacob has fallen asleep with the toy car still in his hand. Carefully I lift him into his bed. He mumbles, "Dad?" as if his father is there in his dream.

With only the motion of bodies in the house, I cannot manage a good sleep on the couch. In the morning, I take Jacob to school then drive into the city. No one says anything when I sit down in Jones's chair and sign his name onto important papers. One day, I even join my coworkers in singing happy birthday to someone. A skinny woman cuts me a big slice of cake and asks after Alice and Jacob. I tell her I will say hello for her. It is the opposite of disappearing. I stay in the house for nearly a month. At night I cannot hear the highway, and the streetlights make it hard to see the stars. The lights in the house are always bright now, and it is exhausting to be such a dim sun in their presence.

"Where do you think your father is?" I ask Jacob one morning.

He pulls his mouth to the right as he thinks it over.

"Space. That's where I would go," Jacob says. He is so young.

One night Alice finally emerges from her room while we are eating dinner. I have made tuna casserole from a recipe I found in a kitchen drawer. The house had all the ingredients.

"I would like you to take the dollhouse away," she says. Her voice sounds very different from what I imagine the pretty woman I used to watch gardening sounded like. It sounds like the buzz of bees. I wonder if I ever know anyone at all.

"I'll take it to the dump," I say. "Or maybe the Goodwill."

"No," she says. "I couldn't bear to throw it away or give it to someone else. It meant so much to him. I only want it gone. Please."

The garage lights are on and the black car shines brightly in its usual spot. Beside it is the blue dollhouse. It appears to be a very nice dollhouse but nothing particularly special. The windows are real glass and behind them are curtains cut from lace. There is no furniture inside. When I lift it, it is heavier than I expect and I am careful not to fall as I cross the street and set it into the back of my truck. I take the highway. Even though it made her think of angels, my wife was afraid of the highway. The truth is, she was afraid to drive at all. She never had a car, and I would drive her everywhere in my truck. Simon would sit between us. Where did they go? I wish I knew. They would say the same about me.

I pull over near the fence that marks the edge of my property. I lift the dollhouse and step into the field. Here, a thing can disappear without burial. The stars glisten above and below, and I feel like a turtle inside a box with pinprick air holes. I walk until I find a spot for the dollhouse where the grass is short and there is protection from a tree. Behind me the highway roars electric. In the house where my wife and I once lived two shadows move behind the curtains, but they are not ours. We have new homes and we live there.

ADAM PETERSON

IS THE AUTHOR OF THE FLASHER, MY UNTIMELY DEATH, AND
THE CO-AUTHOR OF [SPOILER ALERT]. HIS SHORT FICTION
CAN BE FOUND IN THE KENYON REVIEW, INDIANA REVIEW, THE
NORMAL SCHOOL, THE SOUTHERN REVIEW, AND ELSEWHERE

WHEN
WE TASTE
OF DEATH

DAMIEN ANGELICA WALTERS

Two lines of Death on a mirror.

No one could mistake it for something as mundane as cocaine. Death is blood red and the experience depends on the user—what they've eaten, how much they weigh, how many hours of shut-eye the night before, some kind of crazy biochemical magic or madness that defies explanation. Drowning, fire, heart attack, flesh-eating bacteria. There's no way to tell what you'll get.

That's the beauty of it, the powerful, terrible beauty. You'll never know until the drug hits, and once it does there's no way to change your mind and jump off the train. Boys and girls, keep your hands inside the ride at all times. You're stuck here until it comes to a stop.

Unless it never does.

The water has no top, no bottom. You can't swim your way to freedom and there's no life preserver waiting for you on the surface like a bit of cereal in milk. There is no surface. You spin and twist and finally you open your mouth and the water pours in and in and in.

Nate takes a deep breath before he enters the common room. Lila's sitting in a wheelchair, a thin blanket draped across her lap. She looks up and smiles when he walks in, but the smile doesn't reach her eyes. Her shirt partially conceals the IV needle currently connected to nothing, but the smell of the place is a reminder that can't be tucked away. Her limbs are stick-thin; eventually her muscles will atrophy and the chair will be a necessity, not a choice. There's only so much they can do after all, but she's alive and will be for a long time. Long enough, anyway.

Dark shadows mar the skin beneath her eyes and hollows run under her cheekbones, giving her the look of a starving supermodel. A slim silver chain around her neck holds her wedding rings; her fingers are too thin to keep them in their proper place. Nate kisses her forehead, remembering when her skin tasted of forever instead of antiseptic and sickness.

"You look good," he says.

Her eyes say she doesn't believe him, but her mouth remains silent.

"Want to take a walk?"

She gives a slight almost-nod, a gesture that maybe means yes or I don't care, so he pushes her chair out to the gardens. They talk but it's rambling, perfunctory. There's so much he wants to say, to scream, but he taps his fingers on his upper thigh, holds his words, the real words, in.

They don't talk about why she's here or what happens after he leaves.

The box is holding you in. Top nailed shut. Dirt above. Two feet? Six? It could be a hundred. No one's waiting with a shovel and a need to see your face again. You try to scrape a hole in the wood, and end up with your fingernails hanging in shreds of lost hope from the raw skin underneath. No point in screaming. The air is almost gone. You're holding the last breath inside, and once you let it out, that's it. Hold it in as long as you can, it doesn't matter. There's no one but you; nothing but the box, the silence on your lips, and the screaming in your lungs.

A month later, Nate's back. The doctors don't know why it works that way, the drug they have her on, but nothing else does a damn thing. A dose every day and still, she's only Lila once a month. *It is what it is,* his father would say.

It should've been him, not Lila. It was his idea, like most everything in their relationship. He didn't twist her arm or coerce her any other way, but still, if he'd never mentioned it, they wouldn't have started to ride the red, and this wouldn't have happened.

Again, he pushes her around the gardens. There isn't much else to do. She isn't strong enough to walk by his side, at least not for long, and although the common room has an entire shelving unit full of board games, she never liked them. He tried to teach her how to play chess a couple of times before, in the real world, and then after, in this place, but she refused each and every time.

"Hey, baby?"

"What?" she whispers.

"Remember when we broke the bed frame?" He lets out a quick laugh.

There's a long pause. Then she clears her throat, a dry, raspy sandpaper sound. "Why would you even say something like that? Why would you even bring that up?"

"I'm sorry. I didn't mean anything by it. I was just trying to make conversation, trying to maybe make you laugh."

"It's too cold out here." Her words are clipped at the edges. "I want to go back in."

"Okay. I swear, baby, I'm sorry." He stops pushing the chair, bends down. "Okay?"

She nods but refuses to look him in the eyes. He keeps his mouth shut as he pushes her back, and by the time they're inside, she's dozing off. He didn't mean to make her feel bad, but he doesn't understand why she couldn't just laugh it off. No matter the how or why, it was funny when it happened.

Straps hold you in place as a current runs through your body, a thousand volts racing through every vein, every cell, every organ. Your hair sizzles, your skin bubbles, your mouth fills with the taste of rancid peanut butter. You twist and fight against the restraints, but you're held fast in place and the electricity keeps running.

There's no 12-step program, no kind therapist with a comfortable sofa, no plans for what comes after. That would be cruel. There is no after.

The risk is 1 in 100,000 or so they think. A permanent hallucination, the doctors call it. There's nothing they can point to that explains why some people don't come out on their own, why they get stuck, and there's nothing they can do to prevent the ride.

Nate heard of one case where they put a guy in a medically-induced coma as a test and brought him out a week later, figuring he'd tell them he'd been asleep the whole time. No such luck on their part. Once it takes hold, Death doesn't give up.

Still, the doctors and researchers think they can and will eventually break it, the craving. No need to call it an addiction, it's so much more.

The police have cracked down hard, but they can't eradicate it completely. That shit hasn't worked with anything—let me hear you say Prohibition, amen, my brothers and sisters—let alone something this powerful.

The first time Nate brought a vial home, Lila held it up to the light, and for a long time said nothing. He was the curious one. His buddy Corey said it was the most amazingly intense experience he'd ever had. Fucked up, but intense.

Nate cut the lines on the glass top of their coffee table. One for each of them. Corey said one line would be enough to know if they ever wanted to do it again. He was right.

After, he and Lila lay tangled up in sweaty sheets. The sex had been hard, brutal enough to leave bruises on them both, but better than it had been in a long time. More . . . real. The light in her eyes wasn't from the sex, it was the afterglow, Death's perfect finish, a euphoria so precise and clear that anything was possible. She'd held out her hands, turning them over and over again, staring at something he couldn't see, but could imagine without any effort at all.

"Are you okay?" he'd said. "What was it like for you?"

She'd raked her fingernails across his chest, drawing blood, and fucked his questions away. Right when she started breathing his name fast and quick and grinding her hips hard against his, there was a loud crack and the mattress dropped. They were both too close to coming to care, but they'd laughed their asses off when they carried the broken pieces of the bed frame out to the Dumpster.

The next weekend, he bought a second vial.

You feel them on you—many legs like feather-soft kisses but they only have affection for your flesh. Tiny rips and tears, delicate morsels slipping down gullets before you can comprehend just how long it will take them to swallow every bit down. Skin, muscle, the yellow blobs of fat, and deeper, into the bones, playing hide and seek with your marrow.

Nate stands outside the facility for several long minutes. This time he'll talk to her, really talk. They won't tap dance around the minefield of unspoken words, and he won't say anything stupid. He'll just talk to her. It won't change anything, won't put anything to right, but maybe it'll take away some of the wrong. And maybe she'll really talk to him, too.

He's inside for about thirty seconds before a nurse pulls him aside.

"She's having a rough day today," she says.

He waits for her to explain, and she opens her mouth but snaps it shut. There's a trace of condemnation, of judgment, in her eyes, only a hint, but it's enough. He walks away before she can change her mind again about speaking.

A rough day? Fuck. Lila's riding the red too much to really know what a rough day is. She doesn't have to deal with work or bills or anything else anymore. He clenches his fists, pushes away the thoughts, the bright flare of anger.

Lila's running her hands back and forth along the padded arms of her wheelchair as if they're an instrument she yearns to play. There's something different, something new, in her eyes that he can't place.

She's never blamed him, at least not verbally, but he's caught a glimpse of it in her eyes a few times. But it isn't his fault. He never forced her to do it, but he doesn't want to get into a piss and moan match about it. What good would that do? They can't change anything. And hell, he's apologized a thousand times over. Is he supposed to open his veins and offer his blood?

What he sees now isn't blame. He doesn't know exactly what it is, but it makes him want to run away. Instead, they wander through the gardens, she in the chair and he behind it, the silence hanging over them, heavy and oppressive.

That silence is what does it. They used to talk to each other into the long hours of the night. They used to talk about everything, anything. The silence is fucking wrong. They don't have much time together; they should be talking, not this . . . nothing. He brings her chair to a stop beneath the leaves of a maple tree and gets on one knee. He holds her hand for a long time, brushing his fingers over the bony knuckles while she looks off to the side.

"Is it always the same for you?" He keeps his voice soft.

Her head whips around faster than he imagined possible. Her eyes narrow.

"What?"

"The death, is it always the same?"

Her mouth tightens and she pulls her hand away. "I want to go back. Take me back."

"Come on, baby, don't say that. Just talk to me."

"Take me back now."

No matter what else he says, she refuses to speak. He pushes her back, cursing himself for a fool. She always was stubborn; when she didn't want to talk about something, she dug in her heels. He didn't know why he expected her to be any different now, but damn, he wasn't asking for the moon.

The heat presses in, but there's no smoke to carry you away while the flames do their worst. You feel the lick and bite of fire everywhere, all at once, eating your toes, your fingers, your lips, and the tip of your nose. It doesn't stop, only builds, until you're nothing but a steaming misshapen figure puddled on the floor that's no longer recognizable as human and still, the fire burns.

Lila's not in her wheelchair.

"She refused," the nurse says, her voice clipped, disapproving.

Lila's on her side in the bed, facing away from him, facing the bare white wall. What does she see? An endless avalanche of snow raging fury? The foam of a towering wave as it crashes?

"Hey, baby," he says.

She answers with only silence for a long time. Then, "I don't want you to come here anymore, Nate."

He hisses in a breath. "What? Why?"

She rolls over, fixes him with a gaze stronger and more binding than any rope. No tears, only determination. "Because I see it in your eyes every time. You're the one who wanted it. I went along with it because I loved you."

"Don't lie to me," he says. "Don't lie to yourself. You loved it, too. And you could've said no, for fuck's sake."

"Of course you'd say that."

"What the hell do you want me to say?"

"Nothing. I want you to say nothing. Just leave me alone." She shudders. "You have no idea what it's like."

"So tell me, talk to me then."

She laughs, the sound sharp and high-pitched. "That's all you want, isn't it? That's all you've ever wanted. To know what it's like."

"No, baby. I just want you to talk to me."

"Don't kid yourself, Nate. I know you. You've never been able to fool me, and you don't just want to know what it's like. You want it, you want all of this." She waves her hand around. "It should've been you, but I'm the one who's stuck with it."

The only thing he can say is, "Baby."

"I don't want to talk to you anymore. I don't want to see you anymore."

"Please don't say that. I'm sorry, so sorry."

"Enough, okay?" Now her voice is weary, each word holding the slightest tremble. "If you knew, you wouldn't want it at all. You would never touch it again. Just go."

Then she slips under. One minute, she's awake, aware; the next, her eyes go distant, her mouth soft. Strange that something so powerful and chaotic on the inside elicits such external peace. It shouldn't be that way. It doesn't look right. He crouches down next to the bed, watches her face. He touches her eyelids gently, wishing he could see what she sees, could feel what she feels.

When the nurse tells him he needs to leave, he backs out of the room with his hands shoved in his pockets. Lila's right. It should've been him.

Pain hits your chest like a rubber bullet from a riot gun. It reaches in and squeezes tighter and tighter, a vice grip sending lightning bolts of hurt down your arms, your spine, your legs. The air in your lungs refuses to budge because the unseen hands holding your heart keep twisting and twisting, and even when you think there can't possibly be anything left to wring free, the agony keeps digging in, digging deep.

Nate's eyes snap open.

It's incredible, overwhelming, like the most intense orgasm laced with razor blades and barbed wire. No one who hasn't tried it can even begin to understand how so much torment can feel so fucking good. He tries to grab it back, to hold it just a little longer, but it dances away with a soft kiss nearly as excruciating as the Death, and like any goodbye, it carries the sting of small cruelty. He wipes a slick of sweat from his forehead. Punches the cushion once, twice, three times. Rakes his fingers through his hair.

"Fuck," he mutters. "Come on, come on, come on."

His hands are shaking, and the vial tips over, spilling Death onto the coffee table, a Technicolor Rorschach taunting him, teasing him. But he'll get there, he knows he will. If he does enough, he'll get there. Fuck Lila, fuck the doctors, fuck everything.

He cuts another line, hoping this will be the one that pulls him under and keeps him there.

DAMIEN ANGELICA WALTERS

HAS PUBLISHED WORK IN VARIOUS MAGAZINES AND
ANTHOLOGIES, INCLUDING YEAR'S BEST WEIRD FICTION
VOLUME ONE, THE BEST OF ELECTRIC VELOCIPEDE, CASSILDA'S
SONG, NIGHTMARE, LIGHTSPEED, STRANGE HORIZONS, APEX,
SHIMMER, INTERZONE, GLITTER & MAYHEM, AND WHAT
FATES IMPOSE. SING ME YOUR SCARS, A COLLECTION OF HER
SHORT FICTION, WILL BE RELEASED IN EARLY 2015 FROM
APEX PUBLICATIONS, AND PAPER TIGERS, A NOVEL, WILL
BE RELEASED LATER THAT SAME YEAR FROM DARK HOUSE
PRESS. VISIT HER AT WWW.DAMIENANGELICAWALTERS.COM
OR ON TWITTER @DAMIENAWALTERS

FIGURE
EIGHT

BRENDAN DETZNER

You could see the Foundation of the Eternal Light from the expressway. It was on the seventh floor of a crumbling red brick building that had never quite made the transition from warehouse to office space to something else, and which seemed to be pushed and pulled on by every building surrounding it so that it twisted and leaned and appeared to hang from the sky like a vine. The Foundation of the Eternal Light had moved here two months ago. It had spent the previous six months in an isolated ranch house in Warrenville, and a very hard two weeks prior to that in a pair of adjacent garden apartments in a building in Joliet. Each time, brothers and sisters had been lost. There were three of them left now, and Father Jim.

The seventh floor was not meant to be a residence. There was a men's and a women's bathroom and many winding hallways, two looping interconnected circles. Father Jim kept all of the doors locked, and held all of the keys. Father Jim slept on a futon mattress in one of the corner offices. Brothers Michael, Donald, and Neil slept on hallway floors, when they slept.

The first thing they did when they arrived was take a trip to a

nearby hardware store and spend most of their remaining money. Then they unscrewed and shattered all the lightbulbs and painted the walls and the floors and the ceilings and the windows black. Brothers Michael and Donald each were given a candle. Father Jim had a flashlight, a heavy metal cylinder that was like a club. Brother Neil got nothing. Brother Neil was lost, Father Jim told them. Brother Neil needed to be reminded.

Brother Michael didn't know exactly what it was that Brother Neil had done. They knew it must be something, knew that it must be obvious.

Brother Neil's clothes were taken away and he was locked in a closet. He didn't fight; they all told him how much they loved him and cared about him and needed him as they closed the door. When Brother Michael and Brother Donald turned around, Father Jim was gone.

They walked in circles, sometimes together and sometimes apart, stopping to sleep and to eat from the boxes of fried rice that Father Jim left lying around for them. They dripped hot wax behind them wherever they went. By the time their candles burned down to nothing they knew the corridors so well that they didn't have to see.

Brother Neil cried. He banged on the door of the closet and begged for them to open the door. They could hear him weeping. They steeled themselves and ignored him. Brother Michael had been a part of the foundation for three years, Brother Donald for even longer. They'd always known that these days would come, the hardest times, the birth pains. Father Jim had talked about them every day. They'd come from nothing, had had nothing before this. That was what made them special.

If they lost faith now, it would all be for nothing.

Brother Neil eventually stopped crying, stopped banging on the door.

Father Jim was preparing himself, too. He wore all black, so that he could move through the hallways like a ghost. He shaved his head and his face, clumsily so that the razor left thin red lines all over his face and scalp. You could see his jaw line, his sunken cheeks and the sharp curve of bone under skin just above his eyes. Brother Michael wondered if he'd been eating, and immediately cursed himself, dug deep into himself for daring to question Father Jim, who was his only hope.

Michael was thinking about it when Father Jim appeared, inches away from his face. He shone his flashlight into Michael's eyes, and for a moment, he was sure they were going to catch on fire.

"DO YOU WANT TO BE FREE? DO YOU WANT TO BE A SINNER?"

Michael stumbled backwards, confused.

"No . . ." he whispered, not sure.

Father Jim hit him in the ribs with the handle of the flashlight. Michael clutched at his chest and fell to his knees. He gasped for breath. Father Jim shined the flashlight in his eyes again and he shrunk the rest of the way to the floor.

"DO YOU WANT TO BE FREE? DO YOU WANT TO BE A SINNER?"

Michael tried to cover his face with his hands. "Yes . . ."

Father Jim hit him again. Father Jim kept hitting him, kept asking the questions.

"DO YOU WANT TO BE FREE? DO YOU WANT TO BE A SINNER?"

As soon as Michael stopped answering, as soon as he could no longer think a coherent thought, the light went out and Father Jim vanished.

Time went by, it was impossible to tell how much except by cycles of sleep and wakefulness, which became gradually impossible to count or even distinguish between. Michael heard things, insects crawling over his ankles; he heard voices, felt the warmth of sunlight behind him only to find nothing when he turned to face it.

Once, when Brother Michael woke up, he was in Father Jim's resting place. It looked like a dorm room. It was clean, it was safe. Incense was burning, partially covering the smell from outside— Neil's body rotting. Michael pushed the thought away, buried it in a secret part of himself.

Jim had turned his desk lamp so that it faced the wall and didn't shine into Michael's eyes.

Father Jim was kneeling on his mattress, his hands resting on his knees, his eyes closed. He spoke in a voice Michael hadn't heard in a long time.

"You must hate me for the things I've done to you. But you'll never dare tell me."

It was a trap, one that Michael had seen play out many times before. Father Jim would pretend that he was putting on an act, that he was fooling them, that he took satisfaction from their pain. He would dare the person who spoke to wake up and get a clue and leave. Then, the very moment that the person began to break, that they began to doubt that Father Jim was the prophet, he would become Father Jim again and scream at them for their inconsistency.

"This is the very last time that I'll be honest with you," he said, in that same low, reasonable, human voice. "I only started all this for the women. That was the whole point at first, it was all about pussy."

"You were supposed to figure it out. Not right away, but eventually—you were smart, you weren't like the others. You were supposed to leave, so I'd know when I was done. It was never supposed to go this far."

He produced his key ring from somewhere in his robe and threw it down on the ground in front of him.

"I lied. I'm not a prophet. We're not going to be saved. You've been tricked. Get the hell out of here now while you still can."

Father Jim opened his eyes then, and watched Michael carefully. Michael looked down at the floor and folded his hands in his lap. He didn't move.

Father Jim got up, leaned over carefully, and picked up his keys. He opened the door. A cockroach scurried away. The light from the room reached out into the hallway, so that in a fixed radius from the doorway you could see the dirty floor, black paint covered in a layer of dust, speckled with calcified grains of fried rice.

Michael got up and walked back into the darkness. The door closed behind him.

He walked, he slept. He had a dream about a cold breeze.

Michael realized that he wasn't dreaming.

He turned the corner, and saw sunlight shining down from an open doorway. He got closer. It was a maintenance closet—there was a metal ladder bolted to the wall, leading to an open hatch. He climbed up.

The horizon was a dirty orange Creamsicle color, the very beginning of the sunrise joining together with the headlights and the traffic signals and the electric artery running through the center of the expressway.

Father Jim was lying in the middle of the roof face down, with his limbs stretched out and bent in all directions. There was a gun on the ground next to him, and a neat line of blood twisting and curving from his head to the storm drain.

Michael took a closer look. He didn't move any closer, he just looked more intently. It was another trick, another test. Michael would not allow himself to doubt.

"Fuck, man." Michael turned around. Donald was standing on the other side of the roof.

"Bullshit," Donald said. "It was all fucking bullshit. Fuck. Fuck."

"Don't say that," Michael answered, but Donald didn't listen, he was already walking towards the body.

"Fucking..." He reached down and pulled up on Father Jim's shoulder, flipping the body over and revealing the gaping bloody hole in the side of his head. "Just a fucking joke. Just a fucking joke." He laughed nervously.

"We need to wait," Michael said, but Donald was already walking back towards the ladder.

"I've got to get the hell out of here. I've got to go . . . "

"No. Not now. We're so close."

Michael wasn't sure if Donald heard him. In any case, he wasn't stopping.

The flashlight was on the ground near the trap door. Michael had stepped over it without noticing that it was there.

Donald put his hand on the ladder. He had a vacant smile on his face and was whispering something to himself. He was going to swing his feet over and climb down. He was going to leave.

Michael walked over, picked up the flashlight, and swung the handle into the side of Donald's head, all in one swift motion. He did it without thinking, and was surprised immediately afterwards at what he'd done. Donald didn't even hardly seem to notice that he'd been hit. He took a step backwards. He stopped smiling.

"It wasn't for anything Michael. It was nothing."

"Shut up."

"It was bullshit, Michael."

Michael hit him again and he fell down.

For a moment time seemed to speed up and slow down simultaneously. He was swinging the flashlight. He was not yet swinging the flashlight. He'd swung the flashlight, many times, his arm was heavy, he was sitting on the roof with the bodies of two people he used to know, wondering if the cops were going to come. Wondering if anybody was going to come.

"SHUT UP! WE HAVE TO WAIT! WE HAVE TO WAIT!"

He beat him to death while the sun came up.

BRENDAN DETZNER

LIVES, WORKS, AND WRITES IN CHICAGO. HIS WORK IS
SOMETIMES SCARY, SOMETIMES FUNNY, AND USUALLY VERY
STRANGE. HE'S BEEN PUBLISHED IN PSEUDOPOD, CHIZINE,
BIZARROCAST, ONE BUCK HORROR, THE BOOK OF DEAD THINGS
ANTHOLOGY AND OTHER VENUES. HE ALSO RUNS BAD
GRAMMAR THEATER, A MONTHLY READING SERIES. YOU
CAN FIND OUT ABOUT BGT AT WWW.BADGRAMMARTHEATER.
COM AND READ/LISTEN TO MORE OF BRENDAN'S WORK
AT WWW.BRENDANDETZNER.COM.

MY
MOTHER'S
CONDITION

FAITH GARDNER

had moved to the place where honks replaced hawk-cries and high-rises swallowed redwoods, and didn't visit my mother as often as maybe I should have, and this is why I knew nothing of her condition.

Dez and I rode the bullet train to visit, that time of year when every snow-crumbed town that whizzed by us shouted with artificial lights. It had been too long, I thought, Dez on my knee, sucking her pinky. Dez had been barely able to roll over on her belly when I last visited. She had been a hairless pink prize in a fleece blanket when I last visited. And now her tongue had found words, like *mommy*, and *hungry*, and even sentences: *I want*.

Dez wouldn't recognize her grandmother from a stranger, I thought. Time splintered wholes into parts.

After the long wait at the rain-spattered train station, my mother's telephone bleating and bleating with no "Hello" to interrupt, a yellow cab drove us there. The guilt, the fear was a bone-deep thunder. Something was wrong, some tragedy had befallen my mother—a spill down basement steps, a slick-smiled serial killer, a blood clot to the brain—and left Dez and I with no one to greet us at the station. My mind offered horror after horror like picture-post-cards from hell, and I held onto Dez tightly, fidgeting over her shiny shoes, seeing myself distorted and monster-headed in their itty shine. Out the cab window, the forest was an eye-numbing blizzard of green until the cab pulled up to her house.

"Thank you," I told the cabbie, who chewed a toothpick and eyed my stockinged legs before screeching out of the driveway.

I held Dez on my hip and stared at my mother's bungalow, shingled and brown as a pinecone, and listened to treetop shrieks and ear-tickling breezes.

"What's that?" Dez asked, her arms around my neck.

I picked up the hard suitcase from the damp asphalt, looked back at the empty road.

"This here's the world," I said. "Without subways and sky-scrapers."

The fear choked, choked, with every click of my heels that brought us closer to the house. The flowerbeds had been upturned, the garbage was raccoon-ransacked and strewn in the yard. News-papers piled up, weather-torn and wet. And there were no icicle lights hanging from the roof gutters or plastic fat-bellied men in red suits on her lawn.

"Oh God," I said.

"Oh God," Dez said, and laughed.

And with each tiptoe nearer to the stoop, I imagined I grew smaller, smaller, my years shed and left behind like leaves in the driveway, and I was a little girl again, frantic with desire, my vo-cabulary limited to one infinite word: *mother mother mother.*

I pushed her door open.

"Hello?" I asked the wood-paneled walls, the dried flowers in vases, the needlepoint left on the countertop. Dirty dishes in the sink. A tangled pile of mildew-stinky sheets. My eyes filled, and I felt more puddle than person. But Dez was a weight on my hip, and I stood upright, swallowing the pill of fear.

"I'm here," my mother said.

And that's when I saw her—*thank you thank you,* my silent voice gratefully gushing—she was alive. Seated on a blanket-draped couch, hands folded in her lap. But . . . I had to gasp.

She was the size of Dez.

"Mother," was all I could say.

"Mother," Dez repeated.

"Shhh," I told Dez.

I sat next to my mother—my *mother,* whose hope-bright face and careful cloud of hair only reached my chest. Who wore my jog-a-thon shirt I recognized from 5th grade.

"What happened?" I asked.

"Isn't it obvious?" she said. "It happened to my mother. Now it's my turn."

"Why didn't you tell me?" I asked.

"Didn't want to be a bother."

"No," I said, shaking my head.

"You can naysay all you want," my mother said. "What good does it do?"

Her jaw was clenched, her anger sharpening the words.

"You can't live like this," I said. "You need to come home with us."

My mother reached out and squeezed Dez's fist in her own— they were, alarmingly, almost same-sized.

"All right," she said simply.

And I called the cabbie back, and when the three of us sat in the back seat—Dez in her car seat, mother in my lap—we waved goodbye to the bungalow for the last time.

My body seemed to swell. I was a lady King Kong in a cab. Even the view outside the window, the other cars, the rainclouds smeared across the sky, took on a new diminished proportion.

———

My mother disliked my apartment. The late-night thumps of the treadmill upstairs, the hot curry pong that filled the hall, the roaches that scuttled across the linoleum in late hours.

"At my size, they're monstrous," she said. "You've got to get out of this place."

"In your condition, you've got to take what you can get," I told her. "It could be worse."

"It *will* be worse," she promised.

I bought a double-stroller, took Dez and my mother out on daily walks to the park after work. There, she could listen to the creek water and stare at ants as they marched along tree bark. Dogs without leashes, pigeons pecking at lawns.

"I miss my home," my mother said sadly, staring at a Chihuahua in a leopard-print coat that peed on a maple. "This isn't nature."

"Mother," I said. "I'm doing the best I can."

"That nanny treats me like a child," she said. "Yesterday she tried to spoon-feed me."

I sighed. "I'll talk to her about it."

"And Dez keeps pulling my hair," she said. "No matter what I say—you leave the room and she goes straight for a fistful of my hair."

Dez laughed.

"It's not funny, Dez," I told her. "You be nice to Grandma."

"She won't listen," my mother said. "Sometimes I wish you had just left me there to shrivel up in familiarity."

I held my mother's tiny hand in my own.

"I couldn't let that happen," I said. "I love you."

"Part of love is admitting you have no control," she said. "That's something I think you've never understood."

I stared at an older woman hurrying by us, scarecrow tall and thin, in a herringbone coat. She was laughing into a telephone; I watched the silver sky, and I was so miniscule, plankton in a whale's jaws.

"Let me call a doctor," I murmured.

"Not that again," my mother said. "I told you, I get a whiff of a hospital or a specialist, and I'll shoot off like a cat. I may be small, but my legs still work."

"Fine," I said.

I stared at them side by side—my mother with her colorless curls, my daughter with her mop of white-blond—both in pink sweaters meant for Dez. The opposite poles of my DNA, bizarre twins. I knew this was a snapshot in time, a moment born to be lost, but it felt so permanent then that it ached like a growing pain.

———

My mother's mother—my grandmother, that is—had the same condition. Over a short period of years, she shed pounds and inches, lost the ability to drive, open doors for herself, reach countertops. Finally, my mother took her in, made her a basket-bed and a closet-room. And when my mother took my grandmother to the doctor, they kept my grandmother overnight, then over weeks, invited more and more doctors in to see her, filmed her, poked and pricked her, thrust her in the belly of plastic machines, until finally my mother hired a lawyer and demanded the hospital release her poor, small mother, who was trapped inside an incubator like an awful house of glass.

On the way home from the hospital, on the train, my mother clasped the shoebox holding her mother, muttering apologies. She petted her mother's hair and sucked back tears, suggested medicine women and wild herbs. My mother dozed as the train hummed along, and when she awoke, she had missed her stop. She frantically grabbed her luggage and got off at the next station. It was only then, on the platform with the steaming chug of the train as it pulled away from her and left her alone, that she realized she had left her mother on the seat.

The monotone operator on the telephone swore she would check the lost and found. A day later, my mother got news that the shoebox had been recovered—cardboard crushed, dinner napkin that was once a blanket gone, only empty space remaining.

I made a bed for my mother from Dez's cradle, and when summer came, I moved her to the bassinet. She wouldn't let me use the measuring tape.

"Why?" she asked. "No matter what the numbers say, I'm shrinking."

"It's hard for me to notice," I said. "I see you every day."

But it was the comparison that made her dwindling obvious. For as Dez swelled and ballooned—stumbling around the house in new frilly dresses while my mother stooped to Dez's hand-me-downs—my mother was now the obvious runt of the two. I often found my mother hiding in the hamper, or beneath the bed, to avoid Dez and the nanny, and even the Rumba that my mother had started to fear would swallow her up. I thought that was ridiculous—my mother wasn't insectile enough to be swallowed by a sweeping machine.

By fall, I got rid of the Rumba, though, as it didn't seem so crazy anymore. She was almost minute enough to get a limb caught in it. Besides, history haunted like a ghost made of words. I remembered my mother's mistake with her mother. I vowed never to be so careless.

———

As the weather grayed and temperatures dropped to cruel and icy nadirs, I took her out for walks each day, wrapping her in a fleece blanket, cradling her in my arms as we strolled by delis and street vendors. But I was too afraid to let her off on her own, to explore the park lawns or sit on tree branches. There were sharp-toothed dogs and chiding squirrels. She was bird-sized. She was prey.

My mother was only about six inches tall now, and increasingly quiet, and depressed. She stared out the window for hours and napped constantly in my top drawer among stockings and discarded hairpins.

For Christmas, I bought my mother a dollhouse. I placed her inside and watched her mouth, a red O.

"It smells like trees," my mother said, touching the banister. She was wearing clothes I had bought from a Toys R Us, meant for dolls; that meant my mother wore a jean jacket and pink shimmering tutu. She reminded me of a child, the way she giggled as she touched the hung paintings I'd special-ordered. "The details!"

I hadn't seen joy on her in ages. There was a flushed smudge to her cheeks as she ran up the stairs.

"A kitchen!" she said, throwing open the cabinets. "With dishes!"

She stared at herself in the tiny bathroom mirror. "There I am!"

She sat on the bed in the master bedroom. "It fits me," she said, amazed.

Dez was jealous. "I want a dollhouse," she said, stamping her foot and pushing her stuffed monkeys and books to the floor.

"You'll get it someday," I said.

A heavy moment hung in the air like a knife dangling over the room, and I cleared my throat. I saw my mother stare at me with a tiny frightened expression that asked, *what will become of me?* And I looked away with a visage that refused to answer, my refusal replying, *I don't know.*

I often stared at my clock and thought, if I wanted it bad enough, if I concentrated well enough, I could stop the ticking. If we could pause, there would be no tragedy in this. I could freeze everything and just *be* here, just *enjoy* this instead of scurrying to keep up with the invisible hurricane of change.

Her happiness didn't last. Because, she reminded me, the house was well-designed, impeccably decorated with miniatures but . . . non-functional.

"The toilet doesn't flush!" she said, opening the lid. "See? The sinks don't run. The stove doesn't work. I'm living in a model home."

"There's no such thing as a fully functioning dollhouse," I reminded her.

"It's somehow worse," she said, her voice quivering. "Because for moments in here, the proportions are all so right, I forget I'm not normal. Yesterday I spent half my day straightening out the extra room, rearranging it to make it just right for a guest room—when I realized I'll never have any guests."

"I'm sorry," I said, peering in, seeing my enormous bleary eye reflected in the bitty bathroom mirror. "I'm trying my best."

But nothing I did could prevent her weeping. And though her body was miniscule, her sobs, her voice, they were still large enough to fill a room.

"Why's Grandma sad?" asked Dez, who was wearing her new Christmas pajamas. She was a little girl there, suddenly, with her long tangled hair and her nightgown. She wasn't a baby anymore. I could see the startling blueprint of a woman—a lovely brown-eyed half-me woman—in her features.

"That's enough," I said, wiping my eyes. "Go to bed."

I watched Dez tiptoe out of the room, and into hers, where she crawled into her low bed on the floor and covered herself with blankets.

When you watch over someone every day, nearly every shared hour, change seems like a lie. But there was no denying my mother's shrinkage was slipping to disappearance. The cabinets in her dollhouse became unreachable and she could no longer crawl into her own bed without a boost. Her meals consisted of a mere crumb or two. And then she herself was the size of a crumb, an ant, until finally—I had to squint to see her—a flea, a dust speck, and then beyond location.

"Mother?" I called out in the dollhouse halls, and up the stairwell.

I knew she was somewhere, a microbe, a germ-sized woman lost among the impossible largeness of the dollhouse.

"I'm still here," her voice said.

"Where?" I asked, scouring the microscopic floorboards, the pinky-nail sized flower vases and pots and pans.

"I don't know," she finally said. "Nothing is recognizable."

My breath quickened, my stomach tightened up. I had lost my mother! I had lost my vulnerable speck of a mother! Was she floating in the air now, not tethered to gravity? Would she be carried away by the breeze of an open window, like a dot of pollen, never to be heard from again?

"You have to tell me where you are," I pled. "Describe something. Lead me to you."

"I honestly have no idea," she said. "It's indescribable, it's...colorless. I can't even feel my feet. I seem to be floating."

I scoured my room's corners—windowsills, cobwebs, dust bunnies. There was no woman among the grime and grout between tiles.

"Don't be so alarmed," she said. "It's very peaceful here. I feel like I'm finally the right size."

———

I never saw my mother again, though I looked for her each day, and whenever the vacuum cleaner or the Swiffer came out, I told her to yell if the sucking or sweeping disturbed her. She only replied, "It's fine, I'm fine, dear, you go on ahead."

For Dez's third birthday, she inherited the dollhouse. Dez appeared so titanic, towering over the plastic girls she fisted as she shoved them from room to room, her fingers monstrous in comparison to their tiny pinched plastic waists.

I wanted to be despondent, to mourn like a daughter should mourn a mother, but how could I when her voice was still there, clear and ringing as a bird's cry in my ear? I asked questions and she answered, and it didn't matter if I was in the apartment, or in the park, or walking the noisy people-cluttered sidewalks. My mother's voice was there. In the middle of the night, I would call out "Mother?" And she would answer, "Go back to sleep, baby."

It wasn't until Dez got up out of her bed one night, and hung in the doorway twirling her tangled hair around her finger, asking, "Mommy, who are you talking to?" that I realized that voice— that bell-clear comfort I carried with me everywhere—was now mine alone.

FAITH GARDNER

HAS HAD SHORT FICTION PUBLISHED IN PLACES LIKE
ZYZZYVA, MCSWEENEY'S INTERNET TENDENCY, AND CUTBANK
LITERARY MAGAZINE. HER YA NOVEL PERDITA WILL BE
PUBLISHED BY MERIT PRESS IN 2015. SHE LIVES IN
BERKELEY WITH A HUSBAND, A DAUGHTER, AND A CAT.
FIND HER AT FAITHGARDNER.COM.

FRAGILE

MAGIC

ALEX KANE

As soon as he heard the front door slam shut downstairs, Ezekiel Buckner rolled free of his bedclothes and thudded to the floor. He groaned in the unanswering dark, and felt his way toward the door without making too much commotion. Zeke's father wouldn't have liked him wandering about like this, with his leg braces on for the night. His bedtime was past. Daddy would have told him to get his scrawny ass back into bed *right this instant*—but for now, he had the house to himself. Zeke listened as the car accelerated on down the street, the purr of its engine growing distant until all he heard was the gentle clawing of the trees against the siding.

With a squeak of the tarnished doorknob, he escaped into the dimness of the upstairs hallway, wriggling and pulling with his elbows to reach the narrow rug that ran down the center of the hardwood.

His destination called out to him: a dangling length of string, about ten inches or so above the floor, and a set of pale wooden stairs shadowed by the greater darkness that hung above them, like a yawning rectangular mouth filled with midnight sky.

Daddy had left the trapdoor open. For at least the next hour, the frontier of the attic was his to explore.

The forbidden, the supposedly dangerous and unreachable, always seemed to cry out for his inspection. After all, he'd spent most of his seven years confined to the indoors, to his father's notions of safety, to the doctor's unending list of cautionary suggestions.

If he were given the option to trade his childhood for some less hellish existence, Zeke supposed he'd first have to wrap his pristine little life in a layer or two of bubble wrap, throw in a small ocean of Styrofoam pellets, and box it all up in a cardboard package stamped, in bold red ink, FRAGILE.

But of course he had cable television in his bedroom, and since he was privately tutored and didn't go to school with the other kids in the neighborhood, he stayed up late each night clicking through the channels. Drifting toward sleep to the violet flicker of the changing signal, the sound muted to avoid alerting Daddy, he got his education from programs like *Tales from the Crypt* and *The Twilight Zone*. Old black-and-white fright films like *Psycho* and *The Creature from the Black Lagoon*.

So he knew that everyone was fragile in one way or another, that there was no exchanging your lot for someone else's. You made do with what you had. Or you suffered for it.

As Zeke crawled up the first step, a sudden throb of pain ran the length of his right leg the instant he allowed his weight to fall on the knee. He reached upward with a tired, shaky hand, and pulled with all his strength.

He tried to imagine the secrets that had been hidden away from him, the untold treasures waiting to be found in the upper darkness of the centuries-old house. If the rickety stairs that led the way were any indication, the world of the attic was coated in a thick membrane of dust, gray and stringy like tufts of an old man's hair.

The second step brought yet another ache. A duller pain, this time in his left knee. Zeke clattered upward until he could see the floor of the attic, the wooden edges of the steps jabbing him in the ribcage with each jerky motion.

Moonlight slanted in through a single ornamented window at the opposite end of the attic. It cast a silvery-blue light on the dust-caked hardwood, splintered by the fragmented windowpane and the skeletal shapes of the trees outside.

Milk crates, cardboard boxes, and filing cabinets of every shape and size were piled as high as the ceiling would allow, walling in the sliver of illuminated space in the center and making most of the room inaccessible to anyone larger than a mouse.

The pull-down staircase shimmied and creaked as he crept up the last few steps. An undisturbed patch of dust tickled his chin as he crossed the floor, on all fours like some helpless animal. He shivered, imagining for a moment that the dust was not dust but a spider web, that he was about to feel the scurrying of legs like soft needles across his face.

With this thought, he scrambled to get a grip on the handle of one of Daddy's many locked cabinets, then began to pull with all his might. The strain on his leg braces caused a thin metallic snap. He didn't let it worry him. Right now, he was standing up.

Zeke slowly released his hand, taking care not to let his fingers fall too far from the drawer handle, but found that the braces were holding. His legs wobbled, a little nervous in this unfamiliar up-right position, but—

He was standing on his own two legs.

No crutches, no special chair; just a cautionary hand to keep his balance.

He'd spent his childhood in and out of operating rooms and doctors' offices. *Special*, his daddy had once told him. *Your legs are special, bud—and after we get you all fixed up, they'll be as good as anybody's. Hell, probably better.*

Years and years of sleeping in the cold metal braces. Tossing about in the night for hours, hoping exhaustion would knock him out. Sometimes, he'd just give up the prospect of sleep and lie motionless until dawn slipped over the horizon.

He let his left leg glide forward and find its footing in the dark. The sole of the leg brace whispered as it parted the dust, drawing up splinters from the hardwood. He lifted the other leg, got it caught momentarily on the corner of a heavy box, and took another step. Despite the suspicion that he might be dreaming, he kept on walking.

From atop a mostly-empty shelf just beneath the window, he saw a small face eyeing him.

Zeke steadied himself, and then leaned down to get a better look at the figure that had met his gaze. The little wooden man wore a bright red suit, its buttons and lapel painted on in the same brilliant white as the gentleman's enormous eyes and lips. A beige skimmer hat topped his black head, tilted to one side. Zeke took another step closer.

A long lever jutted from the disc on which the small man stood, the same unpainted pine as his shoes and the smooth twigs that served him for legs. It rested on a green fulcrum that sat on the pedestal opposite the wide-eyed figure himself.

With a steady finger, Zeke tapped the lever.

The little wooden man began to dance. His legs trip-trapped a jubilant rhythm that rocked his body left and right, the pivot of his hips keeping parallel to his shoulders. His hollow knees jerked back and forth in skittering arcs like the sticks of a jazz drummer: *tap, tap-tap, trippety-thok!*

"Wow," Zeke whispered. "You can dance?" He'd never seen anyone dancing before, except on TV. It struck him as magical.

He flicked the lever again, and then a third time. Watched with delight as the small man danced some more.

"Do you think you could teach me?"

In just a few short minutes of exploring the attic, he'd already learned to walk. Nothing seemed impossible to him now.

Tap, cluck-cluck—

Zeke picked up the little wooden man and carefully made his way back down the attic stairs.

⸻

"How'd this happen?" his father asked, holding up the leg brace he had broken last night. A single silver wire dangled from the snapped joint, loose and frayed.

"Daddy, I'll tell you, but you can't get mad," Zeke reasoned. "Promise?"

"You had them on, and you were told to go to sleep."

"I know, I—"

"So why *didn't* you?"

Zeke sucked air through his teeth. "The attic, Daddy. I wanted to see the *attic.*"

His father tossed his spoon into the sink, then turned on the faucet and rinsed out his oatmeal bowl. Zeke just kept eating.

"You wanted to see the attic?" The creases in Daddy's forehead deepened. "What for?"

"You can't get mad. Promise." Zeke set his own spoon down, stared at a spot where the sun was reflecting off the surface of the table.

"Okay, fine. I promise." Daddy crossed his arms and cleared his throat. "You can tell me about it, buddy. I . . . won't get mad."

"I only wanted to see what was up there. I didn't want to *do* anything, but I thought I could just look around. Maybe find something of Mommy's."

Right away he wished he could take it back, could close his mouth and hit the mute button. Wake up again and start the day over. He twisted his lips.

"Well," his father said in a voice that was almost a whisper, "did you find anything?"

"Yes. A toy."

"One of Mommy's?"

"Don't know." He hadn't given any thought to who might own it. *Probably yours,* he thought. Instead he said, "But I can walk on my own, now. Without the braces, even—I think."

"Oh yeah?" His daddy nodded almost imperceptibly. Zeke had known this would happen; Daddy never believed him unless he had something bad to tell.

"Watch," he said, and struggled to stand up without the support of his crutches before his father could object. He had rehearsed this moment in his bedroom, standing up and walking about with neither his leg braces nor his crutches to keep him from falling. The nearer he kept the dancing toy, the easier walking seemed to be. Down here in the kitchen, though, his bony legs shook and ached in protest. He gritted his teeth.

"Whoa, *whoa!* Sit down. Right now," Daddy said. He reached out with his arms as if Zeke might fall at any moment.

"It's okay, *watch*." Zeke left the kitchen and headed for the stairs. He figured he'd just go to his room, show his father the toy—he hadn't yet named the small wooden man—and gauge his reaction. *He's gotta see the magic,* Zeke thought. *And then maybe he'll take me out for a walk . . .*

But his daddy didn't want to watch anything, would rather stop the spectacle before it began. He grabbed the back of Zeke's T-shirt and pulled, tried to rob him of his footing on the cold, hard stairs. Zeke's feet, clad only in a pair of old Adidas socks, slipped right out from beneath him, and he collapsed backward into Daddy's arms.

"You're gonna give me that toy you found. If it belonged to your mommy, it belongs to me now. And don't you fool yourself into thinking you can go prancing around without your crutches, because sure as shit, you'll fall and your legs will snap like twigs—and then they'll *never* heal."

Zeke said nothing. His daddy didn't like to be told he was wrong.

———

"I'm going to Terry's real quick," his father said as he finished putting Zeke's leg braces on for bedtime. "You'll go to sleep before I get back, or I'm going to take a hammer to that new toy of yours."

Terry was a doctor friend of Daddy's, who he went to see whenever he needed more of his medicine. Zeke worried that his father took too much, because his pills outnumbered Zeke's own by more than double the prescriptions, and the capsules themselves were bigger, too.

He guessed his daddy must be sick, but since he had never mentioned it neither did Zeke.

Underneath the blankets, he grasped the little dancing man and prayed silently for his father to leave without asking for it, without getting mad at him for hiding it. On his nightstand, the platformed lever and the dowel that held the toy man up while he danced sat empty. "I will," Zeke promised, but he could hear the falseness in his own voice. "But, Daddy . . . "

"Huh?"

Zeke bit down on his lip. "When will I be able to walk on my own?" *Without the magic,* he thought to himself. "When will my legs be all fixed up?"

"I don't know, bud," his father said. "Just go to sleep."

In the chill nighttime gloom, Zeke found his new friend's face suddenly frightening. It was black enough that it disappeared into the surrounding dark, leaving visible only its wide shining eyes and pale-lipped grin. Zeke shivered, pulled his warm blankets tight around him, and then bolted onto the floor, upright and on his feet. Even as his bones ached within the support of his braces, he found a deep comfort in the standing position. He held on to nothing. The influence of the small wooden man at his bedside gave his legs all the balance and stability they needed.

Do you think you could teach me? he'd asked his new friend the night before, in awe at the sight of the dancing toy. The desire had become obsession in the hours since. "Well," he whispered, "will you?"

With ease he crossed to the light switch beside the door and flicked it on.

The dancing man eyed him from across the room, his thin legs hanging motionless. They seemed to call out for Zeke's play.

Zeke had listened as his daddy's car sped off into the night. Again, he was alone in the house, if only for a little while. If he was quick, he'd have time to learn the toy man's dance.

"How do you do it?" he asked. "I don't think my knees'll bend like *yours*."

Carefully, he stretched one leg out, and the sole of his brace hit the floor with a *clack*. He slid his foot back in, tried swinging the other leg outward. Zeke tried to visualize the toy's smooth rhythm—*tap, tap-tap, trippety-thok!*—to feel the divine music of the world coursing through him—*tap, cluck-cluck*—to hear the quiet thrumming of the earth far below.

His bowed legs wobbled, and his knees rubbed against one another as he fought to develop a groove. He found the music thumping in his heart good enough, but his legs didn't obey the overwhelming rush of emotion he was feeling.

"Harder than you make it look, toy man. Way harder," Zeke said. He tapped the lever and watched his friend dance a while.

Then he got back on his feet and tried once more. His bones cried out for relief, for rest, but he did his best to ignore them. The world sung softly beyond the window: the whispering of the wind against the trees, the chittering of the crickets and the locusts, the hissing and rustling of autumn leaves. He listened, he absorbed, he dreamed waking dreams. And when at last he was sure he had the rhythm in him, the bedroom door swung open.

"Damnit, I said *lights out!*" Spit flew from his father's mouth with every word. His eyes were dark and moist, alight with an anger Zeke had never seen before.

"But, but I . . . ," Zeke stammered. Then he paused to take a deep, shuddering breath. "Please don't. Don't be mad."

He ignored his plea, and opened the door to the closet, searched in a frenzy for something on the upper shelf. He found it.

The hammer was all black save for a red band around the grip and some rust on the nose.

"I told you what I'd do. If you didn't mind and stay in your god-damned bed."

"Please," Zeke whispered. "Don't."

"No, no, no. You knew what'd happen." His father raised the hammer, stalked over to the nightstand, and swung.

The little wooden man slammed down on the table, and the dowel that held him up while he danced split lengthwise in half. The platform where he'd stood cracked in a jagged line down the middle.

Again Daddy struck the little man. Wood chips flung across the room—red, black, splintery bare pine.

Zeke winced. The sound of the hammer striking his toy disgusted him, knotted his innards. He wanted to move in and stop him, but he knew it was hopeless; his friend would never dance—or do anything else—again.

"Stop it," he rasped, almost inaudibly. "*Stop . . .*" His legs gave out, shaky and tired, and he collapsed to his knees. The surgical pins that held his legs together felt like knives scraping against the bone.

He heard the *thunk* of the hammer as it crashed to the floor, and as he fought the agony in his ruined legs he opened his eyes to a mess of wood splinters, tiny arms and legs. A small black face caved in by the head of a hammer. Its smile had fled. And in that moment, two things happened: a transference of power—and a payment extracted in full. What magic the doll had held took hold of the boy, all the while draining life from the man. Some prayers were answered, and some dark deeds finally punished.

Elsewhere, in parts unknowable, Ezekiel's mother at last found restful peace.

"Daddy?" Zeke said, forgetting for a moment the evil his father had wrought on his mommy's dancing toy. On his friend.

His father stood silent, fingers empty and trembling; then he twisted at the waist and toppled to the floor in a violent wreck of shattered bone. Blood spurted from breaches in his calves and thighs, where knobby white was poking through, slick with flowing crimson.

Zeke turned his eyes away from the ghastly sight, willed it to cease, to be nothing more than a nightmare of his corrupted mind. He clapped his hands to his ears in the hope that it might silence his father's howling. This couldn't be real.

"I'm so sorry, I'm so sorry, I'm so sorry," he chanted. "Oh, Daddy—*I'm sorry!*" Tears wet his face, and he wished with all his heart for his daddy to be all right. For *everything* to be all right.

He watched as his daddy dialed frantically on his cell phone, listened to the muffled screaming go on and on for another minute or so. In the distance, he could hear the braying of an ambulance. Police sirens. All coming to help his daddy, he supposed. To get him all fixed up like new.

To hell with his mommy's toy, who had been reduced to wood shavings.

To hell with *him*.

Hide-and-seek, he thought. *I'll have to go hide, now. Then they'll chase me, try to yell at me and ask me questions. Maybe even hurt me, like Daddy hurt the dancing man.*

But at least his father would be okay.

Zeke rose to his feet, and without a second's thought he thrust himself out the window, glass cutting away at his arms and cheeks, showering the segment of roof outside his bedroom. Blood warmed the left side of his face, and blades of glass wedged into his flesh. The moon hung low in the sky, its brilliance beckoning him into the night, and Zeke breathed deeply of the world's lush air.

As he made his way across the rooftop, headed toward the triangular peak at the front of the house, flashing red and blue lights drew near, whirling like eager phantoms through the neighborhood's once-quiet streets. By the time they reached him, Zeke Buckner stood towering over the blackening sprawl of the town he scarcely knew, too late to try and make an escape. Police officers slammed car doors, paramedics paraded into the house. Sirens whooped. And to the rhythm of the great cacophony, he began to dance.

ALEX KANE

LIVES IN WEST-CENTRAL ILLINOIS, WHERE HE WORKS AS A
FREELANCER, PLAYS TOO MANY FIRST-PERSON SHOOTERS,
AND BLOGS ABOUT CULTURE AND TECHNOLOGY IN HIS
SPARE TIME. A GRADUATE OF THE 2013 CLARION WEST
WRITERS WORKSHOP, HIS STORIES HAVE APPEARED IN OMNI,
SPARK, DIGITAL SCIENCE FICTION, AND THE YA ANTHOLOGY
FUTUREDAZE, AMONG OTHER PLACES. FOLLOW HIM ON
TWITTER @ALEXJKANE.

THE ~~EYE~~ EYE ~~LIARS~~ LIARS

SARAH READ

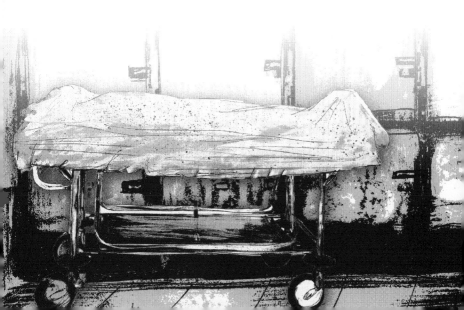

B ending over the corpse, leaning against the cold steel table on which the body rested, Dan squeezed the black spots at the corner of the rotting eye. The blackness oozed out of the pores. It collected in the basin of the temple, pooling as it drained, then evaporating into a black mist. It rose into the air around us, circling the lamp hanging low over the workstation.

"Don't breathe, Greg," Dan said.

The swirling shadow dissipated as it rose, spreading to the dark corners of the ceiling, deepening the shadows. The air tasted sharp and bitter, like Dad's batteries we used to lick in the garage when we were kids.

Dan breathed first.

Looking down at the dead man between us, there were more dark spots, pinprick-sized swellings, reservoirs of foul ink collected under the skin.

"What the hell was that?" I asked.

Dan turned to his tray of tools, waving his gloved hands over them, divining which to use.

"I'm not really sure," he said, rotating the scalpel in front of his

face, examining an edge too fine to see. "My guess would be that it's a waste product of some undocumented parasite. It's always around the eyes, presents as liquid-filled black spots—but the substance vaporizes almost instantly. It's organic, but I haven't been able to collect enough to run any real substantive tests. Once it's vapor, it doesn't test as anything. Nothing."

I rubbed my forehead. The film of sweat had started to cool in the damp basement. I shivered.

"It's just . . . dark air," he said.

He bent back over the body. His face tensed. He always looked ten years older when he cut, like the focus drained the life from him. He looked more like Dad than me, then, but maybe that was the grey lab coat, him holding Dad's tools, bent over Dad's table.

He removed an eye and placed it on a small steel tray. His hand barely moved, but when he straightened, the eye laid open, unfolded between us. A cloudy marble nested in layers of waxy wet tissue. He looked up at me, smiling.

My tongue curled inside my mouth and my throat tightened. The muscles at the back of my knees turned to turbulent water. I tasted bile, felt it burning through my chest, at the back of my throat.

"You don't have to look," he said. He always said that. I never wanted to look but I always did, always watched, first Dad, then Dan. He held the tray out, tapping the bottom of my chin with its cold edge, the eyes sliding across its stained surface.

"Why did you need me here for this?"

"I want you to know what to look for. I need research subjects."

"Dan, that's not really okay. I can't just do that—there are rules."

"Check the dementia patients first—anyone who might be exhibiting visual hallucinations or delusions. Ones who reach a crisis in their condition, then present a few hours of lucidity right before death. The spots start appearing then—during that brief lucid state. I need you to watch them. And bring me the bodies."

He pulled the caps off of glass vials and lined them up, rattling them against the tray, drowning out my protestations.

"Dan, I don't get to decide where—"

"Hold your breath."

I slapped a hand to my mouth. I tasted the powdery residue of the latex gloves I'd been wearing.

He squeezed a black spot against the rim of a vial, collecting the trickle of ink and ramming the cap in place before the plasma turned to smoke.

He exhaled. I didn't.

He held the vial up between our faces. The dark liquid inside sucked light from the room. He swirled the glass tube. The ooze coated the glass, sliding back down it in writhing swirls.

"Whatever this is, it's killing people, Greg. I can't stop it if I can't research it."

"Dad didn't leave you this place so you could play mad scientist."

"Dad didn't leave *you* this place at all," he said, picking up an eye and rolling it in his palm.

"You're supposed to be taking care of these people, for their loved ones. And you're supposed to be taking care of the business." I swept my hand toward a section of crumbling wall, groundwater seeping in through the cracks in the cinderblocks.

"Greg, this stuff's contagious. I don't know how, yet, but it is. Who gives a shit about upselling casket hardware when people are seeing things that aren't there? People are hallucinating, tearing each other apart, dropping dead, and you don't want to help?" He tossed the eye back onto the steel tray. It splashed and rolled, leaving a trail of humor.

"Well, talk to their doctors, put it in your reports."

"No one is going to look twice if I don't bring examples. I need data before I can make a claim like this."

"Your data are *people*, Dan."

"Dead people. And if you don't bring me what bodies you do have, we'll end up with more *data* than we'll know what to do with." His eyes narrowed like the tip of his scalpel, cutting into me.

I sighed and stared at the ooze. "Where does it come from?"

"How should I know? That's the point. Where do fleas come from, or rats? It's just the fucking circle of life." He picked up the corpse's arm and shook the limp hand at me.

I stepped back, stumbling over my foot. "Well someone else has to have seen it; it can't just be here."

"Some old anthropologists in Asia mention something like it, and in other places where they don't embalm or bury or burn the dead. They called them evil spirits, and started burning the people alive at the faintest hint of hallucination. We soak our dead in chemicals, infuse them with toxins, and stick them in the ground—hardly ever get to see what grows when we leave well enough alone." He squeezed the man's jaw and pulled down on his chin. The scent of raw meat and blood rose from the pale mouth.

"Damn," Dan said, "He didn't just *bite* his tongue off, he *chewed* it. Look." He wrenched the neck, aiming the blank face at me. A thin black line of old blood trailed from the corner of the mouth, running over Dan's thumb and dripping onto the table.

I drove back to The Village, hands shaking on the wheel, pressing my chin to my chest to get a better view through the narrow tunnel of my vision. My scrubs stuck to the sweat on my back and legs.

My skin secreted a slippery puddle into the vinyl seat of the van. The plan to stop for lunch on my way back was trashed. I couldn't get out of the van like this. It'd look like I'd wet myself.

The van's parking space sat close to the back entrance of the clinic. I could sneak into the locker room and change, grabbing lunch in the dining room with Miss Bessley, who would tell me again about the dog she'd had when she was eight.

As my sneakers squeaked across the white tile threshold, Tracy walked by, her slate hair pulled back in a braid, the edge of her clipboard pressed against her stomach as she read and walked. The walkie-talkie velcroed to the shoulder of her scrub jacket crackled and beeped, her left eye flinching each time, deepening the grooves that branched across her temple.

"Tracy." She stopped and looked up. Looked me over. I'd forgotten about the wet. "Do you know when those school kids are coming back—the ones with the dogs? Do you remember if they have a collie, like Mrs. Bessley's?"

"Who? What are you talking about?" She looked back to her notes, scribbling across charts.

"The group with the therapy animals, are they coming back soon? Miss Bessley's been lonely, and I thought—" I picked at the damp fabric clinging to my chest, chaffing my neck.

"I wouldn't know, ask the desk." She drew her eyebrows down, "But change your clothes first." She hurried away, her braid swaying, slapping each hip in turn.

In the locker room, I stripped off my damp scrubs and dropped them in the canvas laundry bag and held my underwear under the blow dryer.

There were no XL scrubs left. Stuffing my legs into an L, my balance wavered when the floor nurse called a code grey over the intercom. I pulled on my shoes, grabbed my badge lanyard, and sprinted for the stairwell door.

Floor 3, suite H—Mr. Brunner.

The ruckus echoed down the yellow painted brick stairwell. I scanned my ID at the top landing, and pushed the bar, leaning against the heavy door.

A breeze whipped against my exposed ankles and the scrub seams strained against my thighs as I ran past the row of closed doors to the source of the noise.

"I'll kill you for this, you bitch!" Mr. Brunner had Tracy by her braid, feebly swinging it, "Give it back!"

My hand covered Mr. Brunner's, prying his fingers from Tracy's hair. His hand came away webbed with extracted strands.

"Can I help you find something, Mr. Brunner?" I asked, pushing his wrists down.

"That whore took my lamp. I can't read here in the dark without my lamp!" Sweat collected in the deep lines of his face, beading and dripping from his hairless pate. The loose skin at his neck shook, scattering droplets.

Holding his wrists to his sides, I nodded toward the bedside table. "Is your lamp blue, Mr. Brunner? I see a blue lamp over there—maybe we moved it when we cleaned? Or let me get you settled by that nice bright window."

"No—the leather one, with the brass. It was my father's, from the war. It's very valuable, and *she took it*." He threw himself against me. I wrapped my long arms around him, careful not to squeeze.

The nurse raced into the room, blue gloves in place, flipping a syringe. I tightened my grip as she came up behind the old man and gave him the Ativan.

He writhed against my chest. My shirt split between my shoulders. He went limp. Squatting to scoop up his legs, the seams on my pants gave.

"For chrissakes," Tracy said.

I carried Mr. Brunner to his bed and laid him down.

"Go home and do some laundry. Come back for second shift to make up the hours." Tracy straightened her hair and picked up her clipboard. Her left eye twitched, her cheeks flushed. She flipped to a fresh incident report sheet and turned her back.

Back in the locker room I pulled on my street clothes. I grabbed the canvas laundry bag on my way out.

The tattered too-small scrubs fluttered into the dumpster in the parking lot. No need to fill out a material damage report—Tracy would mention it in hers.

Folding myself into my Civic, I headed home, rubbing at the dark shapes floating across my tired eyes.

The new scrubs were itchy, starched for store-freshness and smelling like dust. I sat in the dark clinic room, watching the blipping lights of Mr. Brunner's monitors, feeling the "do not resuscitate" orders clipped to the foot of the bed stare back at me. The new lamp I'd picked up sat in its box at my feet.

Rubbing my neck, trying to push the soreness out, warm blood rushed into the muscle behind the pressure of my fingers. Thirty minutes left. Then home, sleep for six hours, and come back.

I squeezed a tight muscle in my shoulder. Bright lights flashed in front of my eyes, then the negative, dark spots filling my vision. I pressed my fists to my eyes, opening them to solid dark. Undulating, freezing black clouds rolled around me, and a sharp ringing lanced my ears. Shrill sounds drove through me like knives as the dark wave turned me upside down.

My face hit the cold tile floor jarring my vision back with a white-hot burst of light. Shoes pounded in front of my eyes, smelling like wet rubber and disinfectant. My hands slipped in my sweat as I pushed myself off the floor.

People filled the room, their backs to me. Above their heads, the monitor broadcasted Mr. Brunner's distress signal, emitting the shrill alarms that had cut through me. Squeezing my eyes shut, I rubbed my hands over my face, painting it with salty wet that stung my dry lips. I backed out, watching them do next to nothing, making him comfortable as he passed.

At home, I spent the rest of the night apologizing to the shadow whispering behind my bedroom door.

———

I studied Mr. Brunner's face. Leaning over him, staring closely at his temples and the bridge of his nose, I reached out and smoothed the cold wrinkles, inspecting the depths of the crow's-feet. There was one, two—another on the other side. I texted Dan and then zipped up the bag and rolled Mr. Brunner to the parking lot.

I strapped him down and loaded him up, securing the gurney to the van. Climbing into the driver's seat, my coffee sloshed out of the spout of my travel mug.

Dan's funeral home sat just down the road. Built close enough to The Village for convenience, but not so close as to be suggestive. Dan waited for me outside, wringing his hands. A cigarette butt smoked on the crumbling pavement at his feet, torching the parched weeds growing up from the cracks.

"What took you so long?" He tugged at the back door, pulling the gurney down as I got out. "Hurry, get him downstairs."

In the dark basement lab, leaning in, shining a light in Mr. Brunner's face, we counted spots. Dan pushed and pulled at the skin.

"Gentle," I said.

"What?" The corner of Dan's mouth twitched. "Why, exactly?"

"I know him," I said

"Not anymore." Dan prepared his vials and blades.

I smoothed the sheet over Mr. Brunner's chest, brushed his hair back from his cool forehead. I could hear his voice, whispering about the things his dad had done in the war, asking if I could sneak him another Bond DVD from the office, promising he wouldn't tell Tracy if I watched it with him.

"What the hell are you doing?" Dan pushed my hand away and moved in with a vial.

"He doesn't have as many spots as Alan did."

"Who?"

"The guy from yesterday."

"Oh, no. He hasn't been dead as long. There will be more tomorrow. This is good, really good—I can watch them develop."

I looked away and held my breath as Dan held the vial to Mr. Brunner's eye.

Another body lay stretched out on the next table: a young woman, naked, her eyes removed, barely visible through the darkness. Walking closer, I saw her eyes sitting on a tray next to her head, milky black. The skin around the eye sockets swelled with black pustules.

My breath forced itself out with a moan.

"That's after five days," Dan said. He had sealed his vial.

"She's been lying here for five days?" Her hair fell around her empty face, dark and soft, dry leaves caught in its tangles. The bruises on her throat and thighs were as dark as the shadows where her eyes should have been. The skin along her jaw was red and blue, distended around a small oval with a cross in it.

"No one is waiting for her. I can take my time and get the data I need. I haven't had the chance to observe them this long before—to see what they do when left alone."

"I hope it doesn't hurt. What's this mark here?"

"That's nothing, leave it. And of course it doesn't hurt, she's dead." He shook his head.

"That looks like—"

"I said leave it."

"Is that Dad's ring? Fuck, Dan, did you hit this girl?"

"She already had the spots, Greg, she was as good as dead already. I needed her to come to the lab. She was raving, she wouldn't listen."

"So you killed her?"

"I brought her here to watch her die, to see how it happened."

"You're sick. She's lying here in Dad's room with Dad's ring punched into her face, and you can't even see how sick this is."

"That still bothering you, Greggy? That Dad didn't want his ring pawned for booze? You think you should have it now you're cleaned up?" He pulled it from his finger and held it out. I smacked it out of his hand. It bounced, ringing, rolling into the glue trap in the far corner.

"Wouldn't fit you anyway," he said, bending back to his work. "There was no saving her, but I could learn from her. It's for the greater good, Greg." He pulled one side of his mouth back in a crooked smile.

My fingers flexed. I could feel my heartbeat in my temples. My tongue scraped the dry roof of my mouth, sticking to my clenched teeth. I counted and breathed. Thirty down to one, a breath every five seconds. *I can't change this, I can't change him.*

"Did you run more tests? On Alan?" I asked.

"Who?"

"Alan!" Another ten seconds, another two breaths.

"Right. Yes, look." He went to a cupboard and pulled out a tray of black vials. No. Vials filled with black. "The liquid samples have turned to gas. It appears that the lack of oxygen in the vials slows the reaction, but it doesn't stop it. However, there's no increased pressure in the tube. The reaction doesn't seem to have released any energy." He held the tray under my nose, his eyes rolling with excitement.

"So . . ."

"That's not possible. All reactions have some sort of energy exchange involved. You can't go from a liquid to a gas without it—this is *outside* the laws of chemistry." Saliva collected at the corners of his mouth as he spoke faster, fogging the glass vials with his rapid breath.

I took a step back, tearing my eyes from the tray of dark tubes, and looked for the clock. It perched hidden in the shadows, high up on the wall.

"I need to get back to work. I can't be late again."

Dan lowered the tray, sneering. "Or what? Another job you can't hold down?"

"No. I promised Miss Bessley lunch today."

Dan shook his head, turning to put his tray of dark of vials away.

Collecting The Village body bag, folding it, I watched the girl on the table.

"What was her name?"

"Don't know," Dan said.

Alice Stowe ate three pounds of gravel from the garden. Sometime in the early hours she left her room in her best dress and hat, sat in the gazebo, and ate rocks from a chocolate box. She died that evening, without a single tooth left.

I clocked out, changed, and went to the clinic. She was there, in the cooler, in one of my black bags. I rolled her out and unzipped the bag.

The spots were already there—huge, this time, and swollen. The skin felt cold and taut under my fingertip.

It ruptured. The dark liquid spilled over my finger, filling the space under my nail and pooling in my cuticle. It felt like my finger had been encased in ice. The black smoked off my finger with a soft hiss, the vapors sucking in toward my mouth and billowing on my breath.

I slapped my other hand over my mouth and ran, slipping over the waxed tiles to the sink. Cranking the hot water lever as far as it would go, I held my hand under the steaming stream. The inky shadow mixed with the steam, one swirling around the other, a cyclone of hot and cold. The heat returned to my skin in an agony of needles as vessels rapidly dilated and burst.

When all of the black had washed away or turned to smoke, I breathed again, panting through my tight throat, a high whine echoing off of the sterile walls and steel cabinets. The battery taste of the toxic smoke mixed with the chlorine cleanliness of the clinic.

My fingertip swelled white like a maggot soaked in water. The back of my hand blistered with red, angry burns.

I groped the darkness. The air swarmed thick with shadows that flowed and eddied on unseen currents. My stomach burned as I swallowed the acrid cloud. Black smoke poured from Alice's face, billowing up as if from a chimney, burning the fuel of the darkness inside her.

With my good hand, I grasped the bar of the gurney and shoved her back in the cooler, slamming the door shut.

I swept my hand in front of my face, trying to clear a path through the shadow. It sighed as my hand cut through it, swirling back in to fill the space, caressing my cheek and whispering.

My legs crashed though steel carts of equipment on my way to the back door. I pushed out into the air. The daylight split through me, savaging my eyes, the setting sun hot on my burned hand. Lying on the pavement, I coughed shadow from my lungs.

I pulled my phone from my pocket to call the front desk and tell them to seal the clinic.

There was a text message from Dan, from that morning.

Not waste, eggs. Faces are spawning. Get me out. Nine hours ago.

I rolled over, forced myself up and rushed to the clinic van. It was just a mile down the road—a mile and nine hours too late.

Darkness filled the windows of the funeral home. Pulling up to the back entrance, I turned the headlights on bright and pulled a flashlight from the glove box, using it to break the grimy window by the back door. Wisps of shadow licked the jagged edges of broken glass. Reaching in, my injured fingers fumbled to unlock the door latch, my armpit scraping against the sharp glass.

The high beams penetrated three feet into the darkness and hit a moving wall of shadows. Shapes appeared in the shifting darkness. Faces and shoulders and hands and thighs emerging from the cloud, beckoning. I walked into the middle of it all.

It stung like jumping into a deep lake at midnight in February. The shadow clung to me, sliding across the surface of my eyes, dragging itself over my skin. Whispers started in one ear and finished in the other, too many of them, fading in and out, incomprehensible. I held out my hands and walked toward the basement door. My knees knocked into a stack of caskets, sending the tower crashing, lids flying open. I dropped to the floor, dodging corpses, digging my fingernails into the carpet fibers, tracking the familiar geometric patterns of my childhood. I followed its diamond floral maze to the back wall, sliding my fingers along the chair rail, searching for the door.

I found it. When I pulled it open, the whispers turned to moans.

Clinging to the banister, I felt the edge of each splintered step with my toes.

Halfway down, the thick cloud broke. Above my head, a cumulous of shadow roiled. I thundered down the remaining stairs.

"Dan?"

He wasn't there. Alan, Mr. Brunner, and the young girl were lined up on tables. Their faces concave, drained, covered in black ash. I walked over to the girl. No one would ever recognize her now. It was as if her face had been dead weeks before the rest of her. I turned, gagging.

There. The window of the walk-in freezer gleamed black, opaque as a submarine porthole. Dan's face pressed against the glass. The skin around his eyes was torn apart by erupting fonts of shadow, his eyelids flayed back. His jaw hung open, askew.

I retched. Fell to my knees and puked. Choking, coughing up gobs of tar. Moans rolled out of me, building deep within my center, rattling my bones. I pushed myself back from the caustic puddle, away from the window. The back of my head banged against the edge of Mr. Brunner's steel table.

Mr. Brunner? I forgot to tell The Village.

The cloud on the stairs had risen further, concentrating itself in the highest reaches of the house. I pressed through the thickness of it, feeling cold fingers rake my skin, malevolent hissing in my ears.

The headlights hit me like a hurricane wave. I swam through the light and climbed in the van.

A mile back and too late again.

The Village seethed, a pit of hell. Each lost in their own shadow world, they ripped each other apart—some already bursting at the face, filling the air with spawning smoke.

I took a long roll of plastic wrap from the kitchen.

I held their frail frames as they ranted nonsense and I wrapped their heads in plastic, sealing in the darkness, stemming the flow of shadow. Their eyes pressed against the clear film, rolling in their sockets, spilling ink into the folds of membrane.

I wrapped them up and zipped them into my black bags, dragging them to the clinic, piling them up in a squirming heap.

Tracy stood at the nurse's station, naked, writing notes across her stomach. Her hair hung loose, crimped from the tight braid. The twitch-line by her eye flowed like a river delta of liquid evil. I wrapped her up—all of her, in case the darkness found another way out.

I closed the clinic door and taped around the edges. I poured out the bottles of ethyl alcohol and rolled the carts of oxygen tanks from the gas storage and barricaded the door with them. Down the hall in the kitchen, I lit the burners on the stove, turned on the oven and left it open.

I ran. The air, already dark from those that burst before, swarmed me, raking at my skin with icy fangs. The shadow slithered up through the bowels of the building, collecting on the third floor, a writhing mass of nightmare. Moans echoed down the stairwell.

Walking out into the night, backing away from the building, I watched smoke surge from the chimney, streaming into the sky, obscuring the stars. Out of the corner of my eye, every shadow moved. Black tears ran in smoky tracks down my aching face.

I turned my back and walked, a mile down the road and too late. The ground concussed, a gold light spreading, casting my shadow at my feet. A hot wind flew up behind me, pushing the shadows ahead. I chased them.

Sirens ripped through me, scattering red lights cutting through the dark. They streaked past me toward the gold glow.

I stumbled into the back door of Dad's mortuary, Dan's, mine. I shuffled down the stairs, to the corner of the basement, and pulled the ring from the dusty, sticky glue. I pressed it onto my little finger, forcing it over the knuckle, twisting it into the groove at the bottom joint.

I pulled open the freezer door, catching Dan's body as it fell. He hardly weighed a thing with the evil boiled off. I carried him to a table and laid him out.

I took my knife from the tray. Just like Dad, like Dan. From each shoulder to the base of the manubrium and down to the navel, I cut him open, separating the ribs from the breastbone, laying wide the chest cavity. I pulled the heart from its place and weighed it.

SARAH READ

'S SHORT STORIES CAN BE FOUND IN BLACK STATIC,
REVOLT DAILY, VINE LEAVES LITERARY JOURNAL (WHERE
SHE RECEIVED A PUSHCART NOMINATION), AND IN
THE SUSPENDED IN DUSK (BOOKS OF THE DEAD PRESS)
ANTHOLOGY, AMONG OTHER PLACES. SHE WRITES, READS,
AND KNITS NEAR ROCKY MOUNTAIN NATIONAL PARK WHERE
SHE LIVES WITH HER TWO SONS AND HUSBAND. SHE IS AN
AFFILIATE MEMBER OF THE HWA AND IS EDITOR IN CHIEF
AT PANTHEON MAGAZINE. FOLLOW HER ON TWITTER
@INKWELLMONSTER.

SEARCHING

FOR

GLORIA

W.P. JOHNSON

D ale drove through the marketplace while Stewart pressed his nose to the window of the black Cadillac and stared at the faces, the hot breath of his nostrils leaving a snout of fog. Dale glanced over his little brother's shoulder while keeping a hand on the wheel, pointing out one girl or another. Tufts of dirty smoke rose from a cigarette lodged between his fingers, stretching thin as it snaked throughout the car and shed its gray skin.

"How about that one?" Stewart asked, pointing at a blonde sipping hot cocoa with her parents.

Dale shook his head. "Too young. Plus her nose is flat."

Stewart took out the picture and exchanged glances between that and the girl sipping hot cocoa. Her nose was a bit pugish, while the girl in the picture had a slightly sharper nose. As far as Stewart could tell, they looked similar enough.

"Think he'd notice?"

Dale nodded. "He'd notice right away. And then what? No money, maybe not even a job after," Dale groaned and shook his head. "It's better to wait, have patience. He'd rather have the right girl tomorrow than the wrong girl today." There was a block of silence

and Dale trailed a finger down the pale white scar that crossed his cheek. "This isn't a game to him."

"How long did it take last time?" the boy asked.

"A few months. Once, it took me nearly a year to find the right girl."

Stewart frowned and stared at the picture again. The girl was young, around fifteen years old, with freckles on her nose and milky white skin. She had curly blonde hair that dangled inches from her shoulders and thin lips with crooked teeth. Dale pointed out all of these things to Stewart, adding that she had to be tall and skinny with thin legs, yet she would have to have thick thighs, like a dancer.

"You get it right, you'll take over for me and I'll take another job. More responsibilities, but more money," he said, turning left at the end of the block, then another left after that so they could circle around through the marketplace. "Find the right girl...you can have this car along with half of what he'll give me. Then you'll work full time."

Stewart grinned. The black car, a 1972 Cadillac, was one of the first things Dale bought when he started working for Marcus Winters, kingpin of the north. As they coasted through the marketplace, it left clouds of dissipating smoke and the engine's low groan sounded like a growling beast that slowly lumbered through the streets stalking its prey.

It struck Steward that he didn't even have his license yet. Would Dale teach him that as well? Or would he have to take a driver's test? His reading wasn't so good, but then again he never needed it much in school (when he bothered going) and whenever there was a test he would just close his eyes and focus real hard on Tommy Johnson, the smart kid that sat up front. After a few seconds he would *feel* what the answers were as if Tommy were sitting right next to him, holding half the pencil in his own hand and jotting down words and sentences that Stewart only had a vague understanding of.

"When are we going back home?" Stewart asked after a half hour of driving. They had skipped breakfast and he was starting to get hungry.

"We'll look another hour, then get something to eat."

"Okay." He looked at the picture again.

This isn't a game . . .

Stewart treated the situation like it was a game he was helping his big brother play. At first he had asked who the girl was, why Marcus Winters wanted her, but all Dale ever said was that he wouldn't understand, that he was too young (or to keep his mouth shut and don't ask questions). Sometimes when they drove he closed his eyes and tried to feel Dale, thinking maybe there would be something there, an explanation for what they were doing. But every time he did this with his older brother he found nothing, like he was reaching into an empty box of cereal.

He returned to watching the marketplace, smelling the stench of ice-packed cod, the thin odor of dirt from a vegetable cart, the syrupy smell of overripe fruit and the hot breath of car exhausts. A hundred strangers milled in and out of a dozen storefronts. A skinny blonde girl rushed across the street between the gap of slow moving cars. Dale eased off the gas and watched her skip past, hopping on to the opposing sidewalk.

"Too short," Stewart said.

Dale gave a light smile and scruffed up Stewart's hair. "Yes little brother, too short."

The boy blushed, keeping his nose pressed against the window, wiping away the fog so he could watch the girl as she walked down the sidewalk. For a brief second, he closed his eyes and felt her, catching the briefest glimpse of her thoughts. She was hungry but wasn't sure what she wanted, only that it couldn't cost more than five dollars. She felt in her pocket, feeling a few wrinkled bills and some loose change.

Stewart let himself go, feeling faded memories that went back seconds, minutes, hours, days, letting himself fall deeper and deeper into this stranger until his own thoughts became distant and numb, a shard of sunlight on the water's surface leagues above him.

What a wonderful life she lived. What a wonderful life she would live.

Opening his eyes, he let it all slip away. Then he returned to the streets, searching for the right girl.

They returned home after an hour, sitting down at the kitchen table and drinking burnt coffee. Their mother fussed about them going out without eating breakfast and started cooking them sausage with peppers, onions, and brussel sprouts, filling the room with a noxious smoke that made their eyes wet and their stomachs growl. Stewart wanted pancakes, but he said nothing. Before Dale started working for Marcus Winters, they ate nothing but rice and dented cans of beans.

"Eat," their mother said, setting the two plates down. She dragged the portable heater over and set it next to Dale's feet.

"Thank you, Mama," Dale said. Stewart echoed the sentiments and they ate quietly until she left the room. Dale took off his coat and shifted the heater back towards the middle of the kitchen.

"After this we'll look till dark," Dale said, shoveling a hunk of food into his mouth. "Maybe try north under the subway stations."

"Okay." Stewart brushed aside the brussel sprouts.

"Eat everything," Dale said, gesturing at the food with his fork. "I paid for those sprouts."

Stewart frowned, then slid his fork under the brussel sprouts along with some onions and peppers, shoveling the whole thing into his mouth.

Dale smiled. "Being picky is a luxury. When we didn't have any money, you used to eat whatever was on your plate."

"I remember," Stewart said quietly. "I had to stuff newspaper into my shoes and wear all your clothes."

Dale laughed. "You looked like you were shrinking."

The phone rang, but neither of them got up. Dale sipped his coffee and Stewart did the same, holding back a grimace when the bitter taste made his mouth twist. Their mother called out to Dale.

"What?" Dale shouted back.

"It's for you," she said from the other room. She walked in, standing by the doorway. "It's . . . work."

Dale jumped out of his seat and went into the other room, closing the door behind him. Mother started noisily cleaning, clearing the table and washing dishes. Dale's voice filled their ears in the short moments of silence. Stewart sipped at his coffee again, adjusting to the bitter taste. He leaned back in his chair and closed his eyes, feeling for his mother as she scrubbed the charred bits of onion off a cast iron skillet.

Everything is fine.

Stewart sighed, letting himself fall deeper into her thoughts, reliving the first time he felt her years ago. They were poor and she thought a lot about money, adding and subtracting numbers, paying one bill at a time. Then one day Dale came home with two bags of groceries and a portable heater. Mother wanted to ask how and why, but she didn't and after enough time had passed, she didn't even think it. The only time she ever really fretted at all was the night Dale came home with a long cut over the right side of his face. She said nothing and merely dressed the wounds, but Stewart could feel the way she was screaming inside of her head over the sight of Dale's blood.

He sometimes thought about telling them that he could feel their minds, but deep down he knew that if he did this they would never think freely again and their thoughts would hide from him like cockroaches in the light and he would know less about them had he been a normal boy.

He let himself slip further into his mother's past, going back days, months, years. Feeling the panic when father left and she was pregnant again, feeling the nights when she had to heat up a pot of water to melt the ice in the toilet, nights when they shook themselves to sleep under three comforters stiff from the cold. He shifted forward to the day Dale came home in his first suit and she thought *how handsome!*, and he brought her outside to show her the Cadillac he had just bought.

"*Someone will steal it!*" mother had warned him.

Dale laughed, saying that no one would ever touch it.

"*Even the birds are afraid to shit on it.*"

The birds are afraid of who you work for, she thought.

Then a brief flickering memory of waking up early one morning and kissing Stewart's forehead as he slept while Dale sat at the kitchen table, staring at nothing in particular, smoking, drinking a cup of black coffee while tracing his finger down the long scar on his face.

The door creaked and Stewart's eyes shot open, ripping himself to the surface.

"Come on," Dale said, kicking the chair his little brother sat in. "Got a call."

"We're not looking for the girl anymore?"

Mother ran the water again, noisily scrubbing out the empty sink.

"I'll explain in the car," Dale said, putting on his jacket. He swallowed the rest of his coffee and headed out the front door. Stewart followed on his heels and as he closed the door behind him, he caught a snippet of his mother's thoughts as she started wiping down the kitchen table a second time.

Everything is fine.

They drove out to a bar on the highway half an hour north of the city. Behind them, skyscrapers were a faded row of books that sat on the horizon's shelf, slowly sinking away as they descended upon their exit. The road was absent of traffic and they passed several warehouses before reaching the bar.

The doorman led Dale to an office in the back while Stewart sat on a stool by an empty bar. There was a pinball machine in one corner of the room, but all it did was eat quarters and after a minute of trying to get his money back, Stewart returned to his original post. The place was empty save for the doorman who sat on a stool by the entrance and another man Stewart didn't know. The other man played pool, indiscriminately arranging one ball or another to get the shot he wanted. He chain-smoked, tossing the used cigarettes in an overflowing ashtray that gave off half a dozen tails of smoke.

Everywhere I go there is smoke, Stewart thought. The air in the room stung his eyes and he started blinking, letting them water.

Without trying to, he could feel the jealousy of the stranger playing pool. The man wished he was the one talking to Marcus Winters and the only reason he was playing pool was to give his hands and eyes something to do. The man watching the front door thought of a girl he slept with when he was eighteen. Sometimes he would glance at the man playing pool or Stewart, shifting in his seat whenever they made eye contact.

The door in the back opened and Dale stepped out. Stewart hopped off the stool, meeting his brother halfway. Dale gripped him gently by the arm.

"Jin is going to drive you for a little while," he said, nodding towards the man playing pool.

"Jin?"

"Until you learn how to drive," he said. "I got a few things I need to take care of, so I need you to take over looking for the girl for me."

"Oh . . ." Stewart looked down at the ground and when the cue ball smacked another pool ball, there was a jaw-breaking crack that made his shoulders twitch.

"Hey," Dale said, tilting his brother's chin up. "It's easy, right? Pale skin, freckles on her nose, curly blonde hair."

"Thin legs but thick thighs," Stewart added.

Dale nodded. "No cuts, no bruises."

"No track marks."

"Right, and why is that?"

"Because it isn't what I want," a man said behind them.

Stewart looked up from the ground, looking past Dale as he turned to see the man that had entered from the back office. He wore a gray suit with black leather shoes that were slick like oil against the grimy tiled floor. He took out a silver cigarette case and as he turned it in his hands, it gleamed shards of light that took the glow of the yellow lamp above them and bleached it bone white.

Jin set his pool stick down and took out a lighter, bringing it up to Marcus Winter's face as he lifted the cigarette to his lips.

"Are you the new boy?"

Dale cut in, "This is my brother Stewart."

"Does he talk on his own, or do you have to wind him up first?" Marcus said, taking a drag off his cigarette. "Is he dumb or something?"

Dale blushed. "Nah man, he's real smart."

"If he's smart, then he can—"

"I can talk," Stewart said, stepping up next to his brother. "What would you like me to say?"

Marcus Winters narrowed his gaze on the boy and stepped closer, handing his lit cigarette to Jin. Dale remained frozen, his arms limp by his sides while Stewart took another step closer to Winters, bringing the two a mere foot apart. Up close, the boy could see the crow's-feet around the man's eyes. The pale ghosts of ancient scars crossed his face on a dozen different places, his cheeks the warped surface of a bleached cutting board.

"Your scars . . . "

Winters smirked. "Occupational hazard."

Stewart blinked, feeling a flash of images. The small hands of a girl pushing him away, painted red nails scratching his face. Then there was the cold calculation of rigid thought as Marcus Winters brushed aside this montage of images and returned to his detached assessment of Stewart.

"You look like something has you tongue-tied," Winters said. He knelt down, resting his hands on bent knees, looking into the boy's eyes.

"I'm okay," Stewart said. "I just want to work. Support my family."

"Family is important," he said, smiling. "Do you have any questions about your work?"

"Maybe."

"Stewart," Dale mumbled, reaching out to grab his little brother.

"Shut up," Winters said. "Let him talk." His eyes never left him, never blinked.

Stewart drifted again, letting himself slip into a tiny hole of darkness. The pit of this hole had a shallow pool of sweat and when he looked up he caught the glimmer of a silver switchblade and a bleached bone handle, feeling the hands of two men holding him still as the sharp tip of the blade ran down the side of his cheek, hot blood running down his face.

Dale.

He was inside of his brother, that empty box he had reached his hand into so many times. His brother was sweating and every limb was frozen.

Bring me another girl with bruises, and I'll carve your face off.

Stewart opened his eyes, staring at Marcus Winters.

"Who's the girl?" he asked evenly.

The man's eyes bulged in response with pupils that were dark and glassy, like those of a doll that sat on the edge of your bed and followed your every move. Jin closed in on the boy and a hand reached into his jacket, but Winters lifted a flat palm and gestured that he back away. He inched closer until his slow breath brushed against the boy's face, leaving the stench of warm tobacco.

"You've memorized her face? Her body?" he asked. "*Every detail?*"

"Yes," Stewart said. "She has curly blonde hair, and—"

Winters shook his head. "No need," he said, placing a hand on

Stewart's arm. His fingers gripped him lightly. "All you need to know is that the girl is someone I'm paying you to look for."

Stewart let the only words in his head leave his lips like so much loose change. "What will happen to her?"

The man frowned, narrowing his eyes. "That's none of your business. Look kid, you're new, you don't know how things are done around here, so just listen, shut up, and do your job." He glanced at Dale. "Just like your big brother, okay?" He took his hands off his knees and stood up straight, looking down at the boy. "Understand?"

"Yes," Stewart said. He looked down at the floor for a moment and felt Marcus Winters, searching for an explanation, but there was nothing there except the observation of himself; nothing but a thick surface of ice that obscured what lay below in the darkness. If they left now, he would never find out why he wanted the girl until it was too late. He clenched his body and looked back up at the finely dressed kingpin, already in mid turn to leave them.

"Do you hurt the girls?"

There was a crack and he fell through the thin ice into a cold lake of moments, feeling the girls around him as they banged against the thick ice, fighting for the surface. Everything was small and broken and stained with blood spit from split lips and torn skin, and there were hours of screaming, hours of a yellow light swinging above them, a hundred shadows thrown against a concrete wall, hours of a musty bed they would never walk away from on their own two feet.

Marcus turned back and slipped a hand into his coat pocket. He pulled out the blade and unhinged it. Dale swooped in front of him and grabbed Stewart by the arm and turned him around, backhanding him across the face.

"*Shut the fuck up,*" he said. The second blow was a tightly wound fist. "*You think this is some kind of fucking game?*"

Stewart cried out, but in his mind he exhaled and sank deeper into Marcus Winters, sinking until his toes brushed the murky bottom and the surface was nothing more than a pinhole of light that faded to infinite black by the time it reached him.

My wife was gone and a little girl hid in her room, afraid for what would happen to her. There was no money back then and I wanted to feel big and she was so small, so easy to break, I thought of her in ways I could never tell anyone and it was over so quickly, I could think of nothing else but those few moments when I was in control, believing there would never be anything quite so perfect in my life.

In a matter of seconds, Marcus resumed his cold, calculating thoughts and the memories were buried beneath the ice, but they were like an oil slick that left Stewart's mind slimy and black.

"Listen to your brother," Marcus Winters said, folding the switchblade up and returning it to his pocket. "He knows a thing or two about how things work around here."

Dale dragged the boy by the arm as they left the bar, but he dragged his feet, trying to grasp every last second he could of Marcus Winters, watching the black oil of his past shift in a silent current beneath the frozen glass, hearing the thud of fists as they banged against the thick ice, seeing the girl's face as she screamed her name, her voice lost in the frigid water, her words a bubble of air that smacked silently against the ice.

He could see the name on her lips.

He held on to the name. He held tight as Dale continued to hit him, saying that it was not a game, to not ask questions. He wanted to cry out, to tell him what he felt and saw. He said nothing. He said nothing when his lip and his nose bled and a hard gust of wind bit the tears off his face. He said nothing on the quiet drive home, nothing when his mother cried out over the sight of his face.

The name Gloria was a secret he kept inside of him.

The last embers of night were still lingering in the kitchen when Dale walked in and found Stewart already at the table, stirring a shallow bowl of milky cereal. For more than a week the boy had avoided his older brother, getting up early and leaving the apartment before Dale even awoke. Saying nothing to his little brother, he walked over to the coffee pot and poured himself an inky mug of yesterday's brew. He sat down at the table and sipped the cold coffee, looking at nothing in particular while silence counted the seconds between them. The bruises on Stewart's face were finally starting to fade, but it left the skin on his face worn out, like an old pair of work gloves.

Dale tipped his coffee mug towards the boy. "Once your face looks better, you can start working again."

"They said that?" Stewart kept his eyes on his cereal, sifting the last bits of sludge out of the milk.

"They don't want any attention, with how you look and all," Dale explained. He paused before adding, "But yeah, they said you can work. I had to vouch for you. Convince them that you could be trusted to do your job without questions."

The spoon scraped the inside of the bowl and he let the milk spill out. "Do you think that's true?"

Dale widened his eyes in surprise to the question. "Is there something you want to say to me?"

Stewart set the spoon down and met his brother's eyes. They were neutral and cold and he could see his own reflection in them, bruises and all. When they came home a week ago and his face was still bleeding, they told their mother that he had slipped on ice and fell flat on his face. She didn't believe them at first but eventually she stopped fussing about it. Now the scars were nearly faded, leaving a mask of ten years over the boy's face.

"What happens to the girl?" Stewart asked, keeping his gaze on Dale.

His older brother kept his face still. The long scar on the side of his cheek was a white line that looked gray in the morning light, like a corpse with its eyes clenched shut. He shook his head.

"This isn't a game, little brother."

"I know," Stewart said. "That's why I want to know what happens. Because it isn't a game." He kept silent after, waiting for an answer. A full minute passed by before Dale gave a heavy sigh, looking away as he spoke.

"When I find the girl, I find out where she lives. Then I call some people and give them the address. After that, I wait until he asks me to find another girl."

"But you don't know what happens to her?"

"No," Dale said, shaking his head. "They keep us all separate. The guy I call? I don't even know his name. But he gets her, and someone else probably brings her to Marcus. But I'm the guy that finds her." He dragged a finger over his left eye, closing it. He shrugged. "If I stopped looking, he'd just pay someone else to do it. So I might as well do it myself if I can get paid and take care of you and Mama."

"He kills those girls," Stewart whispered.

"Probably," Dale said evenly.

"He would've killed me if he wanted to," Stewart said quietly.

Dale said nothing and their silence pushed Stewart's eyes over the long white scar on his older brother's face, knowing then that it was a lesson Dale saw every day when he looked in the mirror. Stewart's own bruises would soon fade away altogether, leaving nothing but the memory of his brother's fear, the shallow pool of sweat he kept hidden inside of him.

Stewart leaned in. "You weren't going to stop him."

"No," Dale said coldly. "I would not have stopped him."

Hearing the words sunk in more than Stewart would've thought, and he lost his breath for a moment.

"I'm going to look for the girl," Dale said, "and when I find her, I'm going to find out where she lives and make a phone call. And then after that . . . I don't know what happens to her. But she'll be gone and that'll be that. And there's nothing we can do, so what difference does it make?" He slid his chair back and got up to leave, looking down at the boy. "Mama told me you're out all day but you aren't at school?"

"No," the boy said. When he looked up at Dale, he shrugged.

"If you're not going to work with me, then you're going to go back to school, understand?" he said. His voice was stern and he didn't bother waiting for a response, slipping his jacket on and heading towards the door. "I'm not gonna work and put food on the table just so you can spend all day fucking off with your friends."

The door slammed shut when he left and Stewart waited, listening to the soft footsteps of his brother's shoes as they echoed up the stairwell. He sat there for several minutes before putting on his jacket and leaving, walking down the stairwell and pausing before the front door of the building. He took out a small note in his back pocket and read over the lines. It was scribbled and misspelled, but it would have to do. There was no one he could show it to.

After reading the note a second time and sounding out the words, he felt in his pocket for a loose cigarette he had pilfered from his brother and lit it, sucking in a quick drag before going outside into the cold. The smoke made his lungs feel like cold steel and he coughed less and less the harder he breathed in. The wind shoved him back from time to time, remaining still between its heavy gusts. He took the train north towards a neighborhood in the city he had gone to earlier that week, walking the streets, searching.

The house was only four blocks from the subway stop and the streets were empty without the buzz of shops and restaurants. A lone man shoveled his driveway clean and glanced at Stewart for a short moment, wondering if school had been cancelled that day. The boy trudged through and lit another stolen cigarette, letting his nerves unwind. The wind pulled the smoke off of him and ashes were ripped from their flames like so many grains of sand in a storm.

The house stood before him. He flicked the cigarette aside, letting it die on its own. The embers glowed dimly in the light of morning until it sank down to the filter.

He read the note to himself again.

you dont no me but someone is looking for yor dauter.

He glanced up at the house. The curtains obscured his view of the living room, but when he closed his eyes and reached out, he could feel the girl's mother sweeping the kitchen floor, unaware that someone was watching their house.

if you do not leav the city, they will tak her. if you
go to the polees, they will tak her and hurt you and
no one will stop them.

He felt himself sink deeper and deeper, going back further and further into the past until the present was just a shard of sunlight on the water's surface.

yur girls name is Sandra. you had her when you

were 23. she is a danser and has frekels on her nose,
but not her face.

He folded up the note and tiptoed up the walkway to the house.

if you cannot leave today, die her hair brown.

this is not a game

After slipping the note through the mail slot, he stepped away and waited at the end of her driveway. Waited to feel what the woman would do when she found the note.

W.P. JOHNSON

IS A WRITER OF HORROR, WEIRD FICTION, AND NOIR. HE
GRADUATED FROM TEMPLE UNIVERSITY WITH A DEGREE IN
ENGLISH LITERATURE AND HAS BEEN PUBLISHED BY ONE
BUCK HORROR, KRAKEN PRESS, SHROUD, DARK MOON BOOKS,
PERPETUAL MOTION MACHINE PUBLISHING, PULP MODERN,
FOX SPIRIT BOOKS, AND THUNDERDOME PRESS. YOU CAN
FOLLOW HIM ON SOCIAL MEDIA THROUGH THE MONIKER
AMERICANTYPO. HE CURRENTLY LIVES AND WORKS IN
PHILADELPHIA AND IS WORKING ON HIS FIRST NOVEL.

AND
ALL NIGHT
LONG WE
HAVE NOT
STIRRED

BARBARA DUFFEY

t happened in harvest season. The sunflower fields painted the county yolk-yellow, petals serrating the sky—your mother had taken pinking shears to the horizon. That day, a gray pattern plumed in the southeast, quickly and quietly, so quietly that no one noticed it for several minutes.

"Are the Affenbachs burning their leaves already?" asked Mrs. Nichol. It seemed surreal that they couldn't smell it yet, as if the fire was happening in a mural composed of the scene across the farm road.

"Hmmmm," said Mr. Nichol, as the edges of the smoke turned blue-white, the color of skimmed milk. "Machinery," he said, reaching for the phone.

Mariela was two blocks from school when she first heard about the body in the trunk. She walked through the cloud of smokers every morning, and every morning they said nothing, but this morning they said there was a body in the trunk. She was one block from school when someone stopped to ask if she knew

whose car it was that had caught fire on the farm road in the next county over. She hadn't heard. She hadn't heard of any car. Whose car? Where? What?

It was that girl's car with the body in the trunk. She could still see that girl's shiny pink fingernails clutching her locker door, black as Mariela's own locker down the hall, far enough away that he might have thought Mariela hadn't seen his hand, its scrubbed-clean nails cut to the quick and interlaced with *that girl*'s nails, pink on the black background of that girl's locker. He might have thought Mariela hadn't seen.

Mariela had hated this town in this state with the farm roads every mile west to east, every mile north to south, like a checkerboard. She felt trapped, playing checkers with someone who didn't believe in the king-me rule, someone who made you play back to the front with a single-decker checker. But her parents had brought her because there was work.

Then Mariela had met him at school, and he showed up sometimes at the gas station where she worked behind the counter after school, where she and her co-workers tried to gauge which patrons were too drunk to buy more beer, the stacks of it packed around her peripheral vision so her whole workday seemed framed in red and green diamonds. There he was, smiling, dimpled, framed in red and green diamonds. He seemed a kind of beauty. He got frequent haircuts and always cleaned up before he came back to town from his job at the lumberyard. He started talking to her at work and sometimes she let him buy a 40 when her co-worker was in the bathroom, she too young to sell, he too young to buy.

Then he started talking to her at school. He would meet her at her locker and walk her to pre-algebra. Sometimes she never made it to pre-algebra. She had a vision of those scrubbed-clean nails with their fingers that had been inside her body. She remembered them placed on top of that girl's hand, the promise that they would go inside that girl's body. That girl, who was now just a body, just a body in the trunk of her own burned-out car.

———

What a fucked-up piece of bullshit. Everyone had seen him fighting with Mariela about that girl. Everyone. He tried to think when the fire must have started for the call to go out to the firefighters at four. Couldn't have been too much before four, but early enough that he could still have made it to his job after the fire started. Could have made it to the field from school and then gotten back to Claussen's in time. Fuck. What had he done in his hour after school? What had he done? Why couldn't it have been something better, something that he could at least remember? It had been two days ago. TWO DAYS. Who lost a whole hour just two days later? Maybe this was one of those repressed memory kind of deals. Could he have done it? He didn't think he had done it. Maybe he should get hypnotized and try to remember his repressed memory of his lost hour. He wondered if the hypnotist, or hypnotherapist, or whatever they called themselves, would make him do things he didn't want to do. He had an image of himself clucking like a rooster, as a rooster, as a rooster like his grandmother's crowing around the school, pecking at the sunflowers painted on everything. He wanted to laugh, but something stopped him. The image seemed too right, somehow. He did like that rooster. Envied it, even.

He knew who hadn't been in school that day, though. Mariela. Mariela had had all day to not have an alibi. Everyone had seen how that bitch had shoved him in the hall. Everyone had heard her scream that girl's name and shove him and slap him across the

back of his shoulder as if she were trying to slap herself, awkwardly, and his shoulder had gotten in the way. What a whacked-out
bitch, and now that pretty girl was dead in the trunk of her own
car. Mariela didn't even have a car, but Mariela got to work and
school and the Planned Parenthood clinic in Sioux Falls without a
car, so who knew? This was jacked.

———

The day it happened, the sirens were almost swallowed by your
mother's fabric of sky. The volunteer EMTs took the call. Everyone
chewed sunflower seeds anxiously, and until the snow came, there
lingered a ring of seed shells around the side of the ditch where the
car had been parked. Once they put out the fire, the car was a whale
skeleton displayed on stuck wheels. It still smelled like burning
oil and melted rubber and singed hair. Of course, her skeleton was
inside, and they took it to the morgue in a blue-black body bag.
The day after, the one investigator in town went to the morgue in
the hospital basement and looked at the body. I cannot tell any
child what that body must have looked like. I cannot say how
much muscle might have still attached itself to her bones, muscles
singed as meat.

The investigator looked at the charred car skeleton parked in
the impound lot. He drove out to the farm road and looked at
the ring of sunflower shells. He looked up at the tarp of sky. He
looked up and down the farm road. He drove to the Nichols' farm,
his truck tires crunching on the gravel of their driveway. Nothing
needed paint. Their sunflowers were being harvested by hired help
and Mr. Nichol. They cut the heads off and left them in the shed
to dry, where they would drop their seeds. The seeds would be
sold and bought and become seeds that stayed as seeds and seeds

turned into cooking oil. The farm smelled vegetal like the inside of a stalk, like rotting lemon in impending rain.

Mrs. Nichol told the investigator that she and her husband were in the kitchen when they'd seen the smoke. She told him what time it was because she had been listening to public radio and the tones that marked the hour had just rung as her husband reached into his pocket for his phone. The investigator wrote this down on a notepad application on his own phone. He said that he would have to speak to Mr. Nichol.

Mr. Nichol came back from the sunflower field smelling of pollen. Pollen clung to his Carhartt jacket and the wrinkles of his palm. He confirmed Mrs. Nichol's story.

The investigator drove back to town. Tomorrow, he'd have to investigate at the girl's school. He called the principal. He had programmed the school's number into his phone because it was also his daughter's school.

He would have to ask his daughter if she knew the girl.

———

Mariela wondered what one did with the hatred one held for someone who had died. Mariela knew what the people of this town would do. They would turn the other cheek. They would say, let that girl hit you on your right cheek. Let her ghost do it. Let her ghost slap you on the cheek and wear the bloom of it like rouge. That just made her hate that girl more, hate her for turning him into a murderer. For wasn't that what he was? She imagined the word "murder" in scrollwork ringed with red and green diamonds, like a Christmas card. She vomited in the one-stall bathroom, but that was nothing new. She took a Sprite from the shelf in the cooler, and her co-worker looked at her knowingly. The co-worker was

25 and lived in the USDA Rural Housing Service complex behind the grocery store. She had two children with two different men, so Mariela didn't think she was in any position to judge. Mariela calculated the time it took to drive out to the next county. He could even have gone to sixth period, gone to meet that girl on the side of the farm road, and gotten back to the lumberyard for his shift. She straightened the coils of lottery tickets. She sent her mother a text telling her when she got off work. She wondered if her mom would tell the cop about the cans of gasoline in the garage. She wondered if Taylor would tell her dad about the hall that day.

⸻

Everyone knew Taylor's dad was the cop. THE cop. The one who would come around. He did not plan on being around when the cop came around. Taylor knew him before he knew Mariela. Taylor knew him, and she knew Mariela, and she knew that girl. Fuck. Fuck fuck fuck. Should he go to Mexico? How long would that take? Could you do the same thing, only with Canada? How far was Canada?

He went to the I-90 Travel Plaza. Roosters did not have this problem. Roosters did not have to decide if you would have Internet on the highway or if you would have to buy one of those actual maps. There was one rooster for all the women and all the mornings knew who the rooster was and every morning was the rooster's morning and he told you. He bought a map and he did not tell Mariela he was going and he bought gas at the I-90 Travel Plaza even though it was a dime more a gallon than it was at Mariela's. Tough shit. It was rooster money. It was rooster money and this rooster was gone to Canada and fuck this shit.

The next morning, the sky was milky gray-blue, the edges of your mother's bleach spot. In another state, there would have been thunder. The investigator parked next to the cinder track and walked the half-block back to the entrance of the school, its four double-doors ringed with a mural of sunflowers. He asked the principal about the girl. He asked her six teachers. He asked the girl identified as her best friend. He had asked Taylor at dinner the night before. He knew he had to talk to Mariela and to the boyfriend. He knew neither of them would be in class that day.

He walked slowly down the halls, the linoleum corn-gold and shiny only in the corners around the black lockers. He touched a locker, as if he knew it was Taylor's, softly, superstitiously, as he went by. The smell of overcooked chicken and tomatoes clung to the shiny corners of the halls. He cut through the field behind the school to get back to his truck, the cinders of the track crunching beneath his shoes. He drove to Claussen's Lumberyard, south through downtown to the sunflower fields that lapped up against the back of the Wal-Mart and the Tractor Supply parking lots. He spoke to Mr. Claussen, and then to Claussen, Jr., before he found out that the boyfriend wasn't expected until 4:30 anyway. He drove to Mariela's house, really an apartment in a converted Victorian. It sat kitty-corner from a convenience store advertising walleye for a dollar less per pound than at the grocery store. The investigator bought a Gatorade and waited. He drank his Gatorade. No one came or left the Victorian for twenty minutes. He knocked on the door next to the number of Mariela's family's apartment. The door was an unfinished plank straight from the lumberyard, hung but ill-fitting in the frame. Mariela answered the door. His stomach sprung up his throat, sloshing the Gatorade. Her eyes widened when she saw him. He introduced himself. She led him to their Salvation Army couch, green and thinly padded, its springs outlined on the seat of his pants as soon as he sat down. He asked her where she had been that day. She said she'd been sick at home. He asked her if she had a doctor's note or other documentation she might have used to excuse her absence at school. A decision shadowed her face. They could both see it, hanging there above them, as Mariela's eyes searched the middle distance for the answer. She got up and brought him a note signed in the clichéd chicken scrawl of her big-city doctor, printed on Planned Parenthood letterhead. She had been sick with morning sickness that morning, an acute case. She reddened. The investigator reddened. The Gatorade threatened to make itself known. The investigator nodded, got something out about evidence, and took the note with him. I want to tell you, child, that you are not like that child. Your mother and I cross-stitched you on the selvage of her stomach-hem. Extra, and inside, but wanted.

———

Mariela didn't know what she'd been thinking other than that she couldn't go to school. When the cop showed up, the surprise dissolved immediately into a bath of relief. At least now it would start happening. She could watch it happen instead of imagining it in her dehydrated mind. Last night after work, she'd gone out to the garage and weighed the red containers of gasoline in her arms, held the cans like large dogs, one in the crook of one arm first, then the other in the other, to see if they were lighter than they should be. Her memory of that day was a square of bare wall six inches from the side of her bed. It smelled like Sprite vomit. It felt warm. It had no time other than the changing of the light. At some point, it got dark. She was pretty sure she hadn't done it, but to say she hadn't been delirious would be a denial of the warm light and the bare wall. She did not remember how full the gasoline cans had been.

She didn't know why she should bother. Why was she worried? Didn't she know that he had done it, that he had done it without her?

She didn't, she didn't know. She knew he didn't love her, not enough to burn a thing, not enough to burn that girl.

Canada is farther away than you would think. So.

The rooster would let the hens peck each other to death and would probably fuck the corpses later. Maybe he was messed up for thinking that but you saw some pretty weird shit on the farm. Why should he run away because Mariela had pecked that girl to death? Maybe he shouldn't be on the interstate. Would he be less likely to be found on smaller highways? But then you couldn't get away, just two lanes with a farm on either side. If you wanted a bona-fide police chase, you needed a good four lanes and a few good-sized towns to drive through. A rooster needs his ROOM, know what I'm saying?

Man, if Mariela had killed that girl, she was one stone-cold bitch. He had not anticipated that. He had underestimated her. A begrudging respect for Mariela wafted through the truck cab. He got a little high off it. He thought maybe that baby would be one righteous little dude. One cute-ass motherfucker. Maybe he should turn himself in so at least Mariela would be outside taking care of their cute-ass motherfucker. He didn't want to take care of it. He couldn't even imagine it. It was impossible. He was going to have to take the heat for this. He was going to have to turn himself in for a murder he hadn't committed. It seemed almost noble. If he couldn't be the foreman on a construction crew, he could be a kind of foreman in a family in which he would be absent. He could brag about his kid and hot wife and not have to actually hang out with Mariela every day. At least in jail they fed you. No more of his mother's slapped-together WIC-bread-and-generic-peanut-butter sandwiches. No more spending all his money at McDonald's just to get a big enough hot sandwich to make you full when you closed up the lumberyard. He would live in the State Penitentiary in Sioux Falls and work on becoming the bad-ass motherfucker he should never not have been.

———

The APB went out for the boyfriend around the time he must have turned around. The dispatch desk expected a call from the Highway Patrol near Sioux Falls, or near Rapid City, or near Fargo, or near Sioux City, so when the boyfriend walked into the Public Safety Center and said his name, the volunteer manning the front desk asked him what he had to report. He said, simply, "Myself," and two beats later, the volunteer understood. It was already the most exciting day of her volunteer career. So she should be forgiven. She should be forgiven for turning around and going herself to find an arresting officer, instead of calling to the back like she was trained to do. She should be forgiven for giving him even thirty extra seconds to think. He wasn't a quick thinker, but that would have been enough. It would have been enough for a clearer picture of the penitentiary to condense inside his eyes. It would have been enough time for him to slip out to the railroad tracks that run behind the Public Safety Center, because the Dakota Southern came through right around then, and they never found the boyfriend again.

———

Mariela now stared at the empty green couch. She knew of no one who cared about that girl as much as he did or as much as Mariela did, because hatred is the most concentrated care. Nothing had a frame. Nothing was a square of wall. It was as if the ceiling had been taken off the world and that girl had been sucked out by the force of the vacuum made when the world lost its boundary.

———

He had made it back to the Public Safety Center, which was a remodeled church next to the railroad tracks. Crosses of lighter brick had been built into the top corners of each brick wall. So much for separation of church and state, he thought. So much for that. He could hear a train whistle off to the right, off in the middle distance. It was getting closer, going through town slowly. Getting closer, it crowed its train crow, and he answered inside with his man-rooster crow, and he opened the door. The train got closer and closer, slowly, crowing.

———

The day it happened, your mother had let the world soak too long before she washed it. She had left it too close to the whites she was bleaching, and there was a splash. She hadn't ironed the selvage hem and it puckered the sky at the corners. I wanted it to look its best for you, so I got out the washboard and the soap, as anyone would have done, anyone but the spoiled city folks who don't do chores because their parents never made them, but I am the anyone who would have. So I did. I scrubbed and scrubbed and washed and washed and rinsed, and that's what happens when you do a thorough clean like that—you lose the spores of mold clinging to the fabric, damp too long. You lose the pattern and the print, you bleach the whole thing out to match the spot. You iron away the wrinkles, iron them away, and what's left becomes a plume of smoke rising in the horizon between the sunflowers and the sky. Dirty just in passing until the spot is cleaned away, cauterized, burned entirely out.

BARBARA DUFFEY

IS THE AUTHOR OF THE POETRY COLLECTION *I MIGHT BE MISTAKEN* (WORD POETRY, FORTHCOMING JULY 2015) AND A RECIPIENT OF A NATIONAL ENDOWMENT FOR THE ARTS CREATIVE WRITING FELLOWSHIP IN POETRY. HER PROSE HAS APPEARED IN CUTBANK AND THE COLLAGIST. "AND ALL NIGHT LONG WE HAVE NOT STIRRED" IS PART OF A LONGER MYSTERY NOVEL IN PROGRESS. DUFFEY IS AN ASSISTANT PROFESSOR OF ENGLISH AT DAKOTA WESLEYAN UNIVERSITY IN MITCHELL, SD, WHERE SHE LIVES WITH HER HUSBAND AND SON. YOU CAN FOLLOWER HER ON TWITTER @BARBARANDUFFEY OR ON THE WEB AT WWW.BARBARADUFFEY.COM.

A DULL BOY

DAVID JAMES KEATON

> *"All play and no work makes Jack a mere toy."*
> —PROVERB

'm telling a visibly bored class about immunostaining, the process for using colored dyes to gate out dead cells under a microscope in order to identify rare cellular populations, when the starstruck girl in the front row who has been giving me meaningful looks since day one, slowly and seductively blinks to reveal the words "Red" and "Rum" drawn on her eyelids.

My name is Danny Lloyd, and I'm a professor of biology at Emmanuellatown Community College, although, when I lose my students' full attention, I've succumbed to the theatrics of chemistry demonstrations on occasion. When I was seven years old, I played the part of "Danny" in Stanley Kubrick's adaptation of Stephen King's novel *The Shining*. For months at a Colorado ski resort, I pretended to be a borderline psychotic but otherwise normal 5-year-

old boy. The most distinguishing part of my performance, besides shivering and drooling like a rabid squirrel, was supplying the guttural voice of my index finger, Tony. This is the part of the film that is the most enduring, and that finger still follows me to work, decades later. For the record, I've never named any of my fingers. Not even whole hands, or fists, which seems to be in fashion here in the South, judging by some of the skirmishes in our hallways. When I began studying biology, I wasn't prepared for how self-conscious I'd feel whenever I'd use my finger to point out anything on the dry-erase board. To avoid any jokes, pretty early on in graduate school I stopped using that finger for essentially everything. And trying to indicate to someone to please, "Wait a minute" was always a mistake, even a noble "Watch out!" led to ridicule. And innocently scratching my ear was sometimes interpreted by King fans as Tony telling me a secret. Which was ridiculous because the finger thing wasn't even in the book, and real fans should know this.

I'd managed to lay low through my first several semesters at Emmanuellatown when my full-time teaching career began. Then, one day during the semester before all the rooms were finally outfitted with projectors, I made the mistake of writing something backwards on the overhead. A boy in the back had obviously heard from a friend of a friend of my short-lived movie career, and he shouted out in his best Tony growl:

"Redrum!"

I lost my temper that day, likely lost the respect of that class. But imagine how difficult it would be to kick someone out of the room without being able to point. However, there were plenty more classes to come, and hundreds more chances for that movie to disrupt my life even more.

It was about six years later, right after I received tenure, when technology introduced cell phone smuggling into classrooms. And with most instructors, me included, The Great Texting Cold War had finally begun. The policy on my syllabus was always, "Don't let me catch you texting. If I see this happening, you will lose all points for the day and could be asked to leave the classroom." I also explained that texting while driving was like having a 1.9 blood/alcohol level and illegal for this very reason. How could I have any confidence in their ability to follow my lectures if they were drunk? Someone grumbles something about Stephen King writing *Cujo* while drunk, and I moved on. But this one kid, Kevin, who sat in the back and should have been exhausted at the effort he put into entertaining everyone around him, was harder to catch than most. In fact, I lost a bit of ethos by demanding he stop playing with his phone, only to suffer the embarrassment of his slow, exaggerated removal of a phone that was buried deep in his book bag, which was actually a little plastic box of candy shaped like a phone. He claimed he'd been warming his hands between his legs, and that's why he looked so suspicious. Foolishly, I accused him of being covered in phones. And when he protested the unfairness of it all, I shrugged:

"The trust is gone, Kevin. I've busted you texting way too many times."

Hands were cold, my ass, I was thinking, You want to talk about cold hands? Try eating ice cream for 47 takes while Kubrick makes the guy from The Harlem Globetrotters cartoon cry.

"All work and no play makes Jack a dull boy."

The verse that everyone has recited at least a dozen times, those ten words that show up as jokes on most of my Teacher Evaluations, besides being that famous representation of writer's block in *The Shining*, was spoken in *The Bridge on the River Kwai*, *Buffy the Vampire Slayer*, an Alice in Chains song, *Twin Peaks*, *Melrose Place*, it showed up on the chalkboard during an intro for *The Simpsons*, which means, of course, it was in *Family Guy*, too. But it surprises some people to learn that this wasn't in King's original book either. Although he did jam it into *Pet Semetary*, I'm told.

Less frequently heard is a ten-word variation, the follow-up first recorded in 1825's *Harry and Lucy Concluded* by Maria Edgeworth, where she added, "All play and no work makes Jack a mere toy."

That's a line that could have really haunted someone later in life, so I guess I lucked out.

———

They hired me for that movie because of my name. The boy's name was Danny in the book, and they used my name on the set, "Danny," so I wouldn't get confused.

So I wouldn't get confused? Maybe someone should have told me they were making a movie and there would have been a lot less confusion.

"Jack" and I were the only ones that shared names with our characters. He must get confused easily, too, I figured. I had one up on him though, as there are two Dannys, two Jacks, *and* two Lloyds in that film. My first and last name wraps around his Jack, mere toy or not, whether he had me on his lap or I was spilling Advocaat on his jacket.

Actually that was eggnog, and it was delicious.

I've read in interviews that I was supposedly told they were making a comedy, so I wouldn't be scared. Did they even wonder how my definition of comedy might be affected forever when I watched them filling an elevator with gallons of blood?

———

One time, I made the mistake of Googling my name and came across a blog post where a colleague at Emmanuellatown wrote, "I ran into the kid from *The Shining* today at work. He had the same eyes. I knew him immediately. We're not supposed to talk about it, and it's driving me crazy."

I know there's little oversight in the Arts and Humanities, but I wonder if this instructor has considered how terrifying this might sound.

I understand that people want to talk about the movie all the time. And they never believe me, but I'd never even seen the entire thing until recently. I swear this is true. For my birthday, my sister was supposed to order me a copy of *Shine*, because the music instructor who shares our building's copy machine had been talking about the sudden burst of Rachmaninoff after that film's surprise Oscar wins. He said it was similar to the post-*Sideways* Pinot Noir upsurge (more like Merlot hatred), which was bad enough to endure. But my sister is a lot younger than I am, and she doesn't understand my lack of interest in the film, even if I wasn't starring in it. Actually, in her own way, she's the one who steered me towards my PhD, as she was the only one in real world who insisted on calling me "Doc."

I guess I can understand her obsession, seeing my tricycle up on the little screen, then seeing it parked in our garage. Yes, it's a tricycle, not a "Big Wheel" like so many reviewers claim. That misidentification is why I no longer drive my Dodge 4x4. I thought it was a good choice for someone in Kentucky, but I switched to a Prius when my cousin laughed, "Look, Danny still likes Big Wheels!" Actually, the tricycle was a gift from Mr. Kubrick, and once it was handed down to my sister, it was easy to imagine her imagining herself peddling around those hallways.

But instead of *Shine*, she sent me *The Shining* and feigned ignorance (she made a similar joke when *Shining Through* came out, too), and I immediately printed out the proper return forms, repackaged it, and put it downstairs under our apartment's mailboxes to ship it back. But our vestibule doesn't lock, and someone stole the parcel. I know this because I placed it there at 9:00 p.m., walked down to C.C.'s on the corner for some ice cream, and when I returned at 9:25 p.m. it was gone. Infuriated, I sat in my living room and listened for any clues to the caper, immediately suspecting the kids who'd just moved in above me, and whose distracting bass-heavy sound system was usually all I could think about. So I listened for them to watch the movie, ignoring the much more likely scenario, that they'd sold it back to the Music & Movie Exchange for a quick five bucks of gas money. I sat on the couch all night, staring at the ceiling, careful my head was angled up and my eyes weren't rolling back in my head, never allowing myself that spaced-out look Kubrick had become famous for. I'd successfully avoided the film all my life, but couldn't help catching sight once a year of my own five-year-old face drooling and contorted in seizures.

Eventually, I realized that I would have no idea if they were watching the movie or not. I only knew Jack's angry rant over the typewriter because I was on the set that day, pretending to nap on a nearby couch. And I only knew a spattering of my own lines. So I went down to the Music & Movie Exchange for my own copy. And I watched it.

It was a pretty good movie.

Jack went crazy kind of fast though. Every time a title card said "Monday," "Tuesday," "Wednesday," or "Two Months Later," I imagined it saying, "12:19," "12:25," "12:33," and "Five Minutes Later" instead. Can anyone switch gears that fast from rational to homicidal? Kind of ridiculous.

―――――

Every year, our class takes a field trip to Kackleberry Farms to get some pumpkins for our hydrogen peroxide experiments, a variation on the classic Elephant's Toothpaste demo that you see in most grade schools. Hydrogen peroxide is mixed with liquid soap. Then a catalyst like potassium iodide is added to make the hydrogen peroxide break down quickly, and the foam puts on quite a show. Not enough to fill up an elevator, but it wakes them up for a day nonetheless, even keeps them from texting. More important, no one does a Tony imitation with their clamshell phone.

The formula, $2H_2O_2 \rightarrow 2H_2O_{(l)} + O_{2(g)}$, is deceptively simple, considering how a bit of mad science actually opens their dead eyes for a week of lectures afterward. Something about that foam busting through the eyes and mouth of Halloween pumpkins makes the job fun all over again.

But this year the farm doesn't just have pumpkins.

They have a hedge maze, too.

―――――

Many times, people have congratulated me on my nine-year-old character's ingenuity, when we backtracked over our footprints in the snow to save Danny's life.

Now, I don't want to overanalyze the film. In fact, lately, there have been Post-it notes on my door with "Room 237!" scrawled on them, which steered me towards a recent documentary of the same name. I wasn't surprised by its popularity among my weakest students. From what I've seen, if it wouldn't be such a distraction to show it in class, I could have used it as a hilarious example of horrible inductive reasoning. It's bad enough they're using exclamation points on anything, since it's not only term papers that suffer from that sort of breathless punctuation. Each semester, I explain that students are allowed one exclamation point, whether it's in emails or more substantial assignments. I tell them not to waste it, in case they really need to scream about something important.

But now that I've finally viewed *The Shining*, I realize that it was never backtracking that did this. If you look real close at what I was doing in the maze, if you squint right there in the bottom left corner of your screen, I was actually covering some of them up. I like this idea better.

Once, I had two sets of twins in my classroom. The one set of twins was our turtles. I'd turned the corner at the Science Building one morning, and there in front of my huge off-road vehicle were two box turtles, side by side in the parking lot like they were going to live forever. I took them into our classroom, and with the students, we filled up the empty 20-gallon tank that had been gathering dust in the corner, and gave our new turtles a home. I numbered their shells, "52" and "81" as part of an extra credit assignment. The numbers represented tellurium and thallium on the periodic table, two elements which produced a green flame when burned. Anyone who solved this riddle received fifty points, more than enough to cancel out a texting deficit. Despite the numbers, students would assign their own names, Kevin called them "Cuff" and "Link" every chance he got, and asked me how I could possibly tell them apart.

"Exactly," I'd say.

Someone drowned the turtles a month later, pinning them to the bottom of the tank with our textbooks. I upended the tank into the parking lot, not far from where I'd found them, working their way through the cars for months, the creek they couldn't see mere feet from their heads at all times. I dream of their journey some nights. More often, I dream of the food in the freezer that Scatman Crothers showed Shelley Duvall and me in the film. I would dream of sitting on a sack of coffee beans and eating peanut butter with my hands. Some days the dream comes back, only now I dream of hooking wires to the metal shelves, and applying a series of electric shocks to rows of foods in that freezer, as well as thousands of shelves in hundreds of grocery stores. I would hit the switch and watch the sparks turn the labels first to numbers, then to white, then removing all identifiable features from every product.

My students joked that I'd numbered the turtles so I wouldn't get attached, as if I was going to experiment on them. As if they weren't the experiment from day one.

———

The other set of twins weren't twins exactly. Just two girls of the same height, color, and degree of disinterest. They fought the No Phone rule tooth and nail, more like tooth and claw. They would see my own phone shining through my linen pants, and say sweetly, "Aren't you going to answer that?" They also worked for our campus newspaper, *The Street*, and one of them, possibly both of them, wrote about my brief acting career, violating the unwritten rule of avoiding the topic. The article said things like, "His only other film was an undistinguished role in *Will: The Autobiography of G. Gordon Liddy*, where he again played a boy named 'Danny.'" And, "Rumor has it that they told him he was in an adventure film, not a biography of the Watergate architect" and, my favorite, "Professor Lloyd wears checkered shirts every day, just like the carpet in the Overlook Hotel." I think the little shit was thinking of *Twin Peaks*.

Once the article hit, the jokes were more and more frequent. The "red" and "rum" on the eyelids of the twins mocks me once a week now, and I understand that it's not due to my minor celebrity. Then there was the ridiculous unease when I used terms as innocuous as "Overview" on the top of my semester calendars, waiting for the snickers. Recently, there was one student who claimed he heard me say "gravy" instead of "grading," but I thought he said "Grady." As in Delbert Grady, the smooth-talking Iago of Kubrick's adaptation. I kicked him out, and later swore to my Division Chair that I'd caught him texting. I didn't feel bad about the misrepresentation. It probably saved his life.

I've been thinking about the pumpkin peroxide experiment more and more these days, even during the Spring semester. It's fine to moonlight teaching chemistry when my degree is in biology, but I worry it's probably a little irresponsible to turn my classes into Pumpkin Carving 101 all year round, and Kackleberry Farms isn't open past November. Still, I reserve the van for a brief field trip on Saturday. I borrow the Science Department credit card from Connie, and I make sure that I fill the gas tank up near the school. I wave a couple of the texters up to my desk after class on Friday, and I ask each one if they want to earn some extra credit.

We'd need a lot more pumpkins if we were going to do the experiment every semester, so I figured they had to have some lying around the fields. Unless you gut them, vegetables don't rot very fast at all.

———

There's been talk of a new Stephen King book called *Doctor Sleep*, which is a sequel to *The Shining*. This is another distraction that concerns me, especially after how the author flirted with putting multiple versions of himself into the *Dark Tower* series. And here we have a book that, at least in the minds of the masses, if not the author himself, is a sequel with not just the film adaptation in mind, but with his own miniseries, which he offered as a rebuttal to Kubrick's perceived failures. Combined with King's new fondness for meta-narratives, cracking open this novel feels like a game of Russian Roulette; another demonstration that sort of starts biological, but succumbs to the theatrics of chemistry.

———

Taking the kids to a hedge maze was probably a mistake. Something about that environment opened the floodgates of conversations and questions that I'd managed to duck for thirty years. And something about getting lost in the maze together made them braver than ever, the opposite of what I'd predicted.

My favorite line in the movie is when I say, "I don't want to talk about Tony." I had a good reason then, and I have a good reason now.

We enter the maze at around 2:00 p.m., but the days are short this time of year. The sun is going down, and there's a nervousness in their voices that they're trying to hide. I explain that there have got to be a few lying around in the maze where people have dropped them in exhaustion. And I tell them that I need the mallet to clear away the corn stalks without cutting them down. We're sneaking into a maze a little off-season, you see. No sense in drawing too much attention to our harvest.

The beauty of a croquet mallet is no one who saw the movie thinks it's threatening. Only if you read the book. And it's hard enough to get these kids to read a textbook, let alone one for leisure, especially after its been at the bottom of a fish tank.

It's down to me and Kevin and the twins. Every year there are twins. I try to turn it into a lesson and keep them talking. I come up with a quiz, right off the cuff.

I ask, "What mineral boosts the immune system?" "What process is used to refine grains such as this corn?" "What are the dangers of going on a high-protein diet?" "Is it more dangerous than rampant cell-phone usage?" "What three vitamins are antioxidants? Are they oil or water-soluble? Are we oil or water-soluble?" I throw question after question at them as we back up and retrace our steps.

I carry many chemicals—ammonia, hydrogen peroxide, hydrochloric acid, all of which are much more interesting on blood than on pumpkins. I'll need all my chemicals if I'm going to put the mallet back on my wall for next semester.

They retrace their steps, but I cover mine up.

That night, the foam rolls out of their mouths like jack-o'-lanterns, which is much less alarming than their questions. But there are no screams. They'd wasted their exclamation points at the beginning of the semester, on the first research paper I'd assigned.

Like I said, I turn it into a lesson.

I used to read a lot of articles criticizing the casting, saying that I looked nothing like a young Jack Nicholson. It reminded me of my jealously regarding my younger brothers. The youngest was this lupine, grinning kid, looking and acting exactly like our father. I always felt like the mutant, the anomaly, as I was quiet, tight-lipped, white and smooth as a grub. Then one day, my dad showed me some grainy pictures of him hiding under the table at a wedding reception, and I saw that he started out in the same larvae stage, exactly like me. I was comforted for quite a while, then I was horrified wondering how much scarier my brother was going to get. But the point is, what nobody understands, is that I was chosen for that movie for a reason. Because my father was the one who looked exactly like Jack. He was one who named us all as easily as a boy can name his fingers. Not me.

I know all of these things are distractions, and I'm just as guilty as anyone. But I've figured out why my colleagues avoid the same topic that my students find so fascinating. There's an odd reluctance to congratulate you about anything you did as a child, as if my celebrated acting was accidental, because they lied about which genre I was peddling. But I always knew what I was doing.

DAVID JAMES KEATON

'S FICTION HAS APPEARED IN OVER 50 PUBLICATIONS,
INCLUDING GRIFT, PANK, AND NOIR AT THE BAR II. HIS FIRST
COLLECTION, FISH BITES COP! STORIES TO BASH AUTHORITIES,
WAS NAMED THE 2013 SHORT STORY COLLECTION OF THE
YEAR BY THIS IS HORROR AND WAS A FINALIST FOR THE
KILLER NASHVILLE SILVER FALCHION AWARD. HIS FIRST
NOVEL, THE LAST PROJECTOR (BROKEN RIVER BOOKS),
WAS RELEASED IN 2014.

BRUJERIA

FOR

BEGINNERS

MARYTZA K. RUBIO

Before we begin, did you all place your rum and dulces de tamarindo at the crossroads as instructed? Cigarettes are fine, too. Leyla, did you have a question? Yes, well, we use three coins because three is the number of the gatekeeper, the number of the Trinity, the number that is the basic DNA of our spiritual world. I can't answer that, Leyla. Remember the exhausting and circuitous discussion we had last time "good or evil" came up? The true identity of the gatekeeper is revealed in the Advanced Class.

On your desks, I have given each of you a supply kit with items chosen specifically for you. We may have a visitor from the Jewelry Class next door, the instructor and I have an agreement. If that happens, you may be asked to share your rulers and a pencil. Do not share your gris-gris or your velas, these items are your fates.

Does everyone have a ruler? Does everyone have scissors? A piece of paper, X-Acto knife, duct tape, cutting board, bandage? Spool of wire, two-inch width; spool of wire, half-inch width; copper coil? Agua de violeta, agua de rosa, a live pigeon, paraffin block and tweezers? Check to see that you have one bag of colored sand, glitter glue, and two embroidery needles. I've also brought in an

assortment of oils, hierbas, and plants from my own collection. You may use these items to intensify your petition. Please do not use the ammonia or any of the sealed powders without my assistance. Do not touch the vials of mercury, do not test the sharpness of the knives.

Yes, Denise?

The difference is the smell, that is usually how you can tell them apart.

Yes, you in the back. Carla, is it?

No.

Well, you are misinformed.

Because blood represents life and life is of the highest value. All petitions require fees.

I see.

Well, how about this: Take off those leather shoes and look at them. Now repeat to yourself what you just told me and then decide if you can stay in this class. If not, go next door to the Jewelry Class; the instructor and I have an agreement. Leave your supplies on the desk. Thank you and good luck.

Everyone else, please remove your rings, crosses, and hair pins if you have not done so already. Turn off your electronic gadgets, except you, Anasiria, I know your anklet needs to stay on.

Come in, sir. You are from the Jewelry Class, yes? Welcome. Take Carla's seat. Please take her bag of fates, as it was meant for you anyway, and let's continue.

We will start with Viviana. Everyone please direct your attention to Viviana and her gris-gris. This is a kit for Love, many of you share this aim and will have similar items. Paola, can you see from there? Pull in closer so you have a better view.

Viviana wants to attract love, a new love, a first love.

Yes, sir, you have a question? Why, that is a generous offer, and as the sole male in this class I suspect you will be tempted to ask that of all our students. But the purpose of this demonstration is education, not fulfilling your social desires.

Viviana's kit includes a hummingbird feather, which I won't pass around. Viviana, please hold up your piece of wing. The hummingbird is a fierce warrior, an essential ally for someone who is as shy as our Viviana. I tele-chatted with Viviana last night, and was so pleased she allowed me to make an example of her kit for today's lesson.

No, not telephone, Leyla. Tele-chat.

I'll be brief, class needs to be dismissed before sunset and the logistics of tele-chat can be time-consuming. After crashing our cars in the parking lot of El Super years ago, Viviana and I retained a psychic bond that germinated from our shared susto. I damaged my lower back and her acupuncturist helped me tremendously. Viviana was unharmed—her youth and health are a great armor— but I wanted to offer equally beneficial reciprocation. I have been visiting Viviana's dreams to coax her into this class so she could develop new friendships and confidence. And now, look at her, hair pulled back and a pretty pink lipstick. Soon she will graduate to a pouty red. I am so proud. I am extraordinarily proud of all of you and will miss you when you are summoned to the Advanced Class.

Let's talk about Viviana's pink hummingbird candles. These candles should be burned consecutively; light the next one as soon as the previous one is down to its final layer of wax. This ensures a seamless burning petition. After they have burned out, we will inventory Viviana's suitors and chart the burn pattern of the glass. If the burn pattern is clear, we will then decide if it is best to light one to Oshun as well.

What is the rule for lighting to Oshun, class?

Yes, that is correct.

No, Leyla, she does not have a preference for organic or mass produced honey.

No, Leyla, almond butter is not a suitable substitute for honey under any circumstances. It has no spiritual significance and when burned it smells like rancid milk.

Yes, you, sir.

How clever that your name matches your tattoos, but I prefer to call you "sir."

How does ingesting the honey reach the spirit world? Well, it is the essence of the honey and you ingesting it that provides a mandatory testament to La Bonita that she will not be poisoned by your offering. Transmutation is covered in the Advanced Class, as is transubstantiation.

Excellent question, Paola. For those of you who are at a more . . . progressed . . . state of romantic development than Viviana, you will want something more potent. A red Chuparosa candle, a red Ven A Mi, or even a plain red candle burned over the picture of your intended lover will provide faster results. If you choose to write your names on the glass candle, make sure your name is always on top of his. Always. Full names preferred. Don't assume that the name they tell you is true. People change their birth names, especially in this town, and all candle work is futile without the correct address.

Yes, Anasiria? Well, you are one of my best herbology students, but I wouldn't recommend it to anyone else. Remind me, you're married, yes? Then I guess toloache would be feasible to administer daily, provided the dose is exact. Jimson weed, class, jimson weed. Distilled and dropped into a coffee cup—yes, Anasiria, or vodka—can make men docile and bring them to a perpetual amorous state.

Sir, I prefer you raise your hand rather than interrupt, but yes. You are correct. It is absolutely fatal. Toloache is a relative of belladona, the same plant women used to distill and drop into their eyes to make them dilated and seductive. Don't use belladonna in your eyes. The drops will make you blind and dead. Spaces are infinite in the Advanced Class, but it is best, for all involved, you not rush to your assigned seat.

No, Denise, I do not recommend you seek out toloache in any of its forms. Your hand will slip and you'll fail to administer the exact dose. All that work we've been doing will be lost if you are accused of murder. We are all aligned with you. Have faith that your petition will be heard and toloache will not be needed. When is the hearing? Good, the Listless Lawyer candle included in your kit burns in seven days, be sure to start tonight. Class, I have also included beads in Ogun's colors for Denise to wear on her court date and a Tapa Boca candle for her malhablada sister-in-law. This is in addition to the Dume candle we are burning on Denise's soon-to-be-ex-husband. I brought in two spent Dume candles to show you all how much has changed since the beginning of the semester.

Yes, Leyla, D-U-M-E, not D-O-O-M. They sound the same and if used correctly, will have the same effect.

This candle is from last week. See how the glass is only sooted at the top rim? And here, this solid black one, is from when Denise and I first started working together. All soot and ash. Who can tell me what that means? Yes, that is correct. Obstacles. Now that it has burned clear, I am confident that Denise's rat of an ex-esposo and his complicit mistress will get their due.

What was that, sir? No, it isn't really black magic. Denise has acquired a sizable cache of retribution she can spend without causing harm to herself or her loved ones. Conversely, Denise's soon-to-be-ex husband has accumulated a heavy amount of debt. Denise, please raise your arm for the class to see. Thirteen stitches; the doctors and the fates have blessed her proactive redistribution of fortune.

Yes, Leyla, I agree. The topic requires a proper course all its own. I submitted a proposal for a full-length course on Artes Obscuras, but considering the severe lack of funding in community colleges, it is unlikely the class will take place. If the district continues to make cuts, we may even lose this class. Even if the Artes Obscuras class is approved, I will only be accepting a limited number of students, specifically chosen by me. I am sorry, but none of you will be invited.

No, Paola, that is not why. I care for each of you and know you are all intelligent and capable students. Intelligence and capability are not the issue.

The reason is the cost. The darkness requires a payment that strips the protective layer of your spirit and invites pain and harm in unexpected manifestations.

For example: If you use darkness to win a level of professional achievement you do not deserve, and become lazy in a position that is lucrative yet full of responsibility, the blackness will disintegrate the aura of falseness you have cultivated and depended on throughout your career. Or if you ask dark forces to rip apart a happy couple so the man will love you instead of his wife, he will love you for all eternity and no one will ever rip him apart from you. But you will abuse him. Your children will despise you and grow up to be despised themselves. That will break your heart. His death will break your heart. If you are lucky, the tears of your heartbreak will leech the dark tar from your soul. You will be given an opportunity for redemption, sharing knowledge with strangers and seeking affection from homeless and neglected cats. There is always a sacrifice and you all know what it is.

Now. What can you all tell me about the woman we will be invoking today?

That's right, Denise.

La Anima Sola, the lonely soul chained to the bottom of purgatory, surrounded by the flames of her desperate love. Some may consider waiting in limbo a fate harsher than burning in hell, but only Advanced students know for sure.

Before invoking La Anima Sola, understand that she is a powerful force to harness. She is the middle ground—not dark, not light. She strains her arms for salvation—not dead, not alive. She is permitted to make brief visits to our world to inflict insomnia and obsessive thoughts on an unresponsive or otherwise uncommitted lover. You will soon be granted access to the Anima Sola and may ask her fleet of intranquil spirits to assist you. Please understand that by continuously summoning her, you run the risk of ending up like her.

Other questions?

No, we will never learn how to raise the dead, not even in the Advanced Class.

Security reasons, Leyla.

Yes, that is correct, Viviana. While we cannot wake the dead, it is always important to honor them. Have you all been keeping up with your altars? Cleanliness and disposal of offerings is important.

No, sir. We do not discuss disposal of the dead in this class.

No, sir. The answers you are looking for are found in a chemistry or anatomy class, but your instructors would find that line of questioning disturbing. I would encourage you to register for Analytical Anatomy but the semester is over, your time is almost up.

Let's have a look at your kit, yes?

Ah, you have the Gato Negro kit, your luck is due for a major change! Congratulations. Black cats are magnificent creatures and full of spirited energy.

Class, this is a perfect opportunity for me to point out the folded-up sheet of paper that is included in everyone's supply kit. If any one of you is interested in learning more about the black cat, please pay special attention to that form. I run The Behemoth Foundation, a black cat rescue group, and foster anywhere from four to a dozen black cats at any given time. If you would like to adopt a black cat or just want to volunteer for their care, please be sure to fill out the application included in your supply kit and return to me before the end of class. Be sure to indicate which days are best for an in-house inspection and sign your approval for a federal background check.

I don't understand what my marital status has to do with anything, sir, but I am a widow.

That is an outdated stereotype; I rarely have more than twenty in the house at one time.

Class, let's take a look at our lucky student's kit. Here we have a multi-colored Black Cat candle for him to burn for his deepest and most intimate desires. Sir, will you give us an example of what those are?

Is that really the kind of humor you think ladies would find charming?

I will remind you that our campus security is sparse but vigilant nonetheless.

Anasiria, put down the X-Acto. Viviana, stay close to Anasiria.

You will see this kit also includes a bundle of sage to clear his house of negativity and evil spirits. I don't know why you find that funny, sir. Believe it or not, sage can clear even the dankest of places. Here we also have a prayer card for St. Christopher to protect him on his travels, a horseshoe for good luck, a rosary for his soul . . . Oh, look at this. You also have a small laminated portrait of Sinluz, one of my dearest gatos.

No, sir. You are misinformed.

What they sell in stores is "alleged black cat bone." The repulsive manufacturing methods and ungainly mathematics of the supply and demand are too risky for any business to invest in that cruel harvest.

No, I will not comment on or condone the practices of less ethical independents, but I will say that my cats are treated with love and respect. They are my friends.

That is a vicious and dangerous accusation.

I protect my cats as each of the ladies in this class protect their lovers or their children.

What's that smirk supposed to mean?

Sir, you are out of line.

You have offended me and I will give you a chance to leave.

You need to calm down.

Sit down.

What is that in your hand? Is that one of my knives?

Sit down!

Where did you get that hook?

I did not include that in the supply kit!

I did not include that in the supply kit!

Mujeres! The wire, the needles, the rope coiled around each

of your chairs. Paola, bring me the toloache and vials of mercury. Viviana, please lock the door.

———

Now that your tuition has been paid in full, each of you will have guaranteed success in your endeavors. When you light your candles tonight, you may include a prayer for the lost souls in limbo. La Anima Sola now knows your names. Your classmate murmurs them aloud as he waits.

Release your pigeons before sunset. Be sure to truly want what you ask for, you will receive it and be expected to respect and care for it. It will come in doses or in one rush of fortune, those are things I can't tell you and you can't expect to know. There are mysteries, there are mysteries.

Feed and care for your santos, listen and speak to your ancestors. Keep a record of your dreams and impulses, take time to find the patterns within. Feed stray animals, take care of your fellow man. I'll see you all again in the Advanced Class. I will not be the teacher but we will all be students. We are all required to attend.

MARYTZA K. RUBIO

IS A WRITER FROM SANTA ANA, CALIFORNIA.

HEIRLOOM

KENNETH W. CAIN

leek leather dizzied him, as he traced the camera's contours. He shook his head, his own name escaping him, and returned his gaze to the camera. He'd never seen one quite like this, and even with his lightheadedness, his hands were eager. For now all he could do was look—examining it just as it seemed to scrutinize him through its solitary eye.

What an amazing creation.

Recalling his name, Thaddeus Claremont rose from all fours to his knees with some effort. He scanned the grassy knoll, but saw no one else. Whoever had lost this camera hadn't bothered to stick around. He brushed a light coat of pollen from its side with two gentle fingers, feeling a tingling sensation. The camera hadn't been here long. So why hadn't they come back for it?

Maybe the camera wasn't lost.

Considering this, Thad wondered why anyone would want to intentionally get rid of something so beautiful. He'd used cameras often enough in his line of business, and had come to appreciate photography. The housing on this camera, although worn and aged

like one would expect, wasn't as boxy as those he'd seen in pictures from the early twentieth century.

Again, Thad explored his surroundings. From his spot in the tall grass he saw nothing but trees and bushes, the road where his Cutlass was still running, its door wide open. But he didn't recall leaving the door ajar.

He scanned the field from his car to this place in the grass. How he'd spotted the camera was still a mystery. He remembered the row of pine trees, counting them one by one as he passed. He'd seen the old Miller place, long since abandoned. Trevor Miller had lost his job and his family, left everything behind after going bankrupt. Miller had failed to sell the property and the bank foreclosed. That house was the reason Thad had come here.

After the house, there was New Hope Baptist Church and the graveyard adjacent to the property. Thad had buried his mother there and in passing the graveyard, he'd thought of a childhood myth and held his breath until he fully passed. That was when a glimmer caught his eye. Seeing it now, he thought it was a one in a million chance he should spot the small device in such a grassy field.

Glancing back down, he seized the camera. It was heavier than he'd expected, as if something wanted it to stay right where it'd been left. A slight crack in its lens indicated it would no longer function. This would be no more than a showpiece. He opened the back, finding an abundance of cobwebs and dust inside. The mirror was also broken. He blew hard, forcing air into the housing and the dust stirred, causing him to sneeze. Itchy nose and all, he kept staring inside the camera.

This would be a great place to hide something.

Thad closed the camera and held it tight against his chest, feeling dizzy as he reached his feet. He hurried to the car, as if he were thieving this antique and threw himself into the seat. Before closing the door he placed the camera on the passenger seat with care. There she sat, almost seeming to glimmer, his very own antique camera with its special hiding spot. He longed to find something to put inside it.

Before he left, he found himself staring back out across the grassy field. Something about his departure felt wrong. After a few lingering moments, he threw the car into drive and headed back to his office.

———

It was a tedious drive from the country to the city. He'd made the trip several times, always on business, but it was getting to a point where he considered such trips more of a hassle than they were worth. In the end, he'd gotten the pictures of Harry Edenton with his young mistress, and that would pay the bills for another month, maybe a little longer. This was the reason he made such journeys—for the money. Money always made his problems go away. But sometimes it created new ones. This month's setback came in the form of scotch. He poured himself a tall snifter, drinking as he browsed the photos.

She's going to pay extra for these last few.

He spread them out and then slid the three apart from the rest. They were as good as pornography. Thinking this, Thad thumbed to the last, seeing much of the young woman's pale flesh. He picked it up and lingered on her curves.

She's something else, all right.

His eyes fell back to the sleek vintage camera. Crossing to his shelves, he stared at it a moment longer before picking it up. He opened the back of the camera, the urge overcoming him, and his desire to put something inside it. In went the photo and he closed the back, holding it for a second before placing the antique back on the bookshelf. He admired the camera with a grin.

A knock at the door startled him. Thad gathered the rest of the photos and shoved them back into the envelope, planting the best two at the end. He turned and found Jane Edenton's fuzzy silhouette in the window of his door, his name showing backwards across her face.

"Come in."

She opened the door and stepped inside, pulling it shut behind her. "Thank you. How do you do?"

He lit a cigarette, took a drag, and blew out a fine cloud of smoke. "I do just fine."

Fidgeting, she looked nervous. "Did you get what I asked for?"

He took another puff and let it out slow. "Of course I did."

This seemed to make her anxious. And eager buyers always paid more.

Mrs. Edenton had suspected her husband's infidelity, but she had no interest in a divorce. She had money and that meant she could buy anything she wanted.

"May I see them?" she asked.

Thad picked up the envelope and tossed it across the desk, observing with interest.

Nearly tearing the envelope open, she took the photos out all at once and pawed through them. She'd see the young Miss Harlow, and her long spill of blonde hair. She'd view the nape of her neck, the young woman's bare shoulders, the small of her back. There would be photos of them hugging and kissing, and then she'd see the two at the end. One with the young lady on her knees, and the other with her on all fours.

When Mrs. Edenton came to the last two, her already troubled face flushed. She turned away for a moment. When she looked back, Thad could see her comparing herself to this young woman. She glanced at her own chest, confirming his suspicions, and then sighed lightly.

"These ... these are exactly what I asked for ... "

"I aim to please, Ma'am."

Pained eyes found him. "Do you?"

This he'd also expected. Afterward she'd try to negotiate a lower price, but he wouldn't allow it. Instead, he'd hit her up for extra and hold her accountable for her actions. She'd pay up, too. They always did.

Jane set the photos aside and threw off her long jacket. She was a good-looking woman. What a shame a man would cheat on a woman like this. She unbuttoned her shirt, revealing a hint of the red bra beneath. She slid off her skirt, lacy red panties capturing his attention.

A flash filled the room, blinding Thad before he could make his move. He thought the bright light had come from the antique camera, but that was impossible. The damned thing didn't even have a flash. But he was certain it had originated from that very spot.

His hands shot out, finding soft, warm flesh as he took her into his arms. She came willingly, stepping into him and kissing his neck. Running his hands down her sides, it surprised him how voluptuous she was, having thought her of a thicker build. He kissed her, caught in the throes of passion and forgetting the camera, as well as the large white spot hindering his vision.

Her lips were soft, her tongue breeching his mouth, and his moving to meet it in a dance. Her hands were on his back, easing off his jacket and then in front unbuttoning his shirt. A single hand slid inside, rubbing his chest and working its way down.

With the white haze clearing, he opened his eyes and saw the red strap of her bra. His hands worked their way around and undid the clasp. It came away easy, with him drifting back enough to let it fall free to the floor. That was when he saw it, or rather her.

Standing before him, bare-chested and clothed only in her red panties, was young Daisy Harlow. His eyes stole glances up and down her firm body and she smiled.

This can't be.

He staggered back and her lips formed a pout. She bit one side of her bottom lip, and then moved in on him. Thad backed away until he found himself forced against the wall. She was at him, her hands all over him. It was difficult to resist, trying hard not to think of the woman in his arms. He shook his head.

Her curious eyes searched him. "What is it?"

He held up his palms, hoping she would ease back some. "It's just that…" How could he put this without hurting Jane? Hell, he was going mad, so if he didn't just come out and say it, he would be doing her an injustice. "I see Daisy Harlow."

Her smile waned, her pout seeming to grow. "Well of course you do, silly."

"I . . . " Wrinkles formed on his forehead. "I don't understand."

"What are you talking about, Harry?"

His eyes widened, feeling strained. "What did you call me?"

His tone sounded panicked, as he noticed for the first time that it wasn't his voice at all. Not only that, but this wasn't his office. Shaken, he fell back, surprised when he landed on something soft. She was on him, rubbing him, and he was giving in. She kissed him, and then was at his jeans, prying and freeing. She gasped as he entered her. Thad forgot himself, where he was and what might have happened, surrendering to passion.

When the door opened, they were too caught up in the throes of lovemaking to notice. Her blonde hair tinged with red, but only on one side. Her face, angled up, now nodded down to him. One side of her face remained intact, but the side farthest from the door no longer looked anything like her. A gaping red hole stared down at him.

She collapsed on his chest, with him still inside of her. Her blood-soaked hair flayed across his face. He pawed at his eyes and pushed her aside, seeing a broad-chested man standing near the door, reloading his gun.

Thad ran, a loud crack frightening him as the hot sting of a bullet found his thigh. Stumbling, he hopped on one foot, still trying to escape. Heading for the back door, he was losing blood fast and wasn't sure if he would make it. The click of a gun chamber came again, followed by another explosion. His vision blurred and then cleared, everything going red all at once. He stared at the door, through the window, unable to comprehend what he was seeing. He began to fall, hearing words, something about revenge, but unable to discern whose words they were.

He blinked his eyes and for a moment he was himself again. But then that part of him was gone, forever lost in the dark and never coming back. He tried to open his eyes, but they would no longer respond. He yielded to the sensation, letting it wash over him and chose to doze instead. The sleep was good, never-ending, and all encompassing.

Harry woke in a haze, not feeling quite himself. With some effort he stood, the room spinning around him.

Where am I? Who am I?

He thought long and hard, but only one name came to him, "Thaddeus Claremont?"

That sounded right.

He tried to focus on something, anything, and discovered the aged camera. He staggered toward it, his legs struggling, but carrying him there.

Leaning hard against the shelving, he took the camera and held it tight against his chest. There was something that felt so wrong about it, but another part of him wanted the camera more than anything, whether it worked or not. It would make a good keepsake, but he found himself longing to put something inside of the antique.

KENNETH W. CAIN

IS THE AUTHOR OF THE SAGA OF I TRILOGY (THESE
TRESPASSES, GRAVE REVELATIONS, AND RECKONING), THE
UNITED STATES OF THE DEAD, AND TWO ACCLAIMED SHORT
STORY COLLECTIONS: THESE OLD TALES AND FRESH CUT
TALES. HIS SHORT STORIES HAVE BEEN PUBLISHED,
OR ARE FORTHCOMING, IN SEVERAL ANTHOLOGIES
AND PUBLICATIONS. HE LIVES IN CHESTER COUNTY,
PENNSYLVANIA WITH HIS WIFE AND TWO CHILDREN.
HTTP://KENNETHWCAIN.COM

THE OWL AND THE CIGARETTE

AMANDA GOWIN

Her favorite part of the old house had been the screen door facing the river. She'd stand late at night against the frame and smoke hand-rolled cigarettes, tracing his initials on the window screen with her free hand, faded ink under her fingers with her eyes on the lights of town. All the screens held some trace of his hand, each frame labeled neatly for storage in the outbuilding. With her skin against his mark she didn't ache so much, picking out the light of the White Woman's porch in the distance and knowing that the windows and doors of the Other Woman's were not so carefully claimed, cataloged, possessed. In the Other's house he was a guest, a visitor, and the shape of his body made no welcome mold in that bed, spoke not the word Home in his mind nor on his lips. The dark was a comfort, quiet as it was, with the smoke pulled toward the moon like a drafty white hole in the sky—a tear that needed mending with a little spackle or some thread, nothing that couldn't be patched.

That was before The Fire. After, she stood in the door to the new trailer in the old spot with her hand on an unmarked frame, watching the same distant porch light—and the moon was larg-

er, brighter, and she had no thread strong enough, or mud thick enough to blot that wound in the sky. An owl called and she never had an answer, just the surety that his body rested in a now familiar groove in that bed not a mile away. There was no home to come to, no comfort or reminder of anything holding him to her. Her skin shone in the moonlight, slick ivory and unfamiliar, and she knitted the eyebrows she no longer had at her alien self. A scarf around her head, body against the doorway in posture too familiar to ever change, the cigarette and light of the Other's house were the only things she recognized. The hand that brought the paper to her lips was not her own.

Just the children looked right at her—the daughters of her daughters and sons of her sons. Where her own brood found her hard to look upon, the tiny ones lifted their eyes in wonder. They rubbed her hands and said she was made of silk, white silk, and that her face looked like the moon. Brown fingers entwined in her own and asked her for stories of magic and animals, of the spirits in the trees and the water. She helped them put the beads on string with her legs folded on the vinyl floor while her own children shifted under the weight of memory, more comfortable now on the couch of the Other than in this new plastic house with this new plastic mother. The night the children left she stood in the door and dripped tears, her eyes trained after the taillights, the porch light forgotten, and when the owl asked Who? she pitched her cigarette onto the ground in distaste for the dirt itself and retreated into the trailer. There was nothing to return to, no rocking chair's decades-old song, no blankets of her mother.

The night the Other's porch light did not blink to life, the moon itself was gone, and she wrapped in a coat and crossed the dark. The owl was silent and spoke not a word as she passed; they looked into each other. It swung its head to follow her steps from the dead branch of the half-blackened tree. She crossed the rope bridge on uncertain legs, over the narrow river that hissed and gurgled beneath her.

It should've taken you, he had said of The Fire. Wrapped and trembling in an unfamiliar bed, she had agreed—agreed with a nod that their joined life died that night, died in the tongues that licked the color from her skin and the notion of Home from his heart. He'd closed his good eye and she wished he had taken her bandaged hand or touched the bedpost before he turned away, but he had not. Without hesitation or one false step the back of him disappeared and that was the way she pictured him, all the years after, his slick black head and flannel shirt with soot on the right shoulder blade, growing smaller.

This night she raised her fist and the knuckles rapping at the door were bare bones in the dim light of the house, the skin so tight and shiny.

He's passed, the White Woman said with hardly a breath.

She gazed for the first and only time at the love of her love, the creviced face and gnarled hands, the stricken blue eyes.

Wait—the Other said, but she turned and shuffled back to the bridge, to the divide, away to the owl and the black tree and the spot she was meant to die.

There were two cans in the outbuilding, one half-full of kerosene and the other half-full of gasoline. Her fingers slipped through the cobwebs in the handles and lifted them easily.

The owl widened its eyes at what she meant to do and its wings as it took to the sky made the sound of a sweeping flame. The screen slammed behind her in a creak that was unfamiliar after two decades.

The floors shone like her skin under the liquid; she dragged the furniture of the bedroom into the pattern of the old place. At the edge of the bed she spun a cigarette, lit it and placed it in the dish, all the same. Undressing in the light of the kerosene lamp, she put on her best nightdress and lowered herself into the pillow. Her fingers skittered to the other side of the bed where the groove of him should've been, and tears slid down her head and around her ears like the stems of eyeglasses. All the same, her eyes closed against the room and she fell back through the years to give The Fire another chance.

The rushing sound came in her sleep but she willed her eyes stay closed this time, willed the flutter in her heart be still. But instead of warm came cold, the cold of rain through the open window and the crack of thunder. She sat up in time to see the lightning flick the tree with a finger white as her own, and it snapped with a sound loud as the squall, pitching itself onto the ugly little trailer.

For the first time since the children had come years before, her voice escaped, a croak of surprise and joy. The roof split under the weight and the rain washed the fuel oil from her hands and feet, from the floor. She stood forever and a moment with her face to the sky until the daylight pushed the last of the storm aside.

Across the field, the river spilled its banks. It whipped the two halves of the rope bridge and carried off pieces of the life she did not have.

By and by the sun dried her, and she stood in the doorway, watching only the dragonflies that skimmed the puddles and the banks of the river.

AMANDA GOWIN

LIVES IN THE FOOTHILLS OF APPALACHIA WITH HER
HUSBAND AND SON. HER WORK CAN BE FOUND IN
MAGAZINES AND ANTHOLOGIES INCLUDING BURNT TONGUES
AND WARMED AND BOUND. SHE CO-EDITED CIPHER SISTERS
AND HER FIRST SHORT STORY COLLECTION, RADIUM GIRLS
(THUNDERDOME PRESS), IS CURRENTLY AVAILABLE. MORE
INFORMATION ON HER LIFE AND WORK CAN BE FOUND AT
LOOKATMISSOHIO.WORDPRESS.COM.

DESERT

GHOSTS

MARK JASKOWSKI

n the space between her flicking the lighter to life and her touching the flame to what you won't tell her is your second-to-last Pall Mall—a space so defined you could fall into it, through it, out the other side before you remember to breathe—you realize that this is about to be one of those moments where, most likely, one of you will politely edge away. Maybe she'll hesitate, there'll be a second of awkward hovering—the kind you're no good at all at swinging your way. Then you'll go back to your drink, smiling ruefully, making yourself not watch her walk away and telling yourself it's for the best. Because the alternative is she doesn't walk away, and that's how things start. How, for instance, you might wind up on another front porch in north central Florida, drinking gin and tonic out of a Big Gulp cup while the mattress burns in the backyard.

You know, hypothetically.

But then, there she is, handing your lighter back, smoke snaking out from the corners of her mouth, and neither of you have turned away, but instead lean in closer, smiling at each other and the situation, in a what-have-we-here sort of way. You get the feel-

ing that you fell right through that moment back there, rather than letting it pass. Your smile only widens. You lean in closer so she can hear you when you drawl, "What's yours?" in the right tone to feel like a cowboy, nodding at the bottles behind the bar to avoid explaining if she doesn't get it.

But she does.

She flashes you that wicked little smile you're already thinking of appropriate metaphors for—glass, knives, mostly sharp things now that you're catching yourself at it—and you know before it even happens that when you walk out of the bar with this woman you didn't exactly just meet, but it's been long enough to feel like it, you won't think twice about how she's looking over her shoulder for you, as though you don't know well enough to be nervous, or about her out-of-state plates. You'll just register how perfect it is that you caught a bus down here as she opens the door to her car, and once you start thinking that, man, you're as good as miles down the road.

Eventually, of course, you get nervous about how she'd already thought you should be nervous, about the Texas plates that disappeared from her car by the next time you saw it—after that first night, leaving the bar. Inevitably this happens after you've settled, against any reasonable expectations, into a sort of normalcy. You eventually wonder, too, about how she's paying for that house while only working part-time at the diner she staffed in high school. It's work, sure, but you know well enough that it's not the sort of work that secures you two and a half bedrooms plus car insurance. Okay, so she's very likely uninsured. Gas, though, and food. It's not like you were real reluctant to ease yourself into one of those increasingly rare adult-feeling nine-to-fives, and you remember all these little bills she seems to wave away with a dull ache.

So, she comes home this afternoon maybe an hour earlier than usual, which doesn't send up any red flags at first; restaurant work is a messy business, and though usually running longer rather than shorter, the latter could happen. When you meet her eyes, though, the expression there, over a face held rigid, apparently by neck and jaw clenching, is the dilated darting manner of a person hunted, and the ground gives way on the last few months of your life, leaving you floating in this interminable pause.

⸺

So you're on the road the next morning. The vacation you take is abrupt and open-ended; you pretend the two weeks' leave you secured from your boss via hitherto unknown reserves of charm gives the trip a concrete limit, but the suspicion that they don't is unrelenting, clicking its tongue at you from the back of your mind. She has yet to give you the story in full, but over the course of conversation, fragmented by the rhythm of travel, a vague picture pulls itself together in the background.

Look:

A man. A woman. A trailer in the desert. A plan that culminated in a couple duffel bags full of money strapped to the boards of the crawlspace under the trailer. Some time passes and they almost make good on their plan to skip town. Almost.

Here the details get a bit fuzzy and you're too far out of your element to press it. She eventually left, obviously, and bounced around the country, solo, for a while, carrying the stash they'd put sweat and blood into like an old wedding ring. She could go anywhere within reason, but the whole works had lost its luster when she'd lost the partner in the venture, just fading off into vague language and long looks at the sunset, the way these stories seem to go.

And so she drifted about for who knows how long, skirting big cities for reasons she clearly thinks ought to be self-explanatory to you, until she wound up sitting in a bar on the slowest night of the week in the Florida humidity, borrowing a lighter from a face half-remembered from her past to light his second-to-last Pall Mall.

———

You're double-checking that the car's doors are locked in the parking lot of a motel in the wrong suburb of Louisville, Kentucky when you finally start to wonder why she wound up with you. You had been focusing on *how*, up to now, trying to pin down the shifting haze of how relationships start. It's an exercise in frustration. Hunting down, in retrospect, what happens to make two people drift together the way they do leads you back from the end result, through a whole host of promising moments, perhaps, but always to an indistinct dead end of more of the vagueness, the haze, full of suggestion and general implications, but nothing much concrete or satisfying.

Why, though. Maybe that's a little simpler. In this case, at least, you think it almost must be. The windswept woman in that bar, the smell of highway dust and car exhaust still drifting around her, sees a face familiar enough to be friendly and distant enough to maybe not have caught wind of certain things. Maybe she decides to flirt a bit, see whether that guy could become somebody she could rely on. Somebody she could be sheltered by. A familiar face after that long drifting, man, that must have felt like finding a stuffed wallet on the sidewalk.

You slow to a stop with your fingers on the knob of the mo-

tel room door and run them over badly painted wood to trace the
faux-brass number bolted there. You hadn't really ever thought
about it like that before. It certainly doesn't speak much to the romantic notions you keep chained up in there somewhere, and it
makes this whole deal markedly less about you. The idea that you
might not be at the center of this relationship, or even the center
of its origin, sends a feeling much like vertigo flushing your face
and unfocusing your eyes. You swallow and decide you could use
a minute more of fresh air. You interpret fresh air as another cigarette, as you're wont to do, and pace up and down on the motel
sidewalk. The security guard in his office annex shoots glances at
you over the top of his newspaper and you remind yourself just
what kind of neighborhood you're in, here, how the rooms can go
for twenty-five bucks a night, and try to adjust your demeanor to
definitely non-suspicious. This only seems to raise the guard's attention. You suck down the last of the smoke and turn on your heel
for the door, braced to start a big discussion.

She's sitting there, paper cup of rum in her hand, and another
poured for you, in Jay Leno's castoff light. You swallow a couple
times. Your smile comes easy enough. You sit next to her on the
bed, but just as you're drawing in that steel-yourself, dredging-up-
the-past breath, she leans her head on your shoulder and wraps
her arm around yours and Jay Leno delivers a poor joke poorly and
you both fall backwards onto the bed, spilling spiced rum everywhere, and staring at the ceiling with her head on your shoulder,
you let that loaded breath out in a long wordless sigh.

***

After you check out of the hotel and realize Kentucky's creeping
toward ice already, decide with minimal discussion that heading

southwest feels better, you sit in the passenger seat and watch red cliffs rise up around you like the corners of her mouth and turn off the radio and slip into a silence that you don't spoil by thinking, planning, or wondering at her angle. The red clay glows in the sunlight. By the time the land melts into the hopelessly deep wheat of the Great Plains, you've put your finger on what's different. The present has settled into itself, and you don't much feel like looking behind you.

She pulls off the freeway into a gas station that looms on a ghost street like a sleeping sentry. The road sign says Kansas. One tired pickup in the parking lot. She goes inside while you fill up the tank and returns with two frightening cups full of Dr. Pepper and a dash of milk. You eye the mixture warily. She leans against the car and pulls hard on her straw, wistfully murmuring that the drink reminds her of growing up, of Ohio. The cup tastes like the dregs of an ice cream float, pleasant enough, you suppose, but you don't taste the significance no matter how long you let the muted carbonation sit on your tongue. It's only when you've taken over driving, settled back into the long straight asphalt strip through nothing, that it hits you that she's acknowledged, out loud and explicitly, that she came from a place, that this is something.

The freeway-exit strip mall where you stop for lunch boasts a taco stand, a discount clothing store, and a sporting goods store, book-ended by chain family diners with the kind of façade designed with the suburbs in mind. You stroll around the parking lot, paper trays of tacos in hand, making a production of window-shopping like a nice couple out on the town, killing a Friday evening. She's licked the last of the salsa from her fingers and turned to head back toward the car, but you're stalled in front of the sporting goods store, eyeing a matching pair of bowie knives with leather cases. She turns to look at you, smiling absently, and you hold up one finger, disappear into the store. Through the window, you see her shrug and shake her head and lean against a streetlight.

The clerk rings you up and asks if you want a bag for those. You shake your head, an echo. Outside, you toss her one of the knives with a daffy grin and say that you always were a sucker for the romantic gesture. His-and-hers knife sets. Beautiful. She raises her eyebrows as you strap your knife to your calf, sliding the leg of your jeans down over it. She insists that this might well qualify as asking for trouble, trying to keep her tone stern and cautionary, but she's grinning too hard and eventually slips the other knife into her jacket pocket.

<hr/>

You stop at a motel in Denver, thinking to make Santa Fe the next afternoon. She pops the trunk and tells you she wants to show you something, opens the compartment where the spare tire should be and pats a fat duffel bag, the kind you'd check at the airport for a two-day trip, and smiles. The contents are not a mystery. You think back on the scraps of her history you've gathered together and something visceral tightens, the past week fluttering in the wind like tissue paper and the fear you saw in her eyes that afternoon in her house settling in where your throat used to be. You try to swallow it down. The bag of cash is nothing more than an abstraction made concrete, but seeing it, with all its associations of blood and terror, whatever cold scheming brought it here in the first place, is a very different experience indeed.

The Rubicon is so close. You hover a moment on the edge of flight, but gather yourself, composing your face. She's watching you with the tilted-head expression of a curious hound, waiting to see which way this goes, and you realize that this is not a casual gesture. There's a definitiveness to her that you've only seen a couple times. The important thing is that you know—that you know in a concrete way why if you go back to Florida she won't be coming with you, that you know what it is you're doing out here, on the foreign side of the country.You've already held her eyes long enough to connote indecision, fear, trepidation, so you shrug and smile, brushing away any misgivings, and retire to another motel bed.

A nearly identical motel room in Corrales, New Mexico. Same carpet, same chairs you've propped against the wall to put your feet up on the table, but with the parched smell of dust and colorless shrubbery outside. You go down the hall for ice, and on coming back see three men in secondhand Army jackets knock on the door once, twice, and then force their way in. The last man to go in pauses outside and smooths down the front of his jacket, parts his hair with the edge of his hand. The ice bucket makes a sound like breaking bones on the concrete.

Ice cubes scattered and already melting at your feet, you run. The door gapes only strides away, closing slowly, deliberately, and you push to make it before it clicks shut, thinking, if at all, of how they aren't expecting you to be with her or they'd have left someone watching the door, how the closing door and your own footsteps move slowly, take forever, far too long.

You get one foot between the door and its frame and pause. Remember the knife on your leg. Sounds of a scuffle from inside. Reach down, slowly, pull out the blade. Crash through the door, shoulder-first.

They've got her in the bathroom. One of them turns as you enter but too slowly. You don't so much tackle as run flat into him. A pure hovering moment of confusion as the two of you hang in the air, crash to the floor. The blade of your knife kissing cleanly into his neck, hot spray on your face, your hands.

The second man comes toward you, and you're not going to be able to get the knife up again in time. He's raising a gun from his hip and stops, falls. She's got to him from behind. He twists and twitches on the floor and you're thinking there's one left, that this might work.

Roar of a gunshot, ringing in your ears. The third man, from the bathroom. You can't look, look anyway, and sure enough he's hit her. Turn and scramble out the motel room door.

———

Crossing the border into Arizona, you've got a duffel bag full of cash and a battered once-blue Buick. You've got bloodstains on the cuffs of your shirt, rolled up to the elbow in a primal moment of precaution, and on your jeans. You've got an empty passenger seat and a layer of dust in your throat, in your eyes. The highway blurs as the sun goes down. You can't see properly and claw at your eyes to clear them. You've got a rubbed-raw face, because there's so much blood packed in a body and gas station paper towels are a poor means to clean it. You've got a half-tank of gas and no reason, no reason to stop driving.

The desert stretches forever and then it doesn't. You turn north and lose yourself in a winding stretch of highway carved through the space left between ancient redwoods. You pull into towns and cities as they come, but every shadowy alley, every shape out of the corner of your eye twists into three lean figures, bracing themselves against imaginary wind, following that scent of yours they picked up in the desert and haunting you sure as ghosts. Keep moving.

The air cools and greys until you hit the Willamette River, where the heavy sky and din of cargo ships and industry induce you to check in the first vacant motel you see. You mill around the city, walking in expanding circles as the sun rises, until you see lit neon beer signs in a window and drift that way. The tables are filled with large men, dressed against the spray of water off the docks, and drinking pale beer. You edge into the most vacant corner you can find, on the far edge of the bar, and mumble something to the bartender that he interprets as an order.

A slight figure with a shock of peroxide hair a few seats down catches your eye in the brief flash of her lighter's flame, smoke halo obscuring her face as soon as you look over. It's a face that's dully familiar, a snatch of song you heard on the radio years ago. You take a long, long drink and stand from your stool and walk over to her, slowly and grinning in a hopefully nonthreatening sort of way. You lean against the bar until she looks over, then ask if she can spare a smoke, which she apparently can, reaching into her jacket pocket for the pack she shields from you as she opens it, but you'd swear that there are exactly two smokes left, and hold the lighter a second, two, three, longer than is necessary before setting it to the tip of the cigarette, smiling to yourself and feeling the time stretch itself out of joint, wondering if she might be amenable to a little road trip.

MARK JASKOWSKI

IS A MAN IN A SPORT COAT LISTENING TO SWEDISH DEATH
METAL. HE'S DOING THIS, AT THE MOMENT, IN COLORADO,
WHERE HE STUDIES AND TEACHES. SOME OF HIS STORIES
HAVE LANDED AT COOL PLACES LIKE BARTLEBY SNOPES
AND ELSEWHWERE.

BLOOD

PRICE

AXEL TAIARI

An empath beckons from across the city. Burrowing deep into his brain, the distorted voice rips him out of a fitful sleep with a message spiked with static: *a gate has opened in Ghoulish Bend. Unidentified wayfarers. Grab your gear and report to your squad within fifteen minutes. Acknowledge the message.*

"Yeah, yeah," Efrim mumbles. "Acknowledged. Get out of my head."

He rolls out of bed with a groan and fumbles for his clothes. He feels mostly sober. Lighting up a smoke, he nudges the shape in the bed. The nameless, naked man moans in his sleep.

"Hey, wake up."

"What?"

"Where are we?" Efrim asks.

"My apartment."

"No. In the city. Which district?"

"Bousculaire."

"Fuck."

Efrim slips into his torso-armor, slides on his white combat helmet, and picks up his weapon. Out of the door with no good-bye. Elevator ride, a stuttering descent into ravine-black darkness

accompanied by mechanical pleading. Snow outside, fat flakes the color of volcanic ash. The streets of Nualla-Stem shimmer blue from neon tubes lining wilted buildings, synthetic veins running along the city's cement skin.

Efrim brings his wrist to his mouth, and speaks into it. "Unit 23, serial 4792891-84. I need a ride in Bousculaire, get in on my location."

"Roger. Ride your way in four minutes."

"Thanks."

Grim visions disentangle themselves from a roving fragment of the past and pounce on him. Efrim dashes down a nearby cul-de-sac and sits against a wall, breathing hard. He removes his helmet, draws his gun out of its holster and brings it to his mouth. His teeth clink against the barrel. His finger rests on the trigger. Metal warms up. The ride lands in the main street before he conjures up the courage to end it. He holsters the gun, re-equips the helmet, rides shotgun.

"What's up, Ef?"

Moric behind the handle tonight. Full armor and combat helmet strapped on, thank the gods. Moric is known for having an ugly case of the gutter-mouth and hanging belly-fat. He is also known for roughing up shub'nar, mutants, jentils, camazotzs—any of the chimeric races. A human supremacist. Efrim smiles as he pictures Moric found dead in the gutter one morning.

"Nothing," he says. "You know what this is about?"

The four-person vehicle soars between black skyscrapers. "Just another gate," says Moric. "Bursters won't leave until they get what they want. We got two squads there already. Animists secured the perimeter. The local duke is on the way to initiate a parlay. No one can understand them."

"The intruders, where they from?"

"Where the hell do those things hail from? An alternate plane, a different continent, somewhere below the surface, doesn't matter. They get here, we kick the bastards out before they decide to stay. Look at this goddamn mess. Ain't it grand?"

Efrim leans his head against the transport's window. Governmental dropships waft amidst mobs of viscous purple clouds, their searchlights probing the streets. Scouts buzz around the Core's fortresses, their fuselage camouflaged by mojo, engines spouting blood-red trails in their wake. The city's architecture is a treacherous thing, an uneven landscape of concrete and millennia-old bricks where houses and brothels cower in the shadows of skyscrapers. Temples grow twisted. To the east, the theme park from Eyes Of The Storm illuminates the skyline. To the south, the Old City burns, forever belching multicolored fumes behind a translucent wall taller than anything else in the city, an ethereal barrier woven out of bent reality and kept alive by never-resting shifts of benders and fringe machinery. To the west, at the edge of the city, the Jerkmouth ghettos.

Home before he ran away from home.

"You see that?" says Moric.

Down below, the gate awaits. Ghoulish Bend's shacks and burnt houses seem to recoil from the gate's alien light. The portal is perhaps thirty, forty meters tall—a pillar of energy large enough to swallow a whole building. It pulsates with crackling blue lights, as if its insides were home to a raging thunderstorm. Floral barriers secure the zone.

"Don't get too close," says Efrim. "Land a block away."

"No shit," says Moric.

The transport touches ground in a nearby park. No snow here.

The two men exit the vehicle with their rifles at the ready. Ghoulish Bend is mostly clear of gangs, but rogue elements are always on the prowl, and law enforcement gear fetches a fat price on the black market. Organs are worth even more.

They make their way to the vine barrier. Two animists guard the entrance. The women could be twins: tall and frail, moss-colored hair down to their knees, flowers as garments, eyes and noses bleeding from heavy mojo use.

"Hello, ladies," says Moric.

The animists nod in unison and the barrier splits open. A door-shaped rectangle of vines turns autumn-red then winter-black, crumbling to dust and creating a corridor. Efrim and Moric pass through the foliage, and as soon as they reach the other side, hundreds of fresh stems sprout and intertwine behind them. The breach has vanished.

Efrim and Moric join their squad, a dozen members from the Burnt Gallants—independent enforcers. Efrim recognizes the uniforms from other cells, too: Sky Burrowers, Blackpowder Masons, and a couple of Throne Breachers. Something like fifty men and women in triangular formation with their weapons aimed at the life forms standing by the gate.

Ghoulish Bend's duke, Iravi Zorem, towers over the troops. Two and a half meters tall, as wide as three men. The jentil's crimson robe pulses with glyphs; its fabric spits out butane-blue sparks. Reality benders, wearing black cowls and robes, flank his sides.

Three naked beings face the duke and his benders. The portal's voltaic mouth twists and yawns at their back. No obvious physical differences between the three visitors—asexual at first glance. Reptilian skins, their scales pale as the desert sand. Humanoid-sized.

Four ivory horns spear out of their faces in pairs: two on the forehead, two below the mouth. No eyes, no nose.

The middle one speaks in a guttural language, a string of grunts and throat-rattles accompanied by tremors.

Over the local dispatch, Moric says: "Aside from being wayfarers, anyone know what those ugly bastards are?"

Silence over the radio. Efrim has never seen this particular race before, either. Wayfarers is nothing but a generic term, only describes beings that travel through portals.

Duke Iravi Zorem turns to the reality bender to his right. "Kaliv, act as a relay, please."

The bender takes a few steps forward, turns to face both the intruders and the duke. Her mojo-boosted voice comes loud from beneath her cowl. The air between her and the creatures undulates. "We want our due," she says.

All three wayfarers turn their heads to stare at her. *They can't stare*, thinks Efrim, *without eyes*. They nod, understanding that she is translating.

"Can you use the shared tongue, travellers?" asks the Duke.

The middle wayfarer replies, spits on the ground, a thick gob of mold-green spit.

"We understand your heathen language," the bender translates. "We refuse to sully our mouths with it."

Duke Iravi Zorem chuckles. "I see. Where are you from? What do you need?"

The wayfarer speaks.

"Where we hail from is no concern of yours," says the bender. "The boy. We want the boy who has requested our help. We have come to collect him. You must bring him to us. Or we will bring blood out of you."

The Duke gathers his thoughts, then extends his arms, opens his hands. "You're going to have to be more descriptive. This is a city of over four million people. Who is the boy, what is the help you provided, and what is the payment? Where can we find him? Furthermore, do you understand that your presence here is a breach and you are in no position to make threats?"

The wayfarer laughs, a bone-chilling chuffle crawling out of the back of his throat.

"We wish to speak to a higher authority," translates the bender.

"No," says the Duke, pointing at the ground. His voice drips with ire. "This is my dominion. I hold jurisdiction. There is no higher authority here. The Council Hands do not deal with this matter, and the Arch-Baron is more likely to nuke you than bargain. You," he points to the middle one, "Speak to me. Answer my questions."

Overhead, two dropships float over the area, blocking the moonlight. Their searchlights zero in on the trio. The wayfarers angle their heads up, growl at the skies.

The middle one speaks for a long time. It sounds like no language Efrim has heard around the city, not even the ghetto-slangs.

The reality bender twitches as she absorbs the sounds, processes them, and then regurgitates them. "A boy from the northern parts of the city has requested our help in a private matter," she says. "We have upheld our end of the contract, now it is time for him to follow through. You speak of jurisdiction—that is fine. We are in the right according to our credence. The boy was aware of what he was doing. He accepted the terms. There is no trickery, no hijinks. It is a clean deal. Ask him. There is no room to argue. You will bring him to us. He is a shub'nar. He lives in a yellow house on what is called Daboul Alley. His name is . . . "

The bender turns to the Duke. "I can't pronounce that, your Highness. It's a shub'nar name."

The Duke spins around, addresses the troops. "Shub'nar speakers, raise your hands, please."

Three hands go up, Efrim included. The Duke points at him. "You. Come closer."

Efrim lowers his weapon and detaches himself from the squad. The intruders' heads track his movements with their eyeless glare. He walks over and stands by the bender.

Efrim looks at them and says, "Could you repeat the boy's name, please?"

The middle wayfarer clicks his canines, slaps his forked tongue against them.

"Understood," says Efrim.

"Thank you," says the Duke. "So, that is the deal, we bring you the boy, you leave?"

The wayfarers nod.

"Soldier. Your name, race and rank?"

"Efrim D'am, sir. Human. Senior ensign in the Burnt Gallants."

"How'd you learn to click?"

"Stepfather was a shub'nar, sir."

"You know the locale?"

"No, sir, we lived in Jerkmouth. But I am as fluent as a human can be."

"Take your pilot with you, go fetch the boy. Yellow house, remember. Any shub'nar tries to bar your way, tell them you have carte blanche. They don't move, you shoot. I'll worry about damage control later."

"Yes, sir," says Efrim.

The Duke turns back to the intruders, raises his voice loud

enough for everyone to hear. "And be swift about it, ensign. Our unsolicited guests here are too cocky for my taste. I'm sure some of our biomancers back at the Core would love to dissect their corpses."

———

Headed north into shub'nar territory. The Bloody Sister River glows green in the night. Illegal campfires line its bank on both sides. Rilke is easy to spot from the air: it's the only flooded district. Water from the river snakes through the streets, has been doing that since long before Efrim was born. Decades prior, shub'nar separatists blew up tremendous amounts of explosives to create a network of trenches, allowing the river to take over. The water was contained by cement dams tactically placed around the district, preventing it from spilling further into the city. Efrim remembers his stepfather on one of his drunken rants, clicking his beak madly between swishes of whiskey. *We fucked the government. Fucked them good, you hear? We took over. Water everywhere! They should have seen it coming, we built the dams months before! The day the bombs went off, we cheered, all of us. We swam through the bellies of submerged buildings. It felt like home.*

Moric settles the transport on one of the rare landing pads in the area. He cocks his rifle, removes the security. "Think we should expect trouble from squids?"

"Shub'nar won't like us here, but we're government. They'll let us pass."

"Or drag us below the water and stab us with those wrist-blades."

Efrim smiles. He clicks the blades' names. *Dux'per.* "Yeah, that's always a possibility—especially if you keep using that racial slur."

"I call 'em like I see 'em," says Moric.

Out of the ship and onto a boardwalk. Water laps at wooden shores. No electricity here. Gas lamps and torches cast shadows on the brick dwellings. Beneath the waters, ghostly lights radiate from subsurface lamps—bioluminescent sea anemones twisted by shub'nar scientists to thrive in salt-free environments.

The two soldiers turn a corner and find themselves in a large avenue. A pack of shub'nar on a plank up ahead are standing in a circle. No path around them.

Moric takes the lead, and the plank is narrow enough that Efrim has no choice but to follow. As they approach, the shub'nar turn to them. Their dux'per unsheathe like poisonous claws as long as a human's forearm. Moric holds his rifle in front of his belly.

The four shub'nar eyeball Efrim and Moric. Human-tall, four arms, octopus skin reflecting light. Crow-black diving pants made out of arachnid weave, no shirts, no boots. Tattoos cover their bare chests.

Moric says, "You gentlemen chat shared?"

The shub'nar don't respond, either not understanding or choosing not to.

Efrim slides open his facial visor so they can see his mouth. He knows that his lips' movements will make up for his flawed pronunciation. "I speak the holy tongue," he clicks. "Many blessings upon you. May the sea carry its bounty to your doorstep."

"Many blessings," the four shub'nar repeat back. Their mouth-tentacles wriggle, signing in respect.

Moric snorts. "Tell the squids they should be wearing their communication masks. It's a crime not to wear one."

Efrim considers clicking a more polite version of the sentence when one of the shub'nar clicks, "Tell your fat friend his armor is at least three sizes too small for his whale-body. Tell him we do not wear the devices in our home, no matter what the Arch-Baron might rule as law."

The shub'nar laugh, and so does Efrim.

"What's that one saying?" asks Moric.

Efrim tries to keep his voice cool. "The shub'nar says they are very sorry, o, prosperous one. They did not expect non-shub'nar visitors at this time of night."

"Tell your fat friend," continues the shub'nar, "that if he calls us squids again, I will drink his sugary blood and craft a buoy out of his blubbery corpse for my children to play with."

They laugh again, and Moric raises his weapon. The laughter dies. "They mocking me?"

"No," says Efrim. "They are feeling foolish for breaking the law and joked that they feel quite naked without their communication masks."

"Human," says another shub'nar, flexing his mouth-tentacles, "I am losing patience with your comrade. What is the purpose of your presence?"

Pick your lies carefully. "We are here to enjoy the exotic products offered by your people. We have a transaction planned on Daboul Alley."

"Drugs?" clicks the shub'nar.

"Yes."

"Well, then. Why didn't you say so. Take a left at the end of the avenue, it'll be right there. And tell your friend to watch his mouth, next time."

"Thank you. May the currents steer you towards home."

"No need, friend. We are home."

"Let's go, Moric."

Efrim grabs Moric by the arm and drags the idiot away from his death.

———

Daboul Alley: a crumbling passage. Algae grow on the faded brick walls as crabs scatter across slippery boardwalks. The yellow house lies sandwiched between two tenements with boarded-up doors. Two-floors with broken windows, frayed curtains blowing in the breeze.

Moric knocks on the door. No answer. He kicks it open and enters, weapon raised. Efrim follows.

The stench hits Efrim like a ringed fist. Broken bottles litter the floor. Glass shards glitter under Moric's flashlight beam. Trash, soiled clothes. Fat flies gather on the walls in nauseating swarms.

"Gods," says Moric, shaking his head.

"Yeah," says Efrim. He knows this house. He smells the people who live here sure as he smells the mold lurking beneath the floor. He grew up in a house just like it. Replace the river smell with sewer stench, trade crabs and crayfish for rats the size of cats. Nausea washes over him, the same soul-sickness that hit him earlier that night, had him pondering death.

Kitchen's empty. Dishes piled up in the sink. Rotten food a feast for hundreds of cockroaches.

"Hello," someone clicks.

Moric and Efrim one-eighty, find themselves aiming at a pre-teen shub'nar. The boy barely reaches up to Efrim's chest. He is shirtless and wears ill-fitting pants, ragged things. Grime and mud stain his face, his chest.

Efrim clicks the boy's name, and the boy nods in response.

"Lower your weapon, Mor. Slide up your visor."

"Why?"

"We're scaring him."

"He doesn't look scared to me."

"Lower your damn weapon."

"Okay, okay."

The boy looks up at Efrim. "I am ready to go, sir."

"Go where?"

"To the desert place. Thank you for helping me."

"It wasn't us, boy."

"You sound funny." The boy's tentacles wriggle softly. Laughter.

"What's he saying?" says Moric.

"Shut up, I'll explain later."

"But you are here to take me, yes?" clicks the shub'nar.

"How old are you?"

"In seasons?"

"Yes."

"Eleven winters."

Efrim frowns. Eleven winters. Barely older than when he himself ran away from home, learned to live in the ghetto, found ways to survive the city, what it does to people. Eight winters ago.

"What did you do, kid? What happened?"

"I asked for help and I got it. Now I would like to express gratitude by repaying my debt."

"Where are your parents?"

The shub'nar extends his suction cup-covered arm towards the stairs. "Upper floor."

"Okay, stay here."

Efrim nods at Moric. "His parents are up there. Let's go."

Up the stairs. The smell intensifies and Efrim knows what lies in wait. In the bedroom, he crouches by the rotting corpses, piled atop one another like vulgar ragdolls. Dried blood splatters on every surface. He slaps the flies away, rolls the mother's corpse over. Her torso has been shredded open from neck to crotch. Her breasts have been cut off and are nowhere to be found. Her insides have the consistency of stew. Her beak has been shoved between her legs. Her mouth-tentacles have been ripped off and planted in her eye sockets.

Efrim takes a moment to remove his helmet and then throws up.

"Those wayfarers did that," he says, wiping his mouth. "She was tortured for a long time."

Moric shakes his head. "How'd they get here? And if they can get here, why bother opening a portal downtown?"

"I don't know," mumbles Efrim.

He doesn't close the mother's eyes, doesn't waste time going over the father's body.

Back down the stairs, Efrim kneels by the waiting child. He brushes dirt away from the boy's face, stares into his black eyes. "Why?"

"They were not good parents. They did not honor the blood bond."

Efrim is close enough to see the ugly details on the child's skin: bruises, cuts, scars. An ideogram of abuse. "How did it happen?"

"I prayed."

"You prayed? To whom?"

"I prayed to the blind horned ones who bask in the suns."

"How did you know to pray to them?"

The child hesitates.

"Come on, you can tell me."

"I read about them in a book of prayers. It said they grant wishes to the just. It said they dispense justice. I think I am just. So I clicked the words three times and they helped me."

Efrim turns to look at Moric. "The boy used an incantation. Probably from a black journal. He had his parents assassinated." Efrim swallows hard. "Given how badly they were tortured, I don't think they merely beat him."

"How'd he get ahold of the rites?" Moric asks.

"Boy, where did you get the book of prayers?"

"From a shaman. He is well-known here. He lives close by."

"Is he of your race?"

The boy shakes his head. "No. Bat-kin."

Camazotz, thinks Efrim. "Okay. And how did you pay?"

The kid stares at him for a long time. Eventually, he lowers his head. "I didn't have any money," he clicks.

Efrim nods, understands. He remembers footsteps in the hallway at night.

"I want to go," clicks the shub'nar. "I must repay my debt."

"Let's get you out of this place."

<hr>

They take a detour on the way back, staying out of sight of roaming shub'nar. Two humans trying to escort a young kin away from his home would bring nothing but blood. When they reach the transport, Efrim straps the shub'nar in the back and asks, "The shaman, where does he live?"

The boy tells him.

Moric stands by the vehicle, smoking. "We ready?"

"I'll be right back. You watch him."

"What, you gonna leave me alone with the fucking squid-spawn?"

Efrim hammers the butt of his rifle through Moric's open visor, then slams the weapon horizontally into his throat, choking him and pinning him against the vehicle's shell. Moric's feet are lifted off the ground.

"You do not talk to him. You do not call him a squid. Humanoctopus would be more appropriate, by the way, you dumb cunt. You do not taunt him. You wait for me quietly. I will ask him when I get back. If you so much as look at him or take off without me, I will do worse things to you than what happened to his parents. Are we understood, you fat racist piece of shit?"

"Understood," blurts Moric through broken teeth, blood gushing from his nostrils.

The camazotz shaman sleeps upside down in his tent, surrounded by stacks of books, potions lining the shelves. The bat-kin opens his eyes and Efrim feels his lips widening into a demonic grin as he aims.

"What do you want?" the shaman moans.

"A retribution in blood," says Efrim.

He shoots the shaman in the crotch three times. The camazotz falls to the ground. It feels good, emptying those bullets. It feels a long time coming. He sees a different face, lying there, bleeding to death.

Efrim walks out of the tent smiling.

Return to Ghoulish Bend. They walk past the two animists, the vines open. Efrim turns to Moric and says, "Get lost."

"What?"

"You get lost. You're done. Go home. Bandage your face up, get a bender to fix your teeth and your nose."

"I'm gonna report you."

"No, you won't."

Moric spits on the ground then walks away.

The young shub'nar and Efrim walk to the portal area. More troops, more squadrons have joined the fray. Dozens upon dozens of rifles, canes, and bows are aimed at the three reptile-kin. Two additional ships now patrol the area. The wayfarers do not appear to have moved at all.

Duke Iravi Zorem stomps over to Efrim, and nods at the child. "I'm impressed, ensign. Have you run into any trouble?"

Efrim looks up to the jentil, his head reaching halfway to the man's chest. "Some trouble."

"Shub'nar body count?"

"Zero."

"And your partner?"

"He's a piece of shit and I would like to request that your Highness remove him from the force."

"I will take it under consideration due to your performance. The boy came willingly?"

"Yes."

"Parents?"

"Dead," Efrim says, nodding in the direction of the wayfarers. "They were summoned by the boy."

"I see," says the Duke. "Hired killers. Arbiters, you think?"

"Yes. Or something close to that. Distant *judicars*. Permission to approach them?"

"Granted."

The young shub'nar looks enraptured by the wide-open gate, the electricity raging from its maw, the strangers waiting for him.

"Come," says Efrim, and offers the child his hand. The child grasps it. They walk.

"Hello," clicks the boy. "Thank you for your help."

"Hello, young one," replies the same reptilian who addressed the Duke earlier that night. Efrim blinks. "You can speak shub'nar?"

"Somewhat."

"What is your race called?"

"There is no name in the sea tongue for it, nor in any language you might know."

"Why do you want the boy?"

The wayfarer speaks using a heavily accented shub'nar sub-slang. "We agreed to dispense justice. We found his cause worthy, so we championed him. Now one must be cleansed."

"Hasn't he suffered enough?"

The thing cocks its head to the side. "Of course. Too much. He has suffered the blood price. He has suffered many other prices through his life, but he chose to endure the blood price on his own."

"I'm sorry. I don't think I understand," clicks Efrim.

"He killed his breeders."

"You didn't do it for him?"

The wayfarer chuffles. "If we could freely sneak into your homes, human, why would we be standing here like dumb grass-grazers? No, we only gave him the approval, and a dash of power to follow through. As I told you, we believed his plea to be worthy. Now we will welcome him and nurse him through his soul-debt."

Efrim sees the mother's corpse again. Days and nights of torture. Mangled body parts soaking in puddles of blood. A stain on the boy's soul. "Will he return to the city?"

"That will be up to him, once he has healed."

"I will come with you," says the boy, and he lets go of Efrim's hand. He runs to the wayfarers, and turns back to wave. "Good-bye, funny speaker."

"Good-bye, little one."

The three wayfarers and the boy head towards the gate.

"Wait," shouts Efrim.

Their main speaker stops. The other two and the child disappear through the portal. "Yes?"

Efrim considers his words, then says, "Every night I wish I could have paid the blood price when I was his age."

The creature speaks without facing him. "You carry this boy's ache?"

"Yes."

"What is it you seek?"

Efrim stares down at his badge, his weapon. "Justice," he says.

"Then come with us," the arbiter says, and Efrim walks toward the beckoning light.

AXEL TAIARI

IS A FRENCH WRITER, BORN IN PARIS IN 1984. HIS WRITING
HAS APPEARED IN MULTIPLE MAGAZINES AND ANTHOLOGIES
INCLUDING BASTION, 365TOMORROWS, NO COLONY, CEASE,
COWS, AND SEVERAL OTHERS. HE IS THE CO-AUTHOR
OF THE SOUL STANDARD, A NOIR NOVEL-IN-NOVELLAS TO
BE PUBLISHED BY DZANC BOOKS IN 2015. READ MORE
AT WWW.AXELTAIARI.COM.

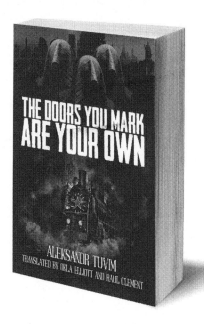